The Night We Met

A NOVEL

The Flight Risk Spy Series: Book One

SHELLY SNOW PORDEA

Published by LBB Publishing. An imprint of Little Black Book: Women in Business

Cover and interior design by Shelly Snow Pordea

Special thanks to editor and friend, Halley Kim

Paperback ISBN 978-1-962417-16-7

Ebook ISBN 978-1-962417-17-4

LITTLE BLACK BOOK
PUBLISHING

Contents

1. Chapter 1 — 1

2. Chapter 2 — 25

3. Chapter 3 — 43

4. Chapter 4 — 63

5. Chapter 5 — 87

6. Chapter 6 — 107

7. Chapter 7 — 117

8. Chapter 8 — 137

9. Chapter 9 — 161

10. Chapter 10 — 173

11. Chapter 11 — 191

12. Chapter 12 — 207

13. Chapter 13 — 221

14. Chapter 14 — 235

15. Chapter 15 — 247

16. Chapter 16   259

17. Chapter 17   271

18. Chapter 18   283

19. Chapter 19   295

About The Author   311

Also by   313

Chapter One

Light flickered and bounced off every surface as dusk fell upon the city. Amanda Hopkins moved through the twilight streets of Rome with an effortless grace, her auburn hair catching the golden rays of a setting sun as it cascaded in soft waves past her shoulders. A few freckles dusted the bridge of her nose, barely visible after years of cockpit sun exposure. She dressed effortlessly—linen pants, a fitted pale pink button-down with the sleeves rolled up, and a light sweater that she draped through the strap of her oversized bag, hinting at a woman who valued fashion with a touch of elegance.

This wasn't Amanda's first time in the ancient metropolis, but it certainly felt like one of the most magical days of her life. Her soft sandals tapped lightly against the cobblestones, their simple design a nod to someone accustomed to movement, not standing still. Tonight, she blended into the city's ancient charm, not as a tourist, not as a woman searching for something, but as someone who was learning to belong wherever she landed.

Amanda was finally content with her place in the world—no longer concerned about achieving more, meeting that perfect someone, or the clanging noise of her biological clock reverberating its dreaded tick-tock like an overpowering gong. She had let that all go. She was finally thirty-five. Not old by any means, but *hopefully* old enough that perhaps her family would stop asking her relentless probing questions.

"Mandy, darlin', when are you gonna hang up your wings and come settle yourself here on the ground with the rest of us?" Uncle Ron would ask with a wink at nearly every family gathering.

She hated that he and Grandpa still refused to call her by her full name. The three syllables of her given name made Amanda feel like she wasn't a bumbling kid anymore, and she wanted her transformation to be recognized. She was, after all, a decorated pilot with more flight hours on her flight log than most of her colleagues of the same age. She had given up the nickname Mandy during high school, and she wished her whole family—and anyone who knew her before the year 2009—would let her grow past it.

Mandy was a kid, but *Amanda?* At fourteen, she was already spending her weekends in flight school, trading teenage drama for airspeed calculations and crosswind landings. By seventeen, she had racked up enough hours to take her first solo flight, and less than ten years later, she was constantly in the skies, effortlessly slipping between private jets and packed passenger planes.

Not that her family cared. They barely acknowledged her time in the sky, too busy obsessing over things like her uterus.

"You're not getting any younger, honey!" Aunt Melissa would say, abandoning any attempt at subtlety, "I had three kids by the time I was your age."

The truth is, Amanda didn't yearn to settle down, have two-point-five kids, and live what most people would label as a *conventional* life. But she always carried a weighty guilt for not being able to tap into those expected desires, and *that* was almost as bad as not having the prescribed spouse and children at her age—or maybe it was worse. She used to hate herself for not feeling maternal or overly romantic. But now, she'd finally done it. She'd reached an age where she hoped people would assume that she was *always* going to be single. She had no cats but considered getting a few, just for the optics.

"It's not real," said a curt voice in a distinctly British accent, fracturing the reverie of a quintessential Roman moment that had been peaceful up until that second.

"I'm sorry, what?" Amanda turned to see the face of a woman in her sixties.

Elegant silver hair slightly brushing her shoulders as she spoke, the woman continued. "The statue. It's not the real one. The original stands in the Vatican. This is just a replica."

The woman wore a pinstripe summer dress with a belt tied around her waist; her figure was perhaps not as slender as it was in her youth, but she was visibly active and fit. She had a navy blazer draped over one arm—everyone knew to be prepared with light layers when traveling Europe in the early summer. She wore desperately impractical shoes for the cobblestone streets, with a wedge heel that Amanda herself wasn't brave enough to don on a leisurely stroll, so she immediately respected this woman, even if she did find her way of striking up a conversation a bit strange.

"Oh," Amanda said awkwardly. "That's… interesting." She wasn't sure why a complete stranger was speaking to her in English while on the streets of Rome, but Amanda likely still stuck out as a foreigner even now after all her travels.

"Yes, it *is* interesting, isn't it? There are others scattered throughout the world. Mere imitations of greatness. Why do you think that is?" The woman asked, but Amanda gave no reply, assuming the question was rhetorical.

They both stood for a few more seconds as the sun crept lower, and Amanda reached for the cardigan draped over her oversized handbag. It wasn't cool enough yet to require it, but she thought it would be a good way of moving herself along and saying goodbye to the stranger who had no appearance of menace but for some reason made her altogether uneasy.

"Well, you have a nice evening," Amanda murmured as she clutched the cardigan in her hand, stepping in the opposite direction of where the woman was standing.

"And you, Amanda, have a lovely evening and a very *happy* birthday."

Amanda stopped, slowly pivoting on her heels and turning to look the woman in the eyes. "Who *are* you?" she asked.

"My name is Katherine," smiled the woman, holding her arm out and offering a handshake introduction.

"And how do you know *me?*" Amanda placed a palm on her chest, reluctant to extend a hand to the woman.

"I can't say that I know you, but I *do* have your dossier," Katherine dropped her hand to her side, abandoning any further formalities.

"My *dossier?*" Amanda's voice remained steady, but her pulse kicked up a notch. She studied the older woman, searching for some indication of what game she was playing.

"Yes." Katherine nodded once, her expression unreadable. She offered no further explanation, meeting Amanda's gape with an unsettling steadiness.

Amanda exhaled slowly. "Look," she said, keeping her tone level, "this whole interchange has been a little odd, and I'm not in the habit of entertaining cryptic conversations with strangers. If you have something to say, say it. Otherwise, I won't feel obligated to keep up the niceties."

"Niceties," Katherine grinned. "Something we've come to expect from a girl from White Pine, Tennessee. You don't disappoint, Miss Hopkins, I must say."

Amanda's eyes widened. It was true. White Pine was the small town where she was born, raised, and ran from as soon as she got the chance. She wasn't ashamed of it, but United States residents probably couldn't point to it on a map, much less people around the world. Everyone in the area claimed to be from Knoxville, Tennessee, when meeting new people, even though White Pine was more than a forty-minute drive from the big city.

Even Amanda introduced herself to new people as a Knoxvillian, but she had a more legitimate claim to it. During her junior year of high school, she had convinced her parents to let her commute to Knoxville for a more robust education, and it was there that she felt her world—and her heart—crack open. She thrived in the challenge, pouring herself into her studies with the same intensity she devoted to her flight hours.

Learning and flying were her twin lifelines—the only things that kept her from sinking into any emotion she wasn't ready to face. Keeping still meant confronting feelings she wasn't sure how to articulate. So, she stayed in motion, soaring through the sky, devouring books, finding time to be occasionally involved in music and theater programs, and chasing knowledge as though it could shield her from everything she didn't want to feel.

And now, with this stranger invoking the place where the roots of her lineage grew long, wide, and deep, she felt an unease settle in her chest like a pressure drop before a storm.

"I don't understand," Amanda managed to say after pushing the lump in her throat down to her chest.

Without uttering a word, Katherine handed Amanda a small photograph, her eyes immediately welling with tears.

"Who *are* you?" Amanda asked again.

"According to your confidentiality agreement, we retain the right to contact you at any point in the future."

"We? *Who* is *we?*" Amanda pressed, but Katherine remained nonplussed.

"Consider this the future, Amanda. Starting today. You'll receive instructions once you reach your room, and I am available to answer your questions as I receive clearance to do so. There's a phone in your room with my number. I look forward to working with you." Katherine nodded without explaining further.

She was the one to turn and walk away this time.

"Wait!" Amanda protested. "That doesn't explain anything. I... I didn't agree to this... whatever *this* is!" she exclaimed.

But Katherine's gait hadn't slowed as she progressed further and further down the open-air piazza, and Amanda stood gripping her cardigan in one hand and the faded picture in the other. She jostled her head as if to shake herself back to reality, tucked the photograph into the front pocket of her bag without glancing at it, and began jogging towards her hotel room.

Nearly out of breath, Amanda rushed up the staircase from the main road onto the terraced entry of her favorite Italian boutique hotel.

"Hi, Bianca!" Amanda greeted the concierge before she paused to catch some air, breathing deeply. "Did someone come by for me today? I'm expecting something, but I wasn't sure if it came," she said, trying to keep herself from appearing panicked.

"Oh, yes, Miss Hopkins," Bianca replied. "Why did you not tell me it is your birthday? I would have brought you breakfast with champagne!"

"Oh, thank you, Bianca. That's not necessary. This is the first birthday I'm intentionally spending *alone,*" Amanda declared with much emphasis, remembering her precise game plan for the day. "And you're supposed to call me Amanda, remember?" She glared at the employee with teasing wide eyes.

"Oh, Miss Amanda," Bianca corrected herself. "But alone? Amanda, I don't like that idea at all!" She declared as her chestnut eyes twinkled. "Perhaps you may change your mind after you see the gifts that are waiting!" she smiled.

"Gifts? Plural? They left more than one thing?"

"Yes, it's supposed to be your birthday surprise. A lovely woman came, but I think she was on a mission for a man." Bianca leaned in closer. "Roses that beautiful can only mean love," Bianca gushed.

"Well, that certainly would be a surprise to everyone, Bianca—including me!" Amanda laughed, allowing some of the oddness of her afternoon to melt away.

"A woman so beautiful as you *must* find love!" Bianca admonished. "It is not always *paradiso,* but in our youth, we must be open and grateful to love and *be* loved," she explained.

"I am happy to be open, but I am not very hopeful," Amanda winked. "I'll go check my room, regardless, okay?" She smiled, feeling less stressed about her chance meeting with Katherine.

"Va bene, va bene. I will see you later," Bianca smiled.

Amanda made her way to the staircase, contemplating. Maybe it was all a joke. An elaborate ruse set up by her siblings because she hadn't come home—yet again—on her birthday. She wouldn't put it past them. The whole family had grown weary of her finding ways to avoid being around them for milestones and celebratory events. It wasn't just that they missed hers, but she was missing their birthdays and special occasions too. Amanda now had two nieces and a nephew, whom, she could admit, stole her heart. But even that wasn't enough to keep her grounded. The skies kept calling.

She rotated the key to the antique wooden door, something she found ridiculously charming about being in a city thousands of years old. Turning keys was something that made her feel connected with humanity. As if an ancient ritual like jostling metal through a lock to unseal a portal into a previously unseen space linked her with souls of the past who had never scanned or swiped anything.

As she glanced around the room, Amanda saw that Bianca wasn't exaggerating. She, too, was taken aback by the beauty the massive roses brought to this space. One vase overflowing with cascading buds and different varieties of the *flower of romance* filled a table in front of the balcony doors. Another, stuffed with bright red blooms, sat on a sideboard at the entrance. Coming in after an evening flight and grabbing a bite before collapsing into bed the previous day hadn't allowed Amanda to appreciate the charm of this room until the sun peeked through velvet curtains. But the morning light was no match for the golden flecks of dusk that now caressed the corners of the room and made each square inch feel mystical.

Every time Amanda had a multiple-day layover in Rome, she booked this hotel, known for its unique decor in each room. She had made her way through five of the eighteen rooms and was determined to spend at least one night in them all. This suite might now be her favorite.

She walked to the bed and saw a long, white box tied with an emerald satin bow, a basket with snacks and drinks, and an oversized blue envelope with her name written in gold calligraphy, sitting on the nightstand next to it. She hoped to find a note from her brother and sister, laced with their sordid sense of humor, which explained away the weird encounter she'd had next to the Trevi fountain. But as she opened the envelope and revealed its contents, her hope was dashed. Amanda lowered herself onto the bed to read.

"The dress is for this evening's dinner, and a mobile phone is under a small partition in the bottom of the basket. Please phone once you are dressed and ready. There's a card with the restaurant's address in the basket. Your reservations are at 8 p. m. You'll need to leave the hotel at least twenty minutes before. I look forward to our first mission together. ~ Katherine"

Amanda left the basket, turning to the box on the bed, and pulled at the fringy edge of the oversized ribbon, unraveling a knot and opening the rectangular box to reveal a floor-length gown. She had worn similar dresses for galas and award ceremonies before, but never for an evening dinner.

Her mind was a train going full steam ahead. *What the hell was going on here?* She hated not having answers. She had no interest in being a pawn in someone else's game. Every instinct told her to demand clarity, to push back against whatever cryptic path Katherine was leading her down. And yet, with no better option presenting itself, she exhaled sharply and reached for the gown.

She suddenly felt self-conscious about her appearance. Amanda Hopkins was the type of woman most people assumed would never have a moment of self-doubt, but thanks to the obligatory awkward middle school phase, she had never fully outgrown her insecurities about trying too hard.

Once the soft rose-colored satin caressed her body, her apprehension eased, at least slightly. Maybe it *was* just a prank. The sense of glamour dulled her nerves about Katherine's intentions as Amanda focused her gaze on the bathroom mirror and smiled. "Thirty, flirty, and thriving," she said with a smirk.

Ever since she could remember, she would sit and watch her mom's favorite movie, *Thirteen Going on Thirty,* not fully understanding the decade or references her mom related to, but connecting wholeheartedly to Jennifer Garner's character—an awkward young girl longing to be a woman. And now, as she stood there, she truly saw herself. It was her birthday, after all—the perfect occasion to appreciate the woman she beheld in her own reflection.

"Let's do this, I guess," she said, bolstering herself for what may lie ahead, leaning her hands on the porcelain of the bathroom sink.

As Amanda made her way through the floral archway of the rooftop bar, a rich scent of espresso and aged whiskey curled upward into the crisp Roman air. A low hum of conversation, clinking of glasses, and the warmth of candlelight surrounded her. She glanced around, scanning for the birthday dinner she had been mysteriously instructed to attend.

She spotted them before they saw her—a small eclectic mix of friends she hadn't expected to see in Rome, all gathered around a table, mid-laughter, wine glasses at each setting. Gold balloons swayed on a chair in the middle, marking a spot for the birthday girl. Her heart skipped a beat.

"Amanda!" someone called.

Suddenly, chairs scraped against the floor, and her closest friends sprang to greet her, wrapping their arms around her as they laughed, their stuttered felicitations filling the air.

"What... how?" she gasped, overwhelmed by the surprise. *"How* are you all here?"

Amanda's best friend, Lyla, grinned as she poured her a glass of wine. Always the planner, always the one who could pull off the impossible with an effortless wave of her hand. *It had been her doing,* Amanda thought.

Lyla was pretty much everyone's bestie—fun-loving and hopelessly romantic. She had spent her high school years trying to get Amanda to loosen up, dragging her to school dances, and occasionally matchmaking her with boys Amanda had zero interest in. Now, she was a powerhouse in the photography world, running one of the most successful film labs in the country, coaching aspiring photographers online, and traveling the world doing what she loved. But despite her success, she had somehow managed to stay untouched by life's harsher edges. No major heartbreaks, no real troubles. Just the kind of charmed existence that made people think of her as the luckiest person they know. And if anyone could pull off a grand surprise like this, it's Lyla. Amanda let a long sigh escape her lips.

"A little birthday magic, you could say," Lyla said with a wink as if their last-minute Roman rendezvous was completely normal.

Amanda took the offered seat, shaking her head in disbelief. She was about to demand answers when her glance landed on a man seated directly across from her.

He was handsome in a way that stirred something deep in her memory—his eyes a hypnotic swirl of gold and hazel, an easy, knowing smile, and the confidence of someone who had, perhaps, just stumbled upon fate itself.

"Amanda," he said, tilting his glass towards her. "Happy birthday... again."

She blinked, then squinted her eyes inquisitively. "Again?" Amanda was almost afraid to ask.

"You don't remember me, do you?" He chuckled, shaking his head.

Amanda frowned, studying him. There was something... familiar.

"Chicago. Four years ago. A little restaurant on Michigan Avenue. Your birthday, just like tonight. A group of friends, a lot of laughter. And me—the guy you bumped into on your way to the bathroom." He paused, watching her reaction. "Except it wasn't just a bump, was it?" he winked.

A forgotten memory churned in Amanda's mind. The dim glow of a bistro, the clink of champagne glasses, the warmth of a fleeting touch. She had turned the corner too fast, and instead of a quick apology, she had found herself caught—his hands had steadied her, fingers lingering just a second longer than necessary. They shared a quick joke—a familiar movie quote—and had laughed it off, but later, when scrolling through birthday photos, she had spotted him in the background of a candid shot, looking straight at her. The moment had stuck with her for a while, but had since become a ghost of curiosity that faded with time, and now came flickering to life again.

"Wait." Her breath came faster. "That can't be real."

He grinned. "Go ahead, check your old birthday posts. I've already checked mine."

Fingers trembling, Amanda scrolled back through years of pictures, her pulse hammering. And there it was. There *he* was, faintly silhouetted in the background—just as she had noticed all those years ago. He lifted his phone, showing his own proof: a photo of himself at that same restaurant, a friend beside him, and in the background—*her*. June, four years prior.

She looked up, stunned. "This is insane."

"I know." Tristan Montgomery leaned forward, lowering his voice until the rest of the table faded into the background. "I've called you the 'Chicago birthday girl of my dreams' ever since. And now, here you are. Again. I knew it was you when they showed me who we were meeting for dinner. The surprise was my idea."

Amanda's stomach flipped. She barely had time to process the uncanny twist of fate—the déjà vu—before Kyle's voice slid into the conversation with a hearty pat on the back, explaining their connection, why Tristan was invited, and the plans the best friends had made for the evening. But Amanda's thoughts remained stuck in the past, her mind flickering back to that night. To that moment. To him.

"Well, hello. How's that for serendipity?"

Before she had a moment to make sense of it all, a woman appeared beside their table, placing her palm on Amanda's shoulder as though they were lifelong confidants. Amanda stiffened. The woman was familiar, but not in the way old friends were. More like a passing shadow in a dream.

"Amanda, darling, happy birthday," Katherine cooed, smiling like she knew every secret Amanda had ever kept. "Aren't you just thrilled?"

Amanda glanced between Tristan, her friends, and the woman who knew more than anyone at the table could have imagined.

"Hmm, thrilled," Amanda murmured, feeling the pull of something bigger than coincidence wrapping itself around her.

"I asked you to phone me before you came," Katherine continued, voice decidedly smooth.

Amanda hesitated, then pushed back her chair, feeling inquisitive glances as she rose. "Excuse me," she smiled somewhat awkwardly at her friends, pushing herself from the table and following Katherine towards the restaurant's exit and into the hallway that led to the building below.

Katherine stopped abruptly, folding her arms. "Where is the phone I left in your hotel room?"

Amanda blinked. "The phone? I... I'm sorry... I just didn't think..."

"This isn't a joke, Amanda." Katherine's tone sharpened, her patience visibly thinning. "I told you to check in."

Amanda exhaled through her nose, feeling stirrings of unease coil in her stomach. "I forgot to check for the phone after getting dressed. It must still be in the basket. I'm sorry. When I saw my friends, I really just thought you were part of a ridiculous ploy to get me here."

"I am not." Katherine stepped closer to Amanda, lowering her voice. "Tristan Montgomery is not some casual acquaintance, a stranger whom your friends randomly decided to include in today's festivities halfway around the world. He is your mark, and I needed to speak with you before coming here." She paused, considering. "Perhaps it is better this way."

Amanda's blood ran cold. "What? Lyla said..."

Katherine's eyes flicked to the dining area before landing back on Amanda. "Now that we're here, a little background. Montgomery is a tech mogul, suspected of espionage, selling cybersecurity trade secrets under contract with the U.S. government to foreign entities. And we need eyes on him."

Amanda shook her head. "This... this can't be right. I was told..."

"You were told exactly what you needed to be told." Katherine's voice softened, but only slightly. "This birthday party, the meet-cute, the charming conversation—it's all a setup. For him."

Amanda swallowed hard. "And what exactly do you want *me* to do? My friends cannot be in on this."

Katherine paused, taking a long breath as if to communicate that her patience was wearing thin. "No, they are unsuspecting pawns. Your friends know nothing. None of them know anything for a good reason. But *you* have orders."

Amanda scoffed. "Orders?"

"Yes. You'll be the flight attendant on his private jet in three days. This is your initial introduction. Get close. Gain his trust. And don't, under any circumstances, let him know we're watching."

"His flight attendant? The least you can do is let me fly the damn plane. Are you serious?"

"Deadly," Katherine responded without elaboration.

Amanda pressed her lips together, glancing towards the restaurant's main floor where Tristan sat, laughing, oblivious. Then, back at Katherine.

"Welcome to the real game, Amanda."

"What if I don't want to *play* your games, Katherine?" Amanda sneered.

"You and I both know this isn't my game or yours. We're both in a position of weakness here. To what lengths would you go in order to protect yourself and those you love, may I ask?"

A tear bubbled up in Amanda's right eye as she swallowed the lump she felt crawling up her throat. "Anything," she whispered.

"Precisely. We both have collateral hefty enough to keep us tethered to *their* game. We're not all that different, you and I," Katherine smirked, walking to the elevator doors and disappearing behind the gliding metal while Amanda stood frozen—paralyzed by the realization that this state of confusion might be her new reality.

"Everything okay?" Lyla's voice jolted Amanda out of her reflection and into the space again.

"Oh, yes," Amanda grinned.

"Who *was* that?" Lyla asked.

"Just a woman I met earlier. I scheduled a few days for myself here, you know, the lonely cat lady on her thirty-fifth birthday trip," Amanda tried to deflect, keeping a friendly banter with her friend playful and unmysterious.

Lyla snickered, tugging on Amanda's arm, steering her towards the birthday party table again.

"We spent some time appreciating art together today, and she told me to call her again. Like, you know, she said we should meet up as if we're lifelong friends, and I couldn't possibly be enjoying myself alone. Anyway... I'm not opposed to talking to new people... I just don't know why everyone objects to my being alone so much, even strangers." Amanda continued without fully finishing a thought, unable to shake her uneasiness completely.

"Well, she is a little weird," Lyla agreed, "but she may just need a little company. She looks like the type who could use a friend." Lyla widened her grin. "Besides, do you ever think that people may just want to be around *you?* Is that so bad?" she grinned.

Amanda pulled her best friend's arm close. "It is not, not at all," she beamed. "I'm glad *you're* here."

"See?" Lyla said. "Bestie knows best," she giggled.

"I don't think that's how the saying goes," Amanda smiled.

"It's *exactly* how it goes," Lyla quipped. "Besides, how else would you have gotten to meet a perfectly gorgeous stranger on your birthday?"

Amanda stopped in her tracks. "Yeah, Lyla, but what the heck? Please tell me—how in the world did this work out?"

"Okay, so I get this crazy deal in my inbox, you know. Flights and hotel with limited dates, and I see it's during your birthday week. Plus, you had just told me that you'd be here in Rome! Like, what are the odds?"

"Super low, I think," Amanda hesitantly replied, eyes widening.

"Right?" Lyla chuckled. "So I jumped on it! And Kyle wanted to come too because who can pass up a plane ticket under fifteen hundred dollars these days? Anyway, we hopped on a plane, and here we are!"

"But… *you* didn't tell me to come here!" Amanda insisted, still trying to piece the puzzle together.

"No, that was all Tristan!" Lyla laughed.

"What?" Amanda leaned back against a bar stool, as the two friends paused on their walk back to the party.

"Yeah, he said he'd have something sent to your room as a surprise and guaranteed you'd show up. He told us all about recognizing you from Chicago, and we were like, 'What?!' Totally hooked. Like, can you imagine the love story that could come from this?"

"Lyla, I love you. I have loved you since the first day of our stupid high school speech class. But stop. I am not the romantic you are, and *how do you even know this guy?*" Amanda's voice was tense and strained.

"Hey, why are you freaking out about this? You heard Kyle talking about Tristan at the table. They have known each other for years. Kyle even knew the story of the dream birthday girl before I did. How could we have known it was you? And when we found out… wow. We thought maybe it's some kind of destiny, you know?" Lyla insisted.

"So you're saying Tristan Montgomery sent me flowers, the card instructing me to meet you all here, and…" Amanda tugged on the tiny bit of slack that was in the fabric clinging to her body, "this dress?"

"That dress was in your room?" Lyla sounded impressed. "Nice."

"Lyla, I'm serious." Amanda leaned in to whisper. "That lady you just saw... she's the one who told me there would be instructions in my room. She scared me with crazy ideas of blackmail and weird cryptic messaging."

Lyla bit her lip. "Man, he's good." She stifled a laugh.

"Okay, well. If you think so," Amanda snapped, pushing herself away from the bar and heading towards the exit.

"Wait!" Lyla protested, barely able to grab Amanda's hand as she caught up to her near the elevator. "I'm sorry. When Tristan said he'd handle it, we thought it would be romantic. Kyle happened to be chatting with him, and when he told us he'd be in Rome this week too, we just thought it would be a chance to finally have two of our closest friends meet. Since neither of you ever stays in one place long enough to cross paths, it sounded like... fate. We didn't think he'd use a scare tactic with some crazy old lady. I promise he's *such* a nice guy."

Looking at her sweet friend pleading in front of her made Amanda soften.

"And... he's rich, if that helps," Lyla raised her eyebrows facetiously.

"Always." Amanda grinned. "And you've known him for *how* long exactly?" she asked.

"I've known him for three or four years!" Lyla said. "But Kyle went to school with him."

"A Cambridge grad, huh?" Amanda could at least be impressed with that.

"I didn't say he graduated," Lyla laughed. "Tristan started his first company while they were there and left early. He's in AI or something. You know me, I don't listen to their shop talk much. They barely ever see each other, but Kyle does enjoy his calls with Tristan. They've reconnected and it's been so good for them, but I kind of keep to myself—busy just running my own little empire," she laughed.

"Okay," Amanda grinned. "At least I know I can trust *you*. If nothing else," she said, not fully accepting the whole situation.

"Of course, you can," Lyla replied, linking her arm to Amanda's and pulling her into the heart of the restaurant again. "Now, let's finish drinking the night away! You're officially up the hill, my friend."

Amanda threw her head back in an open-mouthed laugh. "Why, because my next stop is *over* the hill?"

"Yup," Lyla confirmed.

CHAPTER TWO

"Hello?" Amanda spat out a groggy whisper. Her sleepy eyes twitched open as she answered her cell phone, and the afternoon sun spilled into her room.

"Hey, sleeping beauty!" a voice on the line greeted her. "Are you up yet? It's half past noon!"

"Oh, gosh, yeah. I don't usually party like I'm twenty anymore," Amanda chuckled.

"Twenty-one, you mean, right?" Tristan joked.

"Um, sure, yeah..." Amanda said without a hint of guilt.

"Well, I for one am glad we partied like rock stars last night. I had a wonderful time getting to know you."

"Thanks, Tristan. Me too. It was a weird... and wonderful evening," she sighed.

"Even better than the first night we met," Tristan affirmed.

"I wouldn't call bumping shoulders on the way to the bathroom an introduction," Amanda grinned. "But I am glad we have now officially become friends," she said, hugging the phone close to her ear, not realizing the butterflies in her stomach had more to do with Tristan's voice than Italian wine.

"Mmm, I like that. I'm glad we're *friends.*" Tristan's voice was alight with sarcasm, tinged with suggestion. "So, what are your plans today?" he asked. "You're in town for a few more days, right? You never told me what work has brought you here to Rome, and a couple of hours surrounded by your friends was great, but I'd love to have you all to myself for a little while."

It had been years since a man had been so straightforward with Amanda. She wasn't sure if she found it attractive or pushy. But there was such smooth gentility in Tristan's voice that disarmed and practically disoriented her.

She chuckled. "Well, I don't know if I'm ready to be alone with you, Tristan Montgomery," she bantered flirtatiously, "But I do need some coffee," Amanda said, stretching her arms and legs for the first time that day. "I could meet you somewhere."

"Why don't I come to your hotel? They have a nice restaurant with perfect crepes."

"Oh gosh, nothing sweet," Amanda grimaced. "I need protein."

Tristan laughed, "Okay, then protein it is. They have lovely omelets."

"That sounds great," Amanda agreed. "But, how do you know…" her voice drifted off. Of course, he was the one who sent the gifts and the card. So, he knew *exactly* where she was. A flash of fear sent a chill down her back, but she shoved the fear to the endmost part of her mind without ever becoming conscious of it.

"How do I know what?" Tristan sounded genuinely curious.

"Oh, I was going to ask how you knew which hotel I'm staying at, and then I remembered the birthday gifts," Amanda explained.

"Gifts?" Tristan hesitated. "I did choose the most luxurious bunch of roses I could find, but I think it's generous to call it a gift," he hesitated before continuing, "I think I'd spoil you with showers of gifts if I could, though."

The way he spoke to her both took her breath away and made her skin tingly and not necessarily in a good way. It was dizzying. For Amanda, there had barely been a second thought of the handsome stranger she nudged in a narrow hallway on her birthday four years ago. For Tristan, there was almost an obsession that he may one day meet the girl he swore was the prettiest woman he'd ever seen. So, was this normal? She couldn't be sure. And why her? Was he in on this weird plot with Katherine? Was he really a mark that she was supposed to spy on, even though she's a pilot, and not a spy? She was confident in her skin most of the time, but clearly there were hundreds of beautiful women Tristan must have encountered throughout the years, so her magnetism and beauty alone couldn't be it. And isn't the way you imagine someone always better than the reality?

She swallowed hard. "Tristan," she whispered, unsure of how to respond further.

"Can you be ready in an hour?" He didn't miss a beat.

"I can be ready in thirty. I need coffee ASAP," she laughed. "If you can't be here by then, just find me in the restaurant, I'll make sure I say I'm meeting someone."

"Oh, I'll be there," Tristan said. "See you in a few."

"See you," Amanda confirmed, hanging up her phone and placing it on the bed before she sprang up to get herself dressed.

The room spun, and she caught herself, placing her hands in front of her firmly on the mattress. She took two deep breaths, glancing up at the overstuffed vase on the table by the large balcony doors. Something told her to examine the flowers. Not that she realized that's what she was doing. In her mind, she was just going to savor them. To stop and smell the real-life roses in her charming hotel room. But her subconscious intuition was screaming *inspection* rather than appreciation.

Amanda walked slowly, feeling the lightheadedness of the previous evening melt away as she continued to breathe deeply.

She approached the table, smiling at the simple beauty that roses—her favorite—brought to any space. She turned the vase to see myriad types and colors cascading from every side. The whole vase was crammed with long stems and vines, creating an opulent overflow that threatened to transport her to a dreamlike state until she stopped, noticing a card tucked in the middle. She snatched it from its crevice.

"Happy birthday, friend! You are *so* loved and appreciated. Please enjoy a dinner on us. All arrangements have been made. Love, Lyla, and Kyle."

The same small business card of the rooftop restaurant that had been in Katherine's note was inside of this folded card with the time 8 p.m. written in a blank space labeled prenotazione—the reservation.

Amanda's heart sank. She bolted to the nightstand, emptying the snacks and treats from the basket and searching for more information. She lifted a small flip phone from under a thin velvet lining as her dysequilibrium returned.

Amanda sat on the bed, contemplating what to do when her normal cell phone rang again.

"Hey, Lyla!" she spoke softly.

"Hey, girl, how are you? Did you get enough sleep?"

"Not really," Amanda grinned, trying to sound cheery.

"Yeah," Lyla laughed, "Us either! Do you have plans for the rest of the day? Kyle and I don't leave until tomorrow, and we'd love a little more time…" Lyla's voice trailed off, something that happened often. She didn't always complete her sentences, her mind moving faster than her mouth could keep up with. But Amanda barely noticed, she was used to it.

"Aw, time with lil' ole me?" she laughed. Amanda's Southern accent was strong when she wanted it to be.

"Of course! We didn't come all this way to have only one epic night," Lyla joked.

"It was pretty great, right?"

"Totally," Lyla agreed.

"But?" Amanda pressed. "I feel like there's something you're not saying, and that's not like you at all."

"Isn't that the truth?" Lyla teased. "Girl, I was just trying to give you space to blow me off if you've… you know… made plans otherwise… or if you're not currently alone. You know…" Lyla cackled.

"Oh, gosh. You know as well as I do that I am too old, wise, and mature to make the mistake of taking someone back to my room on day one!" Amanda proclaimed.

"Honey, I am old, wise, and mature enough to know that neither you nor any other human is above pretty much anything," Lyla disputed.

"Fair," Amanda snickered in agreement. She sat down, gripping the flip phone in one hand and her cell phone in the other, when she felt the burner phone vibrate and let out a ring.

"Is someone calling your room?" Lyla asked.

"Oh, yeah, it must be Tristan," Amanda thought quickly on her feet. "We're supposed to meet for coffee. I'm not even dressed. Can I call you back?"

"Sure, of course," Lyla said as Amanda hung up one phone and answered another.

"Hello...?" Amanda responded.

Silence lingered for a few seconds before Katherine spoke. "Did you enjoy your dinner?"

"Erm... Katherine?" Amanda managed to choke out a few syllables.

"Yes, Amanda. Are you ready to take me seriously?" Katherine's gravelly voice was almost soothing.

"I... I'm so confused. I don't think you have the right person for whatever job you think I'm able to do. Tristan thinks he got me to the restaurant last night, you say that you set this up for me to spy on him or something, and I feel like I'm living in a fever dream." The panic Amanda had been keeping to a slow crawl began to pick up its pace.

"Let's just call this an assessment phase. You don't need to know all the answers and explanations yet. The less you know, the better. Being yourself will serve you—and us—very well."

"And..." Amanda had to catch her breath. "Who is... 'us?'" she *had* to ask.

"Mmm," Katherine paused, "I believe you're astute enough to speculate. But it's best you don't know all the players... not yet."

"So, what do you want from me?" Amanda asked as she lifted herself from the bed again, snatching a cotton dress she had hung from the armoire and taking it into the bathroom. "I'm supposed to meet Tristan downstairs in a few minutes for coffee."

"Good. Get to know him better. It will be all the more surprising when you are the one attending his flight in a couple of days. We need him as intrigued with you as possible. If he chases you, there is no room for suspicion that you are, in fact, the one chasing him."

"Chasing? I wouldn't call it that," Amanda said. "And besides, he already remembers me from a chance encounter four years ago. I don't think we have to worry about his interest in me."

"Splendid!" Katherine sounded genuinely pleased for the first time since Amanda had crossed her path. "You'll receive your flight information later this evening."

"I was going to meet Lyla and Kyle for dinner. If I don't spend a little more time with them while they're here, it'll definitely raise suspicion," Amanda said, trying to hold the phone to her ear and brush her hair at the same time. "And this burner phone is crap. How do you even put it on speaker? I need to get ready!"

"You'll receive your permanent line in due time. And good for you, thinking about raising suspicion. You're going to be great at this, Amanda. For now, after this call, remove the SIM and take it with you. Place the phone in a rubbish bin in the hotel foyer, then discard the SIM in the restaurant toilet when you go out this evening. I'll be in touch."

"Wait, that's it?" Amanda tried to keep Katherine on the phone but heard a swift click followed by complete silence—no familiar three beeps indicating the call had ended. It immediately felt as if the conversation never happened.

She looked at herself in the mirror just as she had the evening before. "This is crazy," she said, taking a deep breath.

Amanda only had a few minutes left to brush her hair and apply a bit of powder and eye makeup to her face, so she hurriedly dashed to the bedside, moving items around to find the small crossbody purse she had exchanged her oversized bag for the night before. Thumbing through it, she moved her wallet, lip glosses, and mints, nearly convincing herself that her desired item wasn't there... until her fingers touched the unmistakable texture of glossy paper.

Amanda's high school was one of the only holdouts that insisted on continuing the art of film processing, keeping its photo lab program well into the 2000s. She and Lyla had developed the small, square photo in the photography lab themselves. They were both obsessed with watching how a nanosecond of life could be caught on camera, then slowly emerge, burning itself onto a physical piece of paper, securing a lasting place in history for those to come. Amanda's love of the skies reigned supreme, but Lyla had continued her picture-making passion into adulthood, becoming one of the first sought-after photographers to offer film photos when it became trendy again. She and Kyle built a small but well-respected operation with two lab locations where top photographers from all across the country sent their photos to be developed and printed. Amanda and Lyla's successes afforded them the luxury of staying close, no matter where in the world they landed.

Amanda grinned, looking at her young self in the photo. Most days she could barely remember that girl, but she somehow knew that was the face she carried inside herself daily. It was for her—the young, raw, unapologetic girl—that Amanda lived and breathed. She put the photo back into her purse, rushing towards the bathroom to clean up her look so she could appear as if she hadn't stayed out until 2 a.m., had more wine in one night than she usually drank in a month, and had slept into the afternoon.

"I'm sorry I kept you waiting. It took me a while to look like I didn't get much sleep," Amanda said with wide eyes and a playful tone as she greeted Tristan in the lobby.

"Oh, no trouble at all," he replied with a smooth grin, leaning in to kiss Amanda's cheek. They were in Europe, after all, and Tristan was comfortable adopting habits of the culture he was in, no matter where he went. The Montgomery family had traveled so excessively from the time he was a child that Tristan's natural mannerisms were eclectic and intriguing. He could fit in pretty much anywhere he found himself.

Tristan Montgomery was a man born into a world of privilege but carved his path through sheer brilliance and, perhaps, an insatiable hunger for approval. The son of Harold and Evelyn Montgomery, titans in the global textile industry, Tristan's childhood was a kaleidoscope of opulent boarding schools and rare moments of familial connection. His parents were often elsewhere—in Milan overseeing fabric orders, in Singapore negotiating contracts, or in New York hosting glittering charity galas that doubled as networking gold mines. He spent his childhood in the echoing halls of prestigious European academies—his days filled with fencing lessons and whispered tales of generational wealth shared among classmates who, like him, had more in common with royalty than reality.

But wealth did not mean love. His parents believed in investments, not intimacy. They poured into his education and his carefully curated future, but affection was allocated like rations of wartime. Perhaps this is why he was able to obsessively imagine that one day he'd meet a woman he encountered for only a few seconds. In most scenarios, he presented an impeccable front, but he did not measure his worth only by achievements. He longed for true love and still wanted to make as much money as possible to prove to his parents that he was worthy of it.

By the time Tristan was eight, he was known for his excellence in mathematics and coding, not the most common interest in a world preoccupied with parties and leisure. While his classmates were dissecting Nietzsche and prematurely planning exotic post-graduate gap years, Tristan was tinkering with algorithms on his second-hand laptop, a relic he'd convinced his father to let him keep rather than upgrade. Certainly, the Montgomerys could afford better, but Tristan valued the challenge of making old systems work for new ideas.

By the time he left for university, Tristan had built his first startup, a small but surprisingly lucrative e-commerce site that streamlined fabric sourcing for boutique designers. He sold it for just enough to make him realize he was good at modernizing old ways of doing business—really good. His parents were bemused by his obsession with tech, regarding it as a phase that would burn out when he inevitably returned to the family business. But he wasn't interested in cashmere or couture; he wanted to create something bigger, something lasting, something that wasn't tied to the Montgomery legacy. And, after their legal battles with Gucci, who blamed his parents for stealing design ideas and selling them to a competing brand, Tristan knew he wanted to be far away from that world.

It was during his final year at Cambridge that he met Elise. She was breathtaking. A fellow student studying international relations, with a knack for saying exactly what Tristan needed to hear. She was poised, intelligent, and understood the rules of his world. Their courtship was swift, a whirlwind of gallery openings, weekend getaways to the French Riviera, and champagne-soaked evenings discussing their inevitable futures. They married not long after graduation, a match that seemed perfect on paper. But like a suit tailored for someone else, their marriage never quite fit.

While Elise embraced the socialite lifestyle, Tristan dove headfirst into his next venture: a revolutionary platform that combined artificial intelligence with real-time data analysis, poised to redefine global security, environmental stability, and data protection. His company, Envisage, was a gamble, a high-stakes bet that consumed Tristan's every waking moment, and Elise's patience wore thin as Tristan's obsession grew. She'd married a man who promised a life of luxury and leisure, but what she got was a husband who worked through dinners, missed vacations, and rarely looked up from his screens. By the time Envisage secured its first round of venture capital, their marriage was already unraveling.

Now, at thirty-six, Tristan stood on the precipice of a historic deal—the sale of Envisage to a global tech conglomerate for a staggering sum that would officially cement him as one of the wealthiest men in the world. The divorce papers had been filed over a year ago, though details were still being hammered out. Elise, ever the strategist, was angling for a settlement that would keep her in the lifestyle she believed she deserved. Tristan couldn't pinpoint when it happened, but for his part, he was resigned. Money didn't matter to him anymore; what mattered was freedom—freedom from his past, from his mistakes, and perhaps from himself.

It was a lot to roll over in his head as he sat at a discreet corner table in the lobby of the hotel, waiting for Amanda. She was unlike anyone he'd encountered—he could tell after only thirty seconds with her that very first night in Chicago. And this time, meeting her—spending time with her—he believed that his dream girl was a possibility now more than ever. She wasn't part of his world, not really. She was witty, self-assured, and had a way of looking at him that made him feel seen—truly seen—like he hadn't in a very long time, if ever.

Tristan could admit that he was intense and impulsive, but he didn't consider himself to be the kind of man who believed in love at first sight. But with Amanda? She had a magnetism that drew him in. When they exchanged numbers, he'd found himself texting her even after they said their middle-of-the-night goodbyes—their exchanges a mix of light banter and deeper confessions. He hadn't had time to tell her everything, of course. She didn't know about the marriage, divorce, or the impending business deal that would catapult his name into international headlines. For now, he liked the anonymity, the idea that she saw him as just Tristan, not Tristan Montgomery, heir to a textile conglomerate and soon-to-be tech mogul.

"How much time do we have—should we sit at the bar?" he asked, flawlessly transitioning from his kiss on Amanda's cheek to subtly slipping his hand to her waist.

Amanda's heart warmed. There was no awkwardness to his touch. He didn't linger, just lightly brushed her back, a natural gesture for any couple watching out for each other. Heat rose from her chest, filling her face as she glanced and smiled at him, accepting the invitation.

"Let's get a table, don't you think?" she wanted a little more time—and privacy—than the bar could afford.

"Sure," Tristan agreed, pleased with the idea. "I don't want to impose on your time..."

"Oh, yes, you do," Amanda flirted with a giggle. She could already feel how good she was at the only part of the game she was currently expected to play.

She was a little—okay, a *lot*—weirded out by Tristan's recognition of her, and apparent fixation on her... or the *idea* of her. But she was also intrigued and attracted to him, and she could use this to get very close to him.

As their conversation ricocheted from travel to favorite books to the absurdities of modern life and back again, Tristan found himself leaning in, drawn to Amanda's easy laugh and the way her eyes lit up when she talked about her passions. For the first time in years, he felt a spark of something he couldn't quite name. It wasn't like his usual musings of infatuation. It was... hope, maybe. Tristan felt an almost sadistic comfort in the tension of longing—the familiar ache of waiting for the day he'd meet this dream girl—talk to her, touch her. It was a hammering cadence he had grown used to. And hope wasn't what drove him; it was angst—an anxious energy with no outlet. But now, facing her in the flesh left him unmoored, struggling to find a place to store this unfamiliar sensation.

Amanda was caught in her own internal struggle. She hadn't even been briefed on Tristan's life, his accomplishments, his strengths, or his weaknesses. She had no idea the depths of what either of them had to gain or ultimately lose. But sitting across from him, looking into his eyes, she knew she couldn't allow emotions to get in the way and underestimate him—or herself.

The warm afternoon stretched into dusk as the city's glow cast shifting patterns on the walls. Neither of them knew what lay ahead, but for now, in this moment, they were just two people, caught in a gravitational pull of something that felt bigger than either of them could explain.

Chapter Three

Amanda sat stiffly, hands clenched in her lap in the dimly lit room, her back straight and her eyes fixed on the woman across from her. Katherine exuded an effortless elegance that only deepened Amanda's emerging resentment. Dressed in a tailored navy suit with a silk scarf knotted loosely at her throat, Katherine sipped her tea as though they were old friends catching up rather than what Amanda considered to be adversaries, locked in a game she didn't understand.

Amanda had said her goodbyes to Lyla and Kyle with only twenty-four hours left of her stay in Rome—at least, that was her assumption. Katherine had already told her she'd be given a flight schedule, and she was now instructed to come to a small, beautifully decorated office housed in a three-hundred-year-old building.

"Let's go over this again," Katherine said crisply, placing her cup down with calculated precision. "Smile. Always."

Amanda mockingly gave a toothy grin, but Katherine was unflappable. She—though Amanda didn't know it yet—had every last detail of the strategy memorized. And even though she, too, was a pawn in the schemes her bosses had crafted to gain and retain as much political and social power as possible, Katherine had secured herself a place among the top players. Not the kind that came with trust and respect, but the kind that came from being overlooked. What threat could an older woman be among so many powerful men? They assumed she was loyal simply because they didn't bother to question her. While they played their games, she played hers. Although she couldn't show it, not yet, she had a deep compassion for Amanda, knowing all too well what the young woman's fate could be if she didn't get this right.

"Make him feel like he is the only person in the world. That's your power here. This already comes naturally to you. Lean into your friendly nature," Katherine continued. "There's a reason women are so good at the art of persuasion. You are naturally nurturing, caring, warm... though you may not be displaying those qualities at this moment."

Amanda's jaw tightened. "You do realize I'm a pilot, not a waitress, right?"

Katherine's lips curved into a smile that did not reach her eyes. "And yet, here we are. If you want answers, Amanda, you'll have to play the part. We don't need to be friends here. But I do need you to trust me just a little. You must blend into the world of luxury—be the invisible hand guiding billionaires' whims and desires," Katherine said.

The idea made Amanda's stomach churn. She had spent years working towards her career as a pilot, breaking barriers and earning her stripes in a field dominated by men. She had been battle-tested in the cockpit, a place she felt secure and calm. Rubbing shoulders with the rich, sure, but never having to spend more time than absolutely necessary with them. And now, she was reduced to pouring champagne and fluffing pillows, following Tristan Montgomery around? He was a charming and seemingly gentle man, yes, but nonetheless—a man. And she hated the idea of ensnaring him in some kind of seductress trap or becoming a trophy girlfriend even if it was a temporary role she was playing.

"You could at least tell me what this is about," Amanda said, her voice low but insistent. "Why him? Why me?"

Katherine's expression softened, but only slightly. "Curiosity is natural, but it's a distraction. Your job is to observe, Amanda. Learn everything you can about Montgomery. The rest will make sense in time. Be curious only about the whats and hows, never the whys."

Amanda dropped her head, taking in a deep breath. It wasn't a sign of resignation; it was contemplation. She sped through ideas in her mind, searching for a way out. What was the worst that could happen? That working with Katherine would pull her back into a life she swore she left behind? That her past, the one she had spent years outrunning, would finally catch up?

Hers may have seemed like a glamorous, jet-setting life, but Amanda knew the truth. Every time she boarded a plane, it wasn't just about adventure; it was escape. Another opportunity to take her troubles to the skies and never look down.

She glanced at Katherine again, determining that she'd acquiesce and give this one flight a go, but then she'd reassess. If the risks were too many, Amanda Hopkins knew how to take off—*that* was for sure.

Over the next few hours, the two women continued their training, an exhausting regimen of etiquette lessons, service techniques, and simulated scenarios. Amanda loathed every moment, but beneath her frustration, she felt a growing sense of determination. If Katherine thought she could manipulate Amanda, she was wrong. Amanda would play along, for now. But she was already constructing her own strategies on how to turn the tables.

A private jet idled on the tarmac of Rome's Ciampino Airport, its sleek silver exterior gleaming in the early morning sun. Amanda adjusted her uniform, a crisp white blouse and tailored navy skirt, as she forced herself to smile while the first passenger boarded. She'd been briefed on the manifest: three executives, a personal assistant, and one enigmatic entrepreneur who was running late—Tristan Montgomery.

When he stepped onto the plane, Amanda's breath hitched. He paused at the threshold, his sharp hazel eyes scanning the cabin before they landed on her. For a moment, he looked as though he'd seen a ghost.

"Amanda?" he choked, his voice tinged with disbelief.

She held his gaze, her practiced smile unfaltering. "Welcome aboard, Mr. Montgomery."

It took him a moment to recover. "I didn't realize... this is what you do."

"You never asked," she replied, her tone light but guarded.

Tristan took his seat, his mind racing. They'd spent hours talking about philosophy, music, and books, sharing thoughts and ideas that felt more intimate than any physical attraction. But Amanda had been vague about her career, deflecting his questions with a charming laugh or a clever quip, telling him she was in hospitality, something he assumed she was slightly embarrassed about—never realizing that luxury flight attendant would be on the list of occupations in the field. Now, here she was, in the midst of his circle, something to which he assumed she had never been exposed.

As the jet ascended, Amanda moved through the cabin, performing her duties with a professionalism that belied her inner turmoil. She could feel Tristan's eyes on her, his curiosity tangible. It wasn't just surprise she saw in his expression, it was something deeper, something that made her stomach flip in a way she didn't want to acknowledge. Regardless of her attraction and his charm, she was determined to keep her focus on getting herself out of this mystifying situation.

Amanda adjusted the cuffs of her uniform, still getting used to the fit. Katherine had assured her the paperwork was handled, and that no one would question her assignment. It wasn't unusual for a flight attendant to be assigned to a new crew without introductions, especially in private aviation—crew rotations, quick hires, and discretion were all part of the game. Still, she couldn't shake the feeling that she was playing a role, and sooner or later, someone might start asking questions.

By the time they reached cruising altitude, Tristan couldn't resist any longer. He caught her by the galley, his voice low. "Amanda, what is this? Why didn't you tell me you worked as a flight attendant?"

Amanda's heart pounded as her eyes met his. "Because it didn't matter."

"It does now," he said, his intensity making her pulse speed faster. "It matters because I think… I think I've met the woman I've been looking for."

Amanda's breath caught. These explosive feelings, his irresistible appeal, weren't part of the plan. She couldn't let herself get drawn into his orbit—not when she was intent on getting out of Katherine's web. But as she looked into his eyes, she felt the fragile walls she'd built around her heart begin to fracture.

She forced a smile and stepped back. "Enjoy the flight, Mr. Montgomery. This is, in fact, my job here," she smiled coyly, pressing his shoulder with her fingers, indicating she expected him to move, and pulling off the most convincing act of her life.

Tristan watched her go, his mind racing. Destiny had a strange way of working, and for a man astutely in command of every other aspect of his life, this repeated serendipitous encounter just had to be a sign. He kept his cool, naturally, returning to his seat, but his imagination ran wild.

"Can I get you another drink, Mr. Montgomery?" Amanda offered just moments later. The other guests weren't ignored, but the attention she gave Tristan didn't go unnoticed.

He smiled, "Sure. I'll just take a Coke."

"Certainly," Amanda grinned as she turned to another seat. "And you, Mr. Cavanagh? Can I get you something?" She continued in her duties but her mind raced as she felt Tristan's eyes searing through her uniform, making the warmth of her skin almost uncomfortable. As she turned around to see Tristan's unhidden stares, she blushed. "Those will be right out," she nodded.

As Amanda walked through the airplane aisle, Tristan visualized following her, pressing himself up against her in the tight quarters of the galley, and kissing her passionately.

As many times as Tristan had fantasized about meeting his birthday dream girl, he hadn't obsessed over explicitly sexual encounters—at least, not in his waking hours. His fantasies had always been wrapped in romance—sex felt elusive and almost unattainable with this impossibly perfect woman. He'd imagine a serendipitous reunion in another dimly lit restaurant, a lingering touch at a music festival as they bonded over an obscure band. But now, with her this close, his mind started to daydream about how her lips might taste, how her breath might catch if he touched her the way he ached to.

And he couldn't have known that Amanda's thoughts were slipping in the same direction. That, for just a second, she let herself imagine his hands on her—firm, demanding—the heat of his body pressed to hers, how easy it would be to close the space between them and forget everything else.

Mild turbulence made the jet bounce midair unexpectedly—nothing concerning, but enough to jostle Amanda and Tristan both out of their reverie. Amanda went back to work, passing out drinks, collecting dishes, offering refreshments, and otherwise staying out of the guests' way before preparing for landing.

From her seat in the cabin, she adjusted her scarf and double-checked her poised smile in the mirrored panel beside her. The entire flight had been a delicate dance of avoidance and allure, Tristan Montgomery's gaze lingering on her every time she stepped into view. She touched up her lipstick, remaining nonchalant. Her heart, however, was far from calm.

The plane touched down smoothly on the runway of Athens International Airport as the city bathed in the golden glow of a setting sun. Noisy engines began to power down, passengers began gathering their belongings, and Amanda moved through the cabin, thanking each of them as they disembarked. Tristan was the last to rise from his seat. He moved slowly—as if savoring every moment in her presence.

"Thank you for an excellent flight," he said when he reached her, his voice warm but laced with a deep, unspoken seduction that she recognized from their few short hours together.

"Just doing my job," Amanda shrugged with a polite smile, stepping aside to let him pass.

He didn't move. "It wasn't just a flight, Amanda. Not for me. This has to be a sign," he whispered.

Her stomach twisted. She knew this was coming, but it still threw her off balance. Katherine's instructions echoed in her mind: *Keep him intrigued. Keep him wanting more.*

"And... you believe in signs?" she teased, jovially.

"Not before I met you," Tristan said genuinely. "Never."

"Mr. Montgomery, I'm sure you've had many flights like this one," she said, deliberately repeating his formal title.

He smiled at her deflection, his sharp eyes lighting with amusement. "Stop calling me that. You can call me Tristan, even while working. And no, Amanda, I haven't had flights like this. Nor have I met anyone quite like you, and you know it."

She let out a soft, practiced laugh, shaking her head. "You're impossible, you know that?"

"Perhaps," he admitted with a shrug. "But I'm also persistent."

The rest of the crew filed out behind them, leaving Amanda and Tristan standing alone in the luxurious cabin. Outside the window, a ground crew was preparing to escort him to his waiting car.

"Okay, then, I hope Athens treats you well," Amanda said, making a move to grab her bag and exit the aircraft.

But Tristan gently caught her wrist, his touch light but commanding enough to stop her in her tracks. "Come out with me again tonight."

Amanda turned to face him, her mind racing. She was supposed to build the kind of rapport that would open doors, both figuratively and literally. But part of her wanted to refuse, to take back some measure of control. And maybe playing hard to get would be more effective anyway.

"I can't," she said softly.

His grip loosened, but his gaze didn't waver. "Why not?"

She hesitated. "I'm scheduled to be in London within 24 hours. I don't have the time."

"I'll make sure you're at the airport in time for your next flight," he promised, his voice low and convincing. "Just a few hours, Amanda. That's all I'm asking. That's all I seem to get with you anyway."

She pretended to consider, knowing she'd have to say yes eventually.

Finally, she sighed. "Alright. A few hours. But if I miss my flight..."

"You won't," Tristan interrupted, a victorious smile spreading across his face. "I promise."

Two hours later, Amanda found herself slipping into a black evening dress Katherine had insisted she bring, just in case. It was less intimidating than the first time Katherine dictated what she wore. The thin fabric hugged her figure in a way that felt both empowering and exposing, and she wasn't sure whether that unsettled her more or less than it did the first time. She was uneasy but didn't blame Katherine for it. If anything, she was irritated with herself for how easily she had been drawn in—how quickly she said *yes*, how naturally she played along. And maybe, deep down, she knew how much she hated the insatiably curious part of herself that *wanted* to.

Tristan had arranged for a car to pick Amanda up from her hotel, a sleek black sedan that glided through Athen's bustling streets. When she arrived at the restaurant—another rooftop spot, this time overlooking the Acropolis—he was already waiting, dressed in a shiny dark olive suit that looked as effortless as it was expensive.

"You look stunning," he said as she approached, standing to pull out her chair.

"Thank you," she replied, keeping her mannerisms light. "You don't look too bad yourself."

As they settled in, the city stretched out before them, a glittering sea of lights. The air was warm, carrying the faint scent of grilled lamb, oregano, and citrus from the bustling kitchen. Tristan had ordered champagne that the waiter immediately poured in two flutes lined with mandarin slices and berries.

Tristan lifted his glass. "So why didn't you ever tell me you were a private flight attendant?" he said as they sipped.

"Because you never asked," Amanda replied, her lips curving as if she enjoyed the suspense.

"I suppose I didn't," he admitted, his gaze steady. "But I can't help but feel like there's even more mystery to you than you let on." Tristan squinted his eyes towards her with a tilt of his head.

"Is that so?" she asked, arching a brow.

He nodded. "You're intelligent, well-read, and clearly not easily impressed, sadly for me," he tipped his glass towards her with an animated grin. "You don't fit the mold of someone who simply pours drinks and smiles on command, though. I find you perplexing, Amanda Hopkins."

Her heart skipped a beat, watching the bubbles in her glass rise to the surface and pop miniature splashes of golden liquid into the air. He was perceptive, far more than she'd anticipated. She could only hope that he couldn't sense her discomfort, not with him, but with being forced to carry a secret while wanting nothing more than to inch closer to him.

"Maybe I just enjoy keeping people guessing," she said, raising another sip of the wine to her lips.

"Then you're very... *very* good at it," Tristan replied, leaning back in his chair with a faint smile.

"Did you know they call us *V*-VIP attendants onboard?" Amanda said, emphasizing the first "V" with a smirk, deflecting any unease that threatened to invade the evening.

"Is that so?" Tristan teased, repeating the same phrase Amanda had used with him. Having been part of an elite class throughout his childhood, he did in fact know this tidbit, but he played along.

She chuckled quickly, almost spitting the champagne's airy fizz through her nose. "It *is* so," she managed, barely finishing her swallow. She continued speaking but switched to a scholarly-sounding proper tone. "Apparently, there are far too many very important people in the world nowadays, so when you obtain the lofty qualification of having more money than the posers who splurge on a fancy trip now and then, there's no more fitting description than very-*very.*" Amanda let her cynical flare take over. She figured if she was going to play the part, she might as well bring her personality to it.

Tristan was the one about to lose his composure now. He flung his head back with a hearty gut laugh. "And what would you label these very, *very* important people if not VVIPs?" he asked.

"Hmm..." Amanda contemplated for a moment. "I don't think I've ever thought about that."

"Oh, that's surprising. C'mon. I mean, if you voice a critique, you have to at least come up with a correction," Tristan insisted. "Very distinguished, important people?" he offered.

"Um, VDIP?" Amanda's eyes widened. "That sounds like 'venereal disease in people,'" she giggled.

"Oh my," Tristan laughed. "See? That's why I asked you."

Amanda leaned back in her chair, feigning deep thought. "So, you know how we have government acronyms like PO-TUS and FLOTUS, and who knows all the different code names they have, especially for royals?"

Tristan nodded, happy to be listening to her playful commentary.

"Well, I think we should just be informed that we have a 'POP' manifest on our hands—people of power... but I guess that wouldn't work for royalty since they're just helpless figureheads anyway," she quipped with a short laugh.

"Okay," Tristan nodded, elongating the word and taking a beat. His eyes narrowed as he contemplated his next question, making Amanda squirm in her seat. She wondered if she'd gone too far and put him off. "So, you're into politics?" Tristan asked, hoping to bring the conversation into focus. He may have been smitten, but he was also aware that he needed to be pragmatic if he was going to invite her into his life.

"No," Amanda said with a convincing inflection that diffused any tension. "I just have a general disdain for manipulation and coercion."

The answer was unexpected, and Tristan's face reflected his puzzlement. "Go on," he said, crossing his arms over his chest.

"Okay, take the royals, for example. It's not like they have a choice. Or at least not without devastating consequences. Say what you will about Meghan and Harry and their fortunes, but that guy risked a lot to leave the constraints of the palace. I don't think people give him enough credit."

Tristan wrestled with the words before letting them slip from his mouth. "But there is a reason we don't have a royal family in the States."

"Sure, that's true..." Amanda paused.

"I'm sensing a *but.*" Tristan tilted his head, anticipating that she had an opinion about politics despite her claim.

"Well, to be honest, I don't love our system either." In the few minutes they had been sitting, and on an empty stomach, Amanda had been sipping enough champagne to loosen any restraint on her authentic self. There was a reason her friends in college called her the biggest lightweight they'd ever known. Standing at five foot nine and not being able to knock back two drinks before feeling buzzed made Amanda mindful of her alcohol intake from the time she was in her early twenties.

"I know I'm privileged. It doesn't take making millions to know that most people in the world don't have the opportunity to accomplish what I've achieved, despite my humble upbringing. But... the way the rich and mighty rule the world... the way the one-percenters live," she said with a clear shift in emotion before catching herself. "Um... no offense," Amanda paused.

Tristan leaned in. "None taken. You can be yourself around me, Amanda. I know I've come on strong, but it's just because

I want to get to know you. The *real* you, not some woman I've been dreaming about for the past four years…"

Amanda cut him off. "Yeah, about that… I don't know what to do with that, either. You insisted on being the one to arrange for me to come to my birthday dinner. You told my friends the story about me in Chicago so they would buy into the idea and romanticize the situation, making it almost impossible for me to say no… and…"

Now Tristan cut *her* off. "Manipulation and coercion…" he said in nearly a whisper.

Amanda shrugged. "It could seem that way." She didn't expound, genuinely impressed that he was at least *listening* to the words she was using.

The right side of Tristan's mouth curled upward as he brought a fingernail to his teeth. Since he'd broken the habit of sucking his thumb as a child—a coping practice he adopted after he was sent to boarding school at six years old—he had learned to keep his right thumbnail just long enough to wedge it between the tiny gap in his lower molars. He wouldn't chew on it, just gently press the nail plate between his teeth and into his gums. It was a habit that Tristan was completely unaware of, though anyone who knew him intimately would readily name it as one of his many idiosyncrasies.

Amanda let the silence stretch for over a minute.

"So you're *really* saying you're not into politics," Tristan finally said.

Amanda cackled. "Uh, no. I admit to having opinions, but they're usually the kind I keep to myself. So… let's just say I'm not."

She kept her tone lighter than her feelings, careful not to let anything too sharp slip through.

"Good," Tristan said, his smile easy. "I've got too many intertwining relationships with these so-called people of power to have much of an opinion about parties and political schemes these days. I just want to get my work out into the world. That's the only agenda I have."

He sounded sincere. And maybe he was. But Amanda couldn't ignore the faint suggestion beneath his words—the kind of practiced charm people use when they've learned how to make complicated things sound simple. Even though she was astutely aware of Tristan's ability to persuade, she still *wanted* to believe him.

Their conversation flowed easily, moving from art to philosophy to the best places to eat in Paris. Amanda laughed more than she expected, genuinely enjoying his company despite the shadow of a clandestine mission looming over her.

As the night sky settled into blackness, showcasing amber tones from the city's flickering lights, Tristan knew Amanda would have to get back to her hotel and rest before too long.

"I feel like I've spent my whole life looking for something," he said, his voice quieter now. "Or someone."

Amanda's breath caught, her pulse picking up speed again. She was aware enough to stop drinking after they had finished the first bottle of champagne, but Tristan had ordered another two glasses of red with his entré. Amanda knew he was being more emphatic than he would be when sober, so she decided to simply receive his words with a smile.

For a brief, reckless second, Amanda let herself imagine what it would be like to be free—to not have Katherine's shadow hanging over her. To be obligated to lie and manipulate. To perhaps, instead, lean into this man and his world instead of scrutinizing and betraying it. The irony that she was preaching about her revulsion to manipulation while trying to get close to her mark was not lost on her. And when the moment passed, reality came crashing back.

She glanced at her watch, breaking the spell. "I should go. My flight..."

"I know," Tristan said, his voice reluctant. "But thank you for tonight."

As he escorted her to the car that had been waiting, his hand brushing hers, lingering for just a moment, his words came hushed like a summer breeze. "Safe travels, Amanda," he said as the driver opened the door for her.

She simply nodded, this time initiating a kiss on the cheek herself, saying goodbye, and slipping inside the car. As they pulled away, Amanda watched Tristan through the window, his figure growing smaller in the distance.

For the first time since Katherine had approached her, Amanda felt the weight of what she was doing—not just the danger she was in but the betrayal she would have to inflict.

Because, whether she liked it or not, she was starting to care.

Chapter Four

"Welcome to London," Katherine said, her voice smooth and authoritative. "Your new home."

Amanda had stepped off the train at St. Pancras International, her heels clicking sharply against the polished platform tiles. A chill in the London air bit at her cheeks, a stark contrast to the warmth of Athens. She pulled her jacket tighter around her as Katherine appeared at her side, a sharp figure in a tailored trench coat and heels that looked more like weapons than footwear.

"Thanks?" she said more like a question, reflexively following Katherine to a vintage black Rolls-Royce, its chrome details catching the streetlights. Amanda was surprised to be in a vehicle that would draw so much attention. But that was something she was learning about Katherine—nothing about her was unnoticeable. She was extremely distinct in every way, embodying the old trope of hiding in plain sight. The drive through the city was a blur of landmarks and bustling streets, though Amanda's thoughts were spinning too fast to register any scenery.

The car pulled up in front of an elegant high-rise in the heart of downtown London. "Ms. Harrington," the doorman greeted Katherine with a polite nod before stepping aside to let them enter, but not before offering to take Amanda's roller bag and have it sent to her room.

Harrington? Amanda thought. She filed this surname in her mind for later. A suspicion about aliases hadn't occurred to her until now. "Oh, thank you," Amanda answered the doorman and released her grip on the handle when Katherine's nod of approval met her glance.

A young man appeared, taking the bag in a motion that seemed poetic and reminiscent of stage crews dressed in black, removing props when the lights go down. Everpresent yet veiled. As the gold-framed glass doors slowly came to a close behind them, Katherine ushered Amanda into a lobby lined with polished marble and gleaming gold trim. Ornate grooves glistened in the light of the art deco elevator doors as they belaboredly rolled open.

"This is stunning," Amanda remarked.

"Mmm," Katherine nodded. "This building was designed by Shreve, Lamb & Harmon in the early 1940s. They were the ones who designed the Empire State Building as well. Not as historic as some other structures in this area, but you're

American, so I think you'll appreciate its history as much as anyone." Katherine said. She did not intend the comment to be a slight, but it definitely came out like one.

Amanda rolled her eyes. She was accustomed to being judged for her Americanisms throughout the world. Not that it was all bad—it wasn't. Most people expected her to be friendly, tip well, laugh a lot, and speak only one language. All things which were true and not bad or completely embarrassing. She was proud of her distinctly American openness and candor, but times were certainly changing, and the notion that she was uninformed, inexperienced, or both simply because she's from Tennessee, was enough to get under her skin in a hot second. Plus, she *did* hope to learn Italian fully someday, so there was that. And Duo Lingo wasn't quite doing the trick for her.

"I'm glad you like it because this is where you'll be living." Katherine gestured as the elevator opened at the penthouse floor.

The metal doors slid open, revealing a space out of the pages of an interior design magazine. Floor-to-ceiling windows offered a panoramic view of the city skyline, and the sleek furnishings were a study in muted luxury—cool grays, deep blues, and turquoise—a nod to the art deco era of the place's origin—and soft whites with a smattering of natural woods as accents.

"There are a few documents on the desk," Katherine said, gesturing towards a table in the corner of the open-concept living room. "Take a moment to familiarize yourself."

Amanda inched towards the table, taking in her surroundings before picking up the folder waiting for her. Inside were papers devoid of any logos, addresses, or identifiable markers. A contract that was chillingly efficient in its ambiguity outlined her employment as "Special Operations Personnel" under a generic corporate header. Page after page, Amanda read agreements of mandatory checkpoints, training specifications, and details of a foreign bank account in her name, complete with an initial deposit that made her head spin.

She flipped over the last page, revealing a new international ID underneath. Her photo stared back at her, but the name printed underneath wasn't hers.

"You'll go by that name when necessary," Katherine spoke from behind her.

Amanda turned, holding up the ID. "What? You didn't say I have to go undercover."

"You don't. Not yet. But *when necessary*. As I said," Katherine emphasized the same words she just used.

"But... why do I need anonymity? Is this even legal?" Amanda pressed, feeling the path behind her fading and only uncertainty ahead.

Katherine's lips curved into a faint grin. "Legalities are *flexible* in our line of work, Amanda. The less you're tied to your old life, the better. It's for your safety—and ours."

Amanda felt a cold sweat threaten to arise every time she heard Katherine use the words "us" or "ours." She tried to keep her curiosity to a minimum, but how was she supposed to handle all the mystery around her without at least attempting to unravel it?

"But I've gone by my real name with Tristan... if he's the mark and he already knows who I *really* am..." her voice trailed off. "This isn't about him, is it?" Amanda said with a jolt of realization. "He's not the target, he's the bait! His company... he said that it's going public, and there's a crazy deal about to be made. He's as much of a pawn as I am in this, isn't he?"

Amanda felt her stomach bubble as she sat staring at Katherine, waiting for a response, but Katherine's glassy-eyed grin added to her fear with a chill that raced up her spine.

"Tristan Montgomery is far from an innocent pawn, Amanda. But good for you. You'll likely have a few more goes at it before *all* the puzzle pieces fit, but I have faith in you," she said, pausing momentarily. "And watch yourself, you may even grow to enjoy working with me," Katherine smirked. "I need to take this paperwork back to headquarters signed, so if you don't mind..." she continued, tapping on the table.

Amanda wanted to argue, but she knew it was pointless—for now. She wagged her head in disbelief, picked up the pen, and left her inky signature on every line bearing her printed legal name.

"Rest up tonight," Katherine said after Amanda had scribbled her initials on the last blank space. She snatched the papers from the table, placed them back in the folder, waving it in her hand. "You'll need your strength for tomorrow."

Without another word, Katherine pivoted on her heels and walked to the elevator door, disappearing behind the golden metal.

Amanda sat silently for a few moments before she took a breath and made her way around her new residence. She figured she might as well familiarize herself with her new downtown apartment. "I'll have to get used to calling it a *flat,*" she muttered, amused with herself. Two of her favorite colleagues were British women she shared an apartment with in flight school. They constantly teased each other over vocabulary differences and made a habit of exchanging favorite native candies and novelty foods from their respective countries whenever possible. She could see herself settling in London just fine.

Amanda approached the kitchen, finding a fully stocked fridge with all her favorites. It was remarkable how little she was surprised by this. By now, she knew Katherine to be a fastidious secret agent who made sure that every detail was covered. Taking a bottle of Chardonnay from the wine compartment, she immediately spied glasses hanging on an open shelf to her left and poured herself a glass.

Savoring every sip, she walked from the open area into a bedroom that felt more like a spa than everyday living quarters. Another wall of glass spanned from the left of the massive oak headboard to the built-in closets. An opening led to a marble-lined bathroom that was almost as large as her bedroom back home. Amanda wondered how much time she would actually be spending here since Katherine had told her London would only be her home base. Even though she was used to a life on the move, she was almost sad that she'd likely not be spending more than a few nights at a time here.

"Geez!" Amanda jumped when she felt her phone buzz in her back pocket. "Hello?" she answered.

"Hey, girl! I'm glad I caught you." Lyla's chipper voice warmed Amanda's heart every time she heard it.

"Hey! What's up?"

"Oh, nothing really. I was just checking in on you. I haven't heard from you since we got back from Rome, and that's not like you," Lyla said.

"Oh, yeah, it's been back-to-back flights. You know the drill." Amanda tried to keep it light.

"Okay, yeah, of course," the worry in Lyla's voice eased. "Good... I don't know... I just... don't want you to be upset about us pushing Tristan on you. I thought about what you said, and I was just like... yeah... maybe we were a little inconsiderate."

"It's okay, Lyla, honestly. I... um... I actually spent some more time with him after you left."

"Wait. What? Okay, spill." Lyla was here for it.

"I mean, there's not a lot to tell," Amanda chuckled. "I just happened to be on his flight from Rome to Athens and..."

Lyla interrupted, "Um, I'm sorry, what? How did that happen? Like, you piloted his jet?"

"Not exactly..." Amanda attempted to reply, but Lyla didn't skip a breath.

"What are the stinkin' odds of this, Amanda? If you don't believe in destiny, then let me have enough faith for us both. I mean, hall-e-lujah," Lyla guffawed.

"Oh my gosh, Lyla, seriously." Amanda got caught up in the infectious laugh of her bestie. "Stop... I mean... there's something I've been meaning to tell you, okay?"

"Oh my god, you're pregnant."

"Oh, for the love..." Amanda's exasperated voice let Lyla know she literally *was* trying to be serious.

"Okay, okay, sorry. You know, one of these days it's gonna be true," Lyla tried to joke.

To any other friend, Amanda would have volleyed back the comment, "You first," in jest, but for Lyla, it would cut too deeply. She and Kyle had been trying to get pregnant for at least three years after having put off family planning in their twenties, thinking they'd have plenty of time to form their ideal life later. And while most of their friends were well into their family-establishing years with two or three kids each, Lyla and Kyle were the couple who promised each other they didn't need more, but each night went to bed in silence, dreaming of what it would be like to be a parent.

Amanda knew it helped Lyla to treat the subject with humor, but she could still sense the searing pain behind her friend's words.

"Yeah, someday it might, but not today," Amanda replied. She didn't have the heart to repeatedly discuss that the last thing she wanted to do in life was bring a child into her mess when talking to her best friend in the world.

"Okay, so what is it? No other news will knock my socks off." Her remark was dipped in a crisp layer of charm like a late frost, hiding the delicate interior of an unprepared petal.

"No," Amanda matched her friend's tone. "I just thought that since you guys know Tristan, and now I know Tristan... I should tell you that I wasn't exactly flying his plane... I've made a bit of a shift in my vocation."

"A bit of a shift in your vocation?" Lyla parroted back with a sarcastic flare. "What do you mean? Are you going commercial again?"

"God, no," Amanda snorted. "I've actually shifted to being an attending crew member for a luxury service company..." she elongated the last word, bracing herself for Lyla's response.

"What?" Lyla said, truly unable to grasp what Amanda was saying. "When you say the attending crew... do you mean flight attendant?"

"Yeah," Amanda grimaced, hoping Lyla couldn't hear it in her voice.

"But why?" Lyla asked.

A long pause hung in the air. Amanda couldn't think of an excuse to give Lyla. She wanted to spill her guts. To yell into the phone, "I'm being blackmailed and held against my will!" but she was afraid, and rightfully so, that her original number was being tracked and recorded.

"They offered me a lot of money for much less stress," she lied, knowing that no flight attendant's salary could match what she made as a pilot, but hoping she sold it well enough for Lyla to believe.

"Well, *that's* weird. I don't know what company has that kinda money," Lyla said.

"Oh, there are a few. These billionaires..." Amanda tried to sound like she knew what she was talking about. "They want to have skilled people on board who could, like, fly the plane in case of emergency. We're hosting some of the richest people in the world, you know?" Amanda said. *That sounded totally believable, right?* she thought.

"Dude, that's crazy." Lyla had no reason to think her friend was making up a story. "I guess I never would have thought of that. Flight attendants who are backup pilots? Geez."

"Yeah, it's a whole different world than when I first started flying," Amanda sighed, relieved to have been able to make up a quick excuse. "So... anyway... Tristan was on one of the flights, literally my second one with this company! That's why I haven't even really had time to tell you. When they approached me with the idea... it all came on *so* fast."

And *that* wasn't a lie.

Up before dawn, Amanda was sitting in a plush chair facing the wall of windows overlooking the city, watching the sunrise pass the London skyline while she sipped a morning cappuccino.

A ding of the elevator startled her as Katherine stepped into the apartment, and soon appeared behind her.

"So, I'm to expect no privacy at all?" Amanda stared daggers at Katherine.

"I texted you," Katherine replied. *"Always* have your phone, Amanda," she instructed. "There is no room for idle moments. Not while you're in training."

"Training? Is that what this is?" Amanda scoffed.

"Indeed. Now, be ready in ten," Katherine said.

"Ten minutes? You're kidding, right?"

"Not at all. You'll need nothing more than workout gear and your telephone. Now, go on," Katherine sounded like a counselor hastening campers for their morning calisthenics.

Amanda hesitated, her instinct to resist was warring with something else—curiosity, perhaps. Or was it the thrill of stepping into a world that, up until now, only existed in books and movies? She was *always* up for a challenge.

She sighed, rolling her eyes for good measure, but there was no real fight in it. What else was she going to do—walk away and pretend she hadn't already been pulled into the undertow? Like it or not, she was in this.

With a mix of begrudging acceptance and a strange, bubbling excitement she refused to fully acknowledge, Amanda hurried to her room. She swapped her pajamas for leggings, a sports bra, and a t-shirt, pulled her hair into a ponytail, and returned to Katherine just before the ten minutes were up. Her heart was pounding but she wasn't sure whether it was from irritation or anticipation.

"Okay, I guess I'm ready," Amanda said. "Let's get this training going."

"That's the spirit," Katherine approved.

The women took the elevator down to the lobby before greeting the doorman and settling into the Rolls Royce.

As they left the city behind, the landscape shifted to an expanse of warehouses and industrial complexes on the outskirts of London. Their destination loomed ahead—a windowless structure of concrete and metal, its purpose masked by an unmarked facade. High fences wrapped around the perimeter with security cameras perched on every corner, lenses sweeping the area with quiet vigilance. There were no visible signs of activity as they approached one side of the building lined with what appeared to be loading docks. As their car rolled closer, a heavy door rumbled open, revealing a dimly lit ramp that sloped downward into the underground floor.

As the car descended, entering a cavernous interior like the belly of a warehouse, the heavy steel of the ramp retracted behind them, folding seamlessly into a metal barricade. Amanda turned in her seat, wide-eyed, watching the plates lock into place before facing Katherine.

"This is where you'll prepare," Katherine said.

"To be a flight attendant?" Amanda choked.

Katherine's side grin was becoming all too familiar. "No, today you begin your intelligence training."

"As in *spy?*" Amanda coughed. "Are you telling me that I'm officially in spy training?"

"I encourage you to abandon that word from your vocabulary, my dear. It is frowned upon."

Amanda snorted. "Since when did I become your dear?" she jested, trying to diffuse any tension with humor.

Katherine's eyes narrowed, suppressing a laugh. "Old habits and all..." she said, unwilling to admit she was starting to feel more kinship with Amanda than with any agent she'd been assigned in the past.

Katherine cleared her throat and led Amanda through a heavy steel door. Beyond it lay a towering corridor lined with massive studio spaces on either side. Overhead, an observation deck stretched across the rafters, encircling the entire space like a command center surveying the floor.

"You'll begin your day with firearms training," Katherine said, pointing to the first room. "After that, you'll move to combat and fitness testing, and we'll end the day with a meal in the cafeteria."

"Combat-what, um, cafeteria?" she stammered.

"Yes," Katherine confirmed without any further explanation. "I'll see you at 4 p.m."

Amanda looked at her watch. It was only seven o'clock, and she had barely eaten a bite with her morning coffee. "Four o'clock?" she shouted as Katherine advanced down the long hallway. "They better have filet mignon if I have to go through all this!"

An instructor approached, standing in the vast opening of the firearms room. "Right this way, Agent Adams," he gestured, calling her by the name on her new ID.

"Call me Amanda, please," she insisted.

"Certainly," the man tipped his chin upward in agreement, walking her through the firearms gallery. He pointed out the gear, the target area, and the workspace.

"We'll start at that end," he gestured. "You'll learn the basics about today's weapon, then we'll move down the line. Got it?"

"Got it," Amanda confirmed.

She had been slightly familiar with guns, having to learn how to load a rifle to protect herself from some of the wildlife that roamed the Smoky Mountains. But the man and his staff wasted no time spouting off instructions. Thrusting a Glock into her hands, they showed her how to handle and load, walking her through the basics step by step before leading her to fire at targets.

Nervously shaking, Amanda lifted the gun to nearly eye level before it tumbled to the ground. An instructor shouted for people to hit the deck as everyone around them shot to the floor.

Amanda jumped back, slowly lowering her arm to pick up the gun again, apologizing. "Sorry, I'm so sorry," she repeated.

"You just dropped a loaded gun, Agent Adams," the instructor scolded.

"I'm so sorry," she said again.

"Clear!" he yelled, getting to his feet. "Don't be sorry, be careful," his voice didn't waver. "Both hands. Always. Knuckles locked." He was stern, but had a calming quality that prepared her to try again.

"Okay," Amanda gave a firm nod. Her first shots were shaky, but by the end of the session, she was hitting center mass with alarming accuracy.

"Not bad," Katherine remarked as she watched from above.

"Better than her unpromising start," a shadowed and unsettling voice murmured. The man stood beside Katherine on the dimly lit observation deck, both figures barely visible against the darkened glass that enclosed the space. From their vantage point high above the warehouse floor, they watched Amanda move below, oblivious to their presence.

She hadn't yet learned one of the most vital rules of survival, to scan her surroundings constantly, especially the least obvious directions: up, down, and under. If they had been enemies, she wouldn't have stood a chance.

Katherine's gaze remained fixed on Amanda. "So, do we advance with her training?"

"I see no reason not to," the man replied, his voice low and deliberate. He turned and drifted towards the metal staircase that spiraled down to the warehouse floor, his footsteps swallowed by the hum of the massive space.

"I'll be in my office," he added over his shoulder.

"Sir," Katherine answered, her tone clipped with reverence. She lingered a moment longer, her eyes still on Amanda, as she was escorted to the combat training bay lined with mats and weight stations.

The middle of the floor held a standard-sized boxing ring where Amanda was paired with a wiry instructor who moved like a coiled spring. He didn't hold back, throwing punches and kicks that left her breathless and bruised. Amanda was tempted to flail and scream, demanding to see Katherine and tell everyone that regardless of the consequences, she was out. But like a cottonhead snake threatened by attack, Amanda was determined to defend herself. She was naturally quick on her feet, her innate agility and strength helping her hold her own, bruise after bruise. By the end of the session, she'd managed to flip the instructor onto his back, earning an approving nod.

"You're stronger than you look," he said, offering a hand for her to help him get up from the mat.

"Years of yoga," Amanda replied, wiping sweat from her brow and lifting him to his feet.

He raised an eyebrow in disbelief. "That's *some* yoga you're doing," he smiled.

From the boxing ring, they moved to a room that housed multiple treadmills, pull-up bars, ropes, weights, an obstacle course, and machines with attaching electrodes to measure physical strength. These tests were the most grueling. Amanda ran, climbed, and carried weights until her muscles screamed in protest. The instructors pushed her to her limits, deafening voices relentless in their demands.

"Again!" one shouted as Amanda stumbled on the final stretch of the course.

Gritting her teeth, she forced herself to her feet and finished the run, collapsing onto the mat at the end.

"Impressive," Katherine said as she walked over, offering Amanda a bottle of water. "But this is just the beginning."

Amanda looked up at her, her chest heaving. "The beginning? What happens next?"

"Next," Katherine said, her voice cool and unwavering, "we see if you have what it takes to survive on a *full* mission."

Amanda took a long sip of water, the weight of Katherine's words settling over her. She wasn't just being trained—she was being transformed into an agent.

"Truly, Amanda. You should be proud of yourself today," Katherine said as she watched Amanda bite another chunk of her steak. The cafeteria did indeed have filet mignon, and Amanda wasn't about to skimp on food after the day of protein snacks and electrolyte water she'd had. Once Katherine had joined her at the obstacle course, the women had exited the gargantuan warehouse on its opposite side and entered the campus of London's largest tech company. Perfectly manicured lawns and glassy buildings were in stark contrast to the alloyed boxy structure they had spent the day in. No one would ever suspect that the "training building" in the back was there to train Intelligence officers. Or perhaps Amanda was jumping to conclusions.

"We knew you had the brains and wit, but your physical aptitude was what we were most concerned about. I think today you've alleviated some of that skepticism. Well done," Katherine offered a quick nod of approval.

"And how in the world would you know about my brains and wit?" Amanda probed.

Katherine grinned. "One day, you're not going to meet my every comment with a question, Amanda. If you learn sooner rather than later to do so, it'll be better for us both."

Amanda sat silently, her stare searing into Katherine's skin, causing her boss to shift in her seat.

Katherine let a small puff of air escape through her nose with a huff. "All right," she said, lowering her chin. "A girl who scores sixteen hundred on her SATs and has a photographic memory, landing her a full-ride scholarship to a prestigious American university is what we in the biz call a *sure bet.*"

Amanda dropped her fork to the table with a thud. "I quit college after one and a half semesters and almost flunked out," she said, crossing her arms and leaning back in the chair.

"Only after securing your place at MIT and blowing every-one off so you could return to flight school and complete the hours you had begun accruing since you were a teenager," Katherine countered, assuring Amanda that she conducted exhaustive research before activating her as an agent.

"Well... that's all true," Amanda admitted before returning to her meaty feast.

Katherine allowed a coy, satisfied grin to unfurl across her face. "Finish up," she said. "We need to go to my office before your car arrives in an hour. I'll lay out your next instructions."

"How many offices around the world do you have?" Amanda dug.

"Hmm, another inquisitive retort?" Katherine tilted her head and pushed herself away from the table, standing to her feet and motioning for Amanda to follow her.

The industrial design of concrete mixed with natural woods, and glass with imposing metals, all juxtaposed with towering green plants, carried over from the towering hallways and into Katherine's office in the company's administrative center. The two women sat in chairs opposite a large screen displaying a map of the Western Hemisphere. There was a blinking icon over Iceland and a straight line tracing the flight path from Reykjavík

to New York City. Katherine leaned back in her chair, her expression cool and composed, but her icy blue eyes betrayed the weight of what she was about to say.

"Your next mission," she began, tapping a remote to zoom in on the map, "places you back in Tristan Montgomery's orbit. You'll be his flight attendant once again, leaving Reykjavík tomorrow morning and landing in New York City. Same as before, professional, poised, and approachable, but this time, you'll go deeper."

Amanda raised an eyebrow. "Deeper how? We've already been on two dates. He tries to get me to act less like a professional and more like a girlfriend every time I see him. And he texts me a couple of times a day at this point."

Katherine leaned forward, resting her elbows on the adjacent desk. "Excellent. There's a gala next weekend—a high-profile charity event in Manhattan. Tristan will attend, and you're going as his plus-one."

"Wait, how? Are you going to have him magically invite me? I'll need an excuse to be there." Amanda's pragmatism was something she was incapable of masking.

"Subliminal messaging works even on the most intelligent, my dear," Katherine smirked. "You'll receive an invite, trust me. And this isn't just about him. The gala's benefactor, Julius Babb, is the key to what we're after. You're to make an impression. Charm him. But nothing more; this isn't about seduction, it's about trust. Earn Babb's—and he'll open the doors we need access to."

Amanda's stomach tightened. Julius Babb wasn't just a name in the tabloids; he was a shadowy figure in global finance, rumored to have his hand in everything from the diamond trade and rare earth minerals to cutting-edge cyber defense firms and off-the-books arms deals. His influence stretched across industries few could fully grasp—private space ventures, black-market art dealings, and even the booming world of biometric surveillance. Some whispered that his wealth wasn't just measured in money but in secrets, each one more valuable than the last. His influence was vast and untraceable, a ghost in a suit.

Amanda may have been lax with staying up with trends and news on social media, but she made a point to stay apprised of global happenings, and she had absolutely heard about this scandalous man.

"Why Babb?" Amanda asked cautiously.

"Because he's Tristan's gateway," Katherine replied. "Their relationship is... complicated. They've managed to be subtle about it, but Babb has been mentoring him, funding ventures, and providing connections that Tristan wouldn't have access to otherwise. But there's more to it. Somewhere in Babb's orbit is a black box—and not metaphorically speaking. It's a vault of information, evidence of their dealings, and proof that their actions pose a direct threat to national security."

Amanda's pulse quickened. She shifted in her seat, her fingers curling tightly around the armrests. "Whose nation?" she asked, leaning forward as if closing the distance between herself and the truth might bring clarity. "We're talking about international affairs here. And... you think Tristan knows about this?"

"We're not certain," Katherine admitted, "but Babb and those in his network will definitely have answers. Your job is to get close enough to learn more. The gala will set the stage, but the real opportunity comes afterward. If you do your part, Julius will invite you to come with Tristan on an exclusive excursion to the Caribbean in a few weeks. He wants to discuss the future. That's when we'll make our move."

Amanda huffed. "Should I even ask how you know all this?"

Katherine raised an eyebrow. "Do you *want* to know?"

"Probably not," she let out a nervous laugh. "So, what's the plan? No one walked me through spy gear. Do I get an earpiece? Wear camera glasses or something?"

Katherine scoffed. "We are not private investigators, Amanda. Your dress will be equipped with an undetectable listening device, the entire room has cameras that we will use for monitoring, and agents will be stationed in different locations throughout the night. You mustn't give them one reason to be suspicious. I know you learned about weapons today, but you won't need any for the time being. You'll be in public, unarmed, and safe."

Amanda forced a long breath through her lips and then swallowed hard. "Okay, I guess this is where that trust thing you were talking about kicks in," she said.

CHAPTER FIVE

As Amanda stood on the tarmac in Reykjavík, a biting wind cut through her coat. She made her way up the jet stairs before preparing for passengers to board. Tristan was the last to arrive, stepping out of a black SUV with his usual effortless charm. He paused briefly when he saw her, a flicker of delight crossing his face.

"Amanda," he said with a smile that could disarm an assailant. "I wasn't expecting to see you again so soon."

"Surprise," she replied, her tone light but professional. "Welcome aboard, Mr. Montgomery."

The flight was relatively uneventful, save for the lingering electric energy between them. Tristan's curiosity about Amanda was palpable, his attempts to draw her into conversation carefully masked as a casual interest in the presence of the others onboard. As she served him food and drinks, her fingers brushed against his, the touch fleeting yet enough to set his pulse racing and tighten his jaw. Her reluctance to avoid his gaze was the only indication that both parties were increasingly into each other. Amanda was a pro, offering just enough warmth to keep him intrigued but maintaining a distance that left Tristan wanting more.

"Be my date this weekend?" Tristan whispered as he poked his head around the corner of the gallery where Amanda was preparing for the flight's descent. "It's silly for us to hide anything."

"Hide anything? Is that what you think I'm doing?" Amanda smiled.

Tristan raised an eyebrow. "So, is that a yes?"

"You need a plus-one for something?" Amanda refused to directly answer. "Please tell me it's not for a wedding."

"Are you not the type to enjoy weddings?" Tristan asked.

"Not so much," Amanda scoffed. "I spent an unbearable amount of time in my twenties being a plus-one, not to mention a bridesmaid at weddings where the relationships ended before I turned thirty. Undying love isn't really my cup of tea," she laughed.

"Well, lucky for you, this is a charity gala I need a date for. I've already paid for the whole table, and I'll be surrounded by business partners and their wives all evening. I want to be seen with you." Tristan winked, raising his eyebrows as if to plead, indicating that going without a date would be unthinkable.

He dared not mention that this would be the first signif-icant event he planned to attend without his wife... *ex*-wife.

As a couple, they had personally supported the nonprofit for nearly a decade, but now, for three years running, neither of them had attended, unwilling to show up as a duo to save face. They always made excuses, citing travel or work plans as the explanation for their absence. But this year was different. The divorce was now public knowledge, and Julius Babb had drawn him in close, communicating that he expected Tristan's attendance under no uncertain terms. Tristan's RSVP was immediate upon receiving an invitation—filling the seats came later.

"Fancy," was Amanda's only reply.

"So, that's a yes?" Tristan grinned.

Amanda let the silence stretch before answering, the shadow of a smile showing she enjoyed the suspense. "I'll have to get a dress," she said.

"You'll have time to shop," Tristan assured. "It's not until Sunday evening. I can call in an appointment at Bloomingdales if you'd like."

"No need," Amanda replied. "I have a place." Tristan's brow lowered, eyes sharp with interest and surprise.

"I used to live in the city part-time. I have a friend. I'm a vintage kinda gal, and she just... gets me," Amanda grinned.

"Say no more." Tristan blinked, waving his hand. "I will be pleased to have you by my side wearing anything... or nothing," he leaned in, lingering to see if Amanda's face flushed.

She simply cast him a glance before turning around to secure all the compartments in place.

"It's time to return to your seat, Mr. Montgomery," she said, her back still facing him. "The captain announced our descent if you hadn't noticed."

"I hadn't," he admitted. "I have trouble noticing things when I'm around you," he said, inching closer to her.

She felt herself turn around, as if she wasn't in control of her own actions, magnetically being drawn towards his arms. Neither moved away. Neither moved closer. The tension between them felt like a held breath waiting to be released.

"I..." she whispered, "I think you should pay more attention then," awkwardly incapable of saying anything intelligent in the moment.

A sudden jerk of the plane nudged them together as though the universe was conspiring for them to plummet into each other completely. Tristan curled his arms around the small of Amanda's back, pulling her into him firmly. He leaned his lips as close to her ear as he could, letting his words brush softly against her skin.

"I look forward to spending the evening with you on Sunday," he said, letting his mouth sweep over her cheek before loosening his grip, returning to his seat in a single, effortless move, causing Amanda to sway unsteadily on her feet.

"See you Sunday," she muttered under her breath, biting the fleshy swell of her lower lip.

Soon after touchdown, Amanda pulled out her phone and texted three words: *Need a dress*, with a bright red heart emoji. She was feeling more like the glamorous traveler her friends assumed her to be than someone caught up in espionage.

Tristan had only texted a couple of times from the time they arrived in New York on Friday to Sunday afternoon. He included no flirtation or playful tone like usual—merely listing logistics and instructions about the gala, causing Amanda to wonder if she had done a good job keeping him on the line or if her reaction to his little flirtation wasn't what he hoped it would be. Should she have leaned in for a kiss? If he could be obsessed after a moment, could he become disenchanted with her just as quickly?

"I'm a little concerned that he's not as interested as he was," she told Katherine over FaceTime, spinning slowly in her ballgown. The luxurious vintage evening dress had been waiting for her at the shop, already set aside by her friend Shereen before she even arrived.

"It's lovely," Katherine commented, focused on Amanda's glamorous attire. "You look stunning."

"Isn't it fantastic?" Amanda exclaimed, smoothing the taffeta skirt. "I'll have to hold my breath all night," she joked, the bodice hugging her torso. "Shareen replaced the zipper, so I don't think it'll give, but you can never be sure!" she sputtered.

"I cannot imagine Tristan will be able to stifle his interest at all tonight with you wearing that," Katherine assured.

"I dunno. Let's hope. I was thinking of wearing my hair up. You know, in a big bun at the nape of my neck with these earrings." Amanda held a large beaded sphere to her ear—a flawless compliment to her yellow dress.

"It's perfect," Katherine agreed.

The strangeness of their conversation made Amanda's head spin when she thought about it. Katherine, nearly thirty years her senior and practically a stranger who was blackmailing her into becoming a secret agent for an unknown culprit, was helping her pick out jewelry and hairstyles as if she were a friend offering fashion tips. Amanda blew a short breath through her nose and chuckled at the unbelievable events delivered by the first few weeks of her thirty-sixth year around the sun.

"Well, here goes nothing, I guess," she said, wheels spinning about how she was ill-equipped for this mission. "I'll talk to you tomorrow after I go party it up with the big shots," Amanda downplayed.

"Never let your guard down," Katherine scolded sternly, sensing Amanda's minimizing of events. "This is no game."

"It is or it isn't? First, you tell me this is a game with major players and I have to learn how to play it, and now…"

"Figuratively," Katherine interrupted, "this is a game of risk, Amanda. And in all tangible, absolute reality, it *is* life or death."

Amanda felt a lump move from her gut and slowly rise to her throat. She, more than most, understood the actuality of life-or-death circumstances. Amanda Hopkins had seen things in her small town and knew more than even her closest friends could have guessed. Otherwise, one simple photo of herself wouldn't have been enough to convince her to turn her life upside down. And Katherine must have been banking on it.

"And yet you're sending me in blind, Katherine. Why shouldn't I just run?"

"I don't know all the reasons that are keeping you from doing that, Amanda. I'm not the one calling the tune around here. But my guess is that you do have compelling reasons not to have them chase you down, threaten you, or kill you."

"And how do I know I won't lose my life anyway while trying to save it?" Amanda felt a tear rush down her cheek.

"You don't. We are not in the business of guarantees." Katherine's voice was like a swelling tide, rushing in strong and fierce, yet peacefully soothing in its rhythm. "Now, get yourself ready. You'll have to leave soon."

The grand ballroom at The Plaza Hotel was a sea of glittering gowns and sharp tuxedos—air heavy with wealth and power. The room shimmered under the glow of its iconic crystal chandeliers, their cascading light refracting off gilded moldings and polished marble floors. The gala hummed with the soft strains of a live orchestra, violins weaving through conversations, and laughter that bubbled like champagne in crystal flutes.

Elegant guests, draped in couture gowns and tailored tuxedos, glided across the dance floor, their movements effortless beneath the towering, arched ceilings. Gold-trimmed mirrors reflected silk and sparkling diamonds and refracted light off all surfaces.

Servers in crisp white jackets wove through the crowd with hors d'oeuvres trays and glistening caviar. At the far end of the room, oversized floral arrangements of ivory roses and peonies framed the grand staircase, where newcomers paused to survey the glittering affair before descending into the sea of power and intrigue.

Amanda spotted Tristan just outside the grand space, waiting expectantly.

"I suppose you didn't want me to pick you up because you could make a grander entrance on your own." Tristan extended his hand, leading Amanda from the anterior doors to the inner ballroom.

"Perhaps," she replied coyly.

"Well played," Tristan smirked, leaning in. "You have the whole room staring."

Amanda beamed. She was never one to shy away from attention, landing major roles in plays and musicals throughout high school and local community theatre. Pretentiously flaunting vintage gowns was her grown-up way of upstaging people, and she enjoyed every second of it.

She couldn't have been more pleased with her choice of evening wear, the lemony flecks on her dress danced in this room aglow with gold. Amanda had never been to The Plaza's grand ballroom, but she'd done her research days ago, scrolling through the hotel's online gallery to imagine how she might stand out in the space. Her auburn hair, bright eyes, and golden dress would make her glow like a sunflower in a field at dusk, impossible to overlook.

Now, standing beneath the shimmering chandeliers, she felt like she'd stepped straight into the scene she'd envisioned: something out of *The Sound of Music*, where Julie Andrews blushed in Christopher Plummer's arms as Fraulein Maria and Captain Von Trapp surrendered to their undeniable attraction. Amanda's eyes glinted with quiet delight. Tonight felt like the start of something just as meant to be, and she was ready for it.

Tristan slid his hand to her waist, pulling her into his side whenever he got the chance. He was practically glued to her throughout the evening, introducing her to key players in his world. She laughed at the right moments, asked thoughtful questions, and kept his attention and intrigue firmly on her.

"This isn't like any charity gala I've ever been to," Amanda commented after her second champagne. "Where are the tables and the auctioneer and the video we'll watch where they ask us to donate more money?"

Tristan grinned. "Well, dinner's in another room—and they will have tables—so don't worry about that," he teased. "I'll bet you won't have had food as delectable as what we will eat tonight at any other benefit either. Julius Babb doesn't play around. But the auction will be after our bellies are full and the wine has been flowing for at least two hours," he laughed.

"Okay, and what exactly are we raising money for?" Amanda was genuinely curious—she was not thinking about any covert operation.

"Global warming?" Tristan's inflection made it sound like it was a question.

"Wait. You don't know." Amanda let out an awkward, breathy chuckle that wavered on the edge of uncertainty when Tristan noticed Julius Babb approaching.

"Julius," Tristan said warmly, clasping the older man's hand. "I'd like you to meet Amanda."

Julius Babb carried his years with a quiet authority that demanded attention. Nearing seventy, his once jet-black hair had faded to a distinguished silver, cropped close to his scalp with a precision that mirrored his meticulous nature. His skin was sun-weathered yet smooth for his age, seeming to defy nature itself. Hints of olive undertones mingled with a warm bronze suggested that he lived a life spent between continents. His deep-set eyes revealed he was always one step ahead, with the faintest arch in his brow that challenged anyone to prove him wrong. Whether by wealth, wisdom, or sheer force of will, Julius moved through a room as though it belonged to him—and, more often than not, it did.

Babb's piercing gaze swept over her, his expression inscrutable. "A pleasure," he said, his voice smooth but guarded. "Tristan always did have an eye for elegance."

Amanda extended her palm for a handshake, but Julius clasped her hand and brought it to his lips, lightly grazing her knuckles with a kiss, a quiet dominance hidden beneath the gesture.

"The pleasure is mine. I've heard so much about you," she said.

They chatted for a few minutes, Amanda effortlessly navigating the conversation with the poise she'd been trained to maintain. Not that there was time to instruct her about how to act around powerful men, but Amanda had a history of flying with them and capturing their gaze when wives or girlfriends weren't around. She never crossed a line, but she most certainly dallied with it.

As Tristan crossed the room to get another champagne flute for his date like a true gentleman, Julius turned to address Amanda directly.

"Tristan speaks highly of you," he said, his voice measured.

Amanda turned, her smile practiced. "That's kind of him. He's been... very generous."

Julius studied her for a moment, his eyes sharp and calculating. "Generosity is a double-edged sword, don't you think? It can mask ulterior motives."

Amanda's pulse raced, but she kept her expression calm. "I suppose that depends on the person. Tristan strikes me as someone who is genuine."

Julius's lips curled into a faint smile. "Genuine, yes. But naïve, perhaps. The world doesn't reward kindness as much as it rewards strategy."

Amanda tilted her head, feigning curiosity. "Is that how you see the world? A game of strategy?"

Julius stepped closer, his voice dropping. "It's not about how *I* see the world, my dear. It's about how the world *is*. And in this world, the ones who survive are the ones who know how to adapt."

When Tristan returned, Julius suggested the three of them discuss things further over drinks on his yacht in the Caribbean.

"That is... generous," Amanda couldn't help herself.

"Yes, I am *genuinely* a very generous person," Julius smirked with a hint of appreciation for Amanda's wit sweeping his expression.

"A true friend," Tristan confirmed heartily with a toast.

"To generosity," Amanda said, tipping her champagne, sensing Katherine's invisible approval from wherever she was monitoring the event.

Julius raised his glass to hers in a silent toast before walking away, leaving Amanda with a sense of confusion and unease that settled deep in her chest.

Tristan followed Amanda's gaze. "You're curious about him, aren't you?" he whispered.

Amanda tilted her head. "He's... fascinating. A little intimidating, too."

Tristan laughed. "That's Julius. He likes to play the mysterious benefactor, but he's brilliant. He sees opportunities where no one else does."

"But who is he?" she asked. "You never really told me what he does other than being the host of this charity event."

"Who really knows all that Julius Babb does? He's got a reputation of being one of the richest, most demanding, and yet most generous men in the world... and there's always a type of mystery that comes with that. Some people trust him. Others don't." Tristan shrugged as if his answer explained things to an acceptable degree.

Amanda tried to hide her befuddlement at his reply, tipping her glass for another sip. "So... what about you?" she asked, keeping her tone light. "Do you trust him?"

Tristan's expression was delayed for a nearly undetectable momentary flash, but he recovered quickly. "He's been a good friend to me. And his vision for the future is... inspiring."

The way Tristan spoke was passionate but vague, as though he was still analyzing whether to plunge in and trust her not just with his lusts, but with his secrets.

Back in her London office, Katherine paced the room as Amanda sat FaceTiming her, studying the dossier spread out on the table. Photos of Babb, Tristan, and others filled the pages, alongside satellite images of the villa in the Caribbean where they'd be staying.

"Well done last night. You really wowed them," Katherine congratulated.

"I guess," Amanda shrugged. She wasn't ready to ask her catalog of questions or take inventory of her suspicions. Spending time with both Julius and Tristan, she felt torn between the need to uncover more and her growing instinct to shield Tristan. She was mission-minded now.

"So what next? Do I just keep attending fancy soirees and going on exotic vacations now?" she asked, holding the photo of a sparkling white villa with its terracotta roof. "I know where I'm going, but not why. You're practically sending me in blind again."

"Your job isn't like the movies, Amanda. A good agent will always do their best to be authentic. We are economic with the truth, not everyday liars."

Amanda scoffed. "You know, where I'm from, that's called cognitive dissonance."

"Congratulations on learning buzzy vocabulary from Instagram therapists," Katherine grumbled. "Survival demands things like *cognitive dissonance* if that's what you wish to call it. But the only way to get to the facts is to be real, which demands not knowing too much. Not every day is a car chase and shootout."

"And you think that's what I want?" Amanda's voice rose with incredulity. "I didn't agree to this for the action-adventure. I want my life back. I've been here before, you know. Or did they not tell you?" Amanda said. Her trust in Katherine functioned like a yoyo, dropped on an invisible string one moment, only to be yanked back up the next.

"What do you think?" Katherine probed.

Ever since seeing the old photo Katherine had slipped her in Rome, Amanda had come to one conclusion only. There was one, single, solitary individual who could be behind her personal blackmail. And if Katherine was working with or for him, Amanda knew it was no joke.

"My nondisclosure is from one person only. And since he's the governor now... the power he has must be more than the last time I dealt with him—with that whole damn family. Don't think I haven't heard the rumors about him wanting to run for President in the next election, either."

"This situation is much bigger than just him. It's much bigger than all of us. And I wish I could give you all the answers, I do. But even I don't have those. I move when they tell me to, stay when they say stay, and I have long stopped counting the years, but the weight of them presses into my bones with

every assignment. I do not wish the same for you, Amanda."
Katherine seemed almost teary as she then fell silent.

She had never meant to become a spy. That part was an
accident, or maybe just a series of small, calculated betrayals,
each one pushing her deeper until there was no way out. The
job had started as a favor, then a duty, then a life sentence. And
now? Now, it was a leash. Go when they say go. Stop when
they say stop. Disappear when they decide you should.

The dream of retirement used to be a beacon, something she
could inch towards, one last job at a time. A cottage by the sea,
a garden where nothing needed to be hidden or decoded, a life
without burner phones and cryptic messages disguised as casual greetings. But the closer she got, the more they tightened
their grip. Just one more mission. One more loose end to tie.
One more favor to repay.

She could feel time slipping through her fingers like grains
of sand, but she knew the truth: She belonged to them. No
matter how many times she packed a bag and imagined walking away, the call always came. And she always answered.

Because after all these years, after all the secrets and stolen
lives, there was only one thing more terrifying than being told
where to go. Not being needed at all. And if she could save a
young woman from her same fate, she was going to do everything in her power to do it.

Amanda took a deep breath. "So what do I need to know?"

"We think the vault might be in the Caribbean," Katherine said, her voice surprisingly steady. "We believe that it contains everything we need—names, dates, transactions. If we get it, we'll have the leverage to neutralize a threat."

Amanda frowned. "A threat... like nuclear?" She wasn't surprised that her mind went directly to the thought of total destruction.

Katherine remained silent.

As a child, Amanda had devoured history with an insatiable curiosity, her mind absorbing every detail, every fact, every image as if they were burned into the pages of her memory. But some lessons had left more than knowledge behind, some had imprinted themselves so deeply that even now, years later, they lingered like shadows at the edges of her thoughts.

She could still remember the first time she saw the images. Black-and-white photographs of flattened cities, skeletal buildings standing like charred tombstones, and the hollow-eyed faces of survivors who had seen their world end in fire. Her teacher's voice had droned on about dates and political tensions, about strategies and deterrence, but Amanda hadn't heard any of it. She had been too lost in what she was seeing, too horrified by the realization that this wasn't just history. It was a reality capable of repeating itself.

The concept of war had always been abstract, something that happened in stories or in places far from her quiet childhood world. But nuclear war? That was different. That wasn't soldiers on battlefields or treaties drawn up in distant rooms. That was the sky opening up and swallowing entire cities in an instant—an invisible force capable of turning everything and everyone to dust. The fact that the same weapons still existed, waiting like sleeping giants that could wake at any moment, terrified her.

For most kids, monsters lived under the bed or in dark closets. But for Amanda, monsters were real, embedded in everyday society, lurking in the knowledge that one decision, one moment, could wipe everything away. And for a girl with a mind that never forgot, those images wouldn't fade. They stayed sharp and vivid, a reminder of just how fragile the world really is.

Amanda rubbed her forehead as if to clear her mind. "Okay," she shook it off, "so... you think Julius will just have this box or vault out in the open?"

"Of course not," Katherine replied. "But Tristan might know where it is, even if he doesn't realize its importance. Pay attention to what they say, what they don't say, and what they try to hide. Your job is to be there when the cracks start to show."

Amanda nodded in both agreement and understanding. She was beginning to see that she could possibly do this one thing. Whatever it was, whether by nuclear war or financial extortion, these men seemed intent on overtaking the world. She couldn't be sure yet. But she did know that the players in the game were more powerful than they were during her last entanglement with them when she was only a teenager. And failure wasn't an option. She was stronger now. More mature. She was being compliant for now, but she wasn't going to give them what they wanted without getting something first.

Chapter Six

"It's time," Julius said, gazing out at the ocean, his words heavy with meaning. "We're moving the operation."

Tristan straightened in his seat, a flicker of curiosity crossing his face. "Moving? Where to?"

The sun had dipped low over the Caribbean, painting the sky in hues of orange and lavender. The sea sparkled like molten glass, calm and endless, stretching to the horizon. Amanda lingered by the edge of the infinity pool, a tall glass of mint and cucumber water in her hand, admiring the view while keeping her ears sharp. Tristan and Julius sat a short distance away on the villa's terrace, their voices low but carried by the still afternoon air.

Julius swirled his glass of freshly pressed lemonade, leaning back in his chair like a king surveying his domain. He was dressed casually in linen pants and a loose shirt, but the weight of his presence was anything but relaxed. His voice was smooth and calculated. He turned to Tristan, quieting the conversation just enough for Amanda not to hear what he was saying.

"Tenerife. The Canary Islands have… *unique* advantages. Discretion. Access. A more agreeable regulatory environment, shall we say." He gave a faint smile, a careful mask rather than a true expression.

Tristan leaned forward, his elbows resting on his knees, speaking in an earnest tone, increasing the volume of the conversation.

"Tenerife, huh? That's ambitious. But I get it. If we're scaling this, we need a solid foundation. Still…" He paused, his brow furrowing slightly. "I thought we were building something *here*, Julius. This place has so much potential."

Julius waved a hand dismissively. "The Caribbean was always a stepping stone. You know that. Tenerife is a better fit for… what we're building."

Amanda's pulse began to speed up. The way Julius said "what we're building" sent a chill down her spine. She couldn't tell if he was testing Tristan or if the cryptic phrasing was deliberate.

Tristan didn't seem to flinch. Instead, he smiled, a touch of excitement lighting up his features. "I get it. We're all that much closer to Europe there. A bigger stage. More reach. And with what we've been developing, we can make a real difference, Julius. I know the public doesn't see it yet, but this technology… it's going to change everything. Access to clean water, food security, renewable energy—this is what the world needs. We can do so much good with it." Tristan emphasized each word.

Amanda casually lowered herself into the pool, perching her arms on the side and kicking her feet softly as she turned to face them. Julius didn't notice her. He watched Tristan carefully, his expression unreadable. He took a slow sip of his lemonade, letting Tristan's words hang in the air.

"And that's why I chose you," Julius said finally, his voice low and deliberate. "Because you believe in what we're doing. Your conviction is... refreshing."

Amanda noticed the faintest flicker of something in Julius's eyes. Was it approval? Amusement? It was impossible to tell. He leaned back, his tone growing lighter.

"Tenerife will be ready soon. We'll finalize everything there. For now, I think I need to add a little something more flavorful to this cup of lemonade." He winked as he rose, signaling the end of the conversation.

Tristan nodded, a confident smile on his face, but Amanda could swear she saw the briefest shadow of uncertainty in his expression as he glanced towards the ocean.

As Julius walked inside, leaving them alone, Amanda propped herself out of the pool again, approached the shelf of towels near the seating area, and wrapped one around her waist before she approached the chair next to Tristan.

"Everything all right?" she asked, tilting her head as if she hadn't heard a word of their conversation.

Tristan turned to her, his easy charm sliding back into place. "Yeah. Julius just has big plans, as always."

Amanda smiled, placing her hand on his arm. "And you and Envisage are part of them, I take it?"

Tristan smiled, his tone playful but with an undercurrent of pride. "Of course. He knows I'm the key to making it all work."

Amanda kept her smile steady, but her mind raced. The pieces were starting to take shape—Tenerife, the technology, the hidden operation. But there was a difference between collecting puzzle pieces and understanding how to put them together. She could only imagine what the Hansen family from Knoxville, Tennessee, would have to do with this big of an operation. But they were the only ones who forced her into blackmail from the time she was seventeen, leveraging an NDA she didn't even read closely before she signed. Those pieces from her past didn't seem to fit anywhere. Not yet. They were a wealthy and powerful family, yes, but from what she could remember, this kind of opulence was definitely *not* in their inheritance. Still, they had to be involved.

"Well, I'm going to head back to my room to get ready for dinner." Amanda stood, moving her hand from Tristan's arm to touch his shoulder lightly.

He swiftly placed his palm on top of her hand, grasping and tugging in a quick, unexpected motion. Amanda lost her balance and gripped the back of the chair before tumbling into his lap. They hadn't even shared a proper kiss yet, and now she was fully pressed into his body, feeling every muscle. Her eyes widened.

"Oh, gosh, I didn't mean to make you fall," he laughed impishly.

"You most certainly did," Amanda said, placing both palms on his chest, pushing on him before standing to her feet, pretending she was perturbed.

"Well, I didn't think it would work," he smirked.

Amanda laughed. "I'll see you at dinner," she smiled, bending low to kiss his forehead.

Tristan reached up to clasp her hand before she went. "See you at dinner," he repeated before pressing her fingers to his lips.

Amanda hurried down the hallway towards her room, out of breath from emotion. No part of her wanted to play hard-to-get with Tristan anymore. They'd only known each other for a few weeks, but that was still longer than most of the relationships she'd had in the past five years. She was more comfortable longing for companionship than experiencing it, and would usually gratify her need to be with someone within the first week and push them away by the third. Perhaps the suspense of delayed gratification was more powerful than she thought.

Once she closed the door behind her, she leaned her head against the solid wood, hand to her heart. She blew out a long breath before picking up her Katherine phone, as she now referred to it, and pressed *call.*

"Hey, Katherine. I don't think it's here. The vault..." Amanda tried not to sound breathy.

"Are you okay?"

"Yeah, yeah. I just kind of took the stairs quickly," she deflected.

"You are not out of shape, Amanda. Please don't make this hard for the both of us. I need you to tell me everything," Katherine said firmly.

"No, it's nothing, I just... had a moment with Tristan that took me by surprise is all. I'm a little out of breath. But it's not, you know... *that.*"

Katherine let out a short laugh. "Okay, sorry, go on."

"So, yeah. I heard Julius tell him that they are moving the operation to the Canary Islands. I'm not sure they would have a vault here if they are building operations there, right?"

"Have you looked around the premises for anything?" Katherine asked.

"Not really. It's our first day here. I haven't been able to without it being obvious. It's only us and Julius. Another couple is joining us tonight. Anton and Clarisse, he said. So, there will literally only be five of us in the house," Amanda explained.

"What? Anton and Clarisse Filby?" Katherine asked.

"I don't know," Amanda replied.

"But... our intel revealed a processing center in the Caribbean, and a large gathering of executives scheduled for this week," Katherine said.

"Wait. I thought I was just looking for a vault, not here for another event," Amanda said.

"Never mind," Katherine swept her words away like unwanted dust. "Just observe what you can. Keep your eyes and ears open, and report back every day, just like you are now. Julius is known to collect cigars and antique books. If you can make your way into his study without raising suspicion, do it. You may find something there."

"It feels pretty unlikely to me," Amanda sighed. "In a digital age, surely we can track him better than me skulking around in private studies and closets."

"In a digital age, Amanda, analog is the safest method," Katherine explained.

Amanda hadn't even considered that.

The whole world had hurtled forward, trading ink for pixels, whispers for encrypted messages, and human instinct for artificial intelligence. Information moved at the speed of light now—instant, limitless, and dangerously traceable.

Everyone had spent decades adapting, learning the rules of an age that prized convenience over caution. But the deeper the world waded into the digital tide, the more agents of espionage used methods of the past—a time when secrecy was an art form, not an algorithm. During World War II, spies had embedded entire messages into the tiny ink smudge of a microdot, tucked inside an innocent-looking letter. A whisper of information, invisible to all but those who knew where to look. That was security. *That* was control.

Now, every keystroke left a footprint, every encrypted file a trail waiting to be cracked. Digital locks could be broken, and networks breached with satellite tracking even in the dead of night. But paper? Paper didn't ping off cell towers. It didn't betray its sender with metadata or timestamps. It could be burned, buried, or lost to the wind. A single slip of old-school papyrus tucked inside a yellowing book was safer than a thousand firewalled servers.

"They keep everything they need close and protected from our scanners," Katherine continued. "Just keep your eyes peeled."

Amanda's mind raced as she agreed to follow the instructions before hanging up the phone. Paper. Microfiche. Steganography. Could this be the way the world really works?

While billionaire techies are distracting the population with their swipe-tap-scroll apps, are they Morse-coding it through suboceanic wires?

She ran to the bedside nightstand, lifting the estate's embossed pen from the table, quickly unscrewing it, and suddenly disappointed that she didn't find a tiny scroll of secret information in its shell. Even though her days felt uneventful, save the grandeur, and were practically normal in every other way, Amanda was beginning to understand the false sense of security normality can bring.

CHAPTER SEVEN

AFTER DRESSING IN A flowery chiffon dress that plunged tantalizingly low in both the front and back, Amanda emerged for the evening with a lightness in her step that even she couldn't explain. Her understanding of this treacherous game had broadened, and she was more alert—and more alive—than ever.

The Caribbean breeze filtered through an open terrace as she walked to sit beside Tristan, a glass of chilled rosé in her hand—the sun dipping low, casting golden light across the villa.

"So, what's on the docket for tomorrow?" she asked. "You know I only have three days here."

Tristan leaned back, completely at ease, his smile relaxed.

"You don't have to leave, you know," he said, his voice soft but insistent.

Amanda was caught off guard. "Tristan, I have flights on my schedule. My life doesn't just... stop," she said, knowing she was expected back in London for a full report.

He tilted his head, studying her. "You could come and work for me. You'd have more freedom, no rigid schedules, no more jumping time zones every other day."

She set her glass down firmly, leaning back in her chair with crossed arms. "Are you serious? I just met you a few weeks ago, and you think I should drop everything to what? Come work for you?"

Tristan frowned, his confidence faltering. "I didn't mean it like that..." he choked.

"Oh, I think you did." Amanda stood abruptly, pacing to the edge of the terrace. Despite the common assumption that she had the personality to match her red hair, she was generally cool-headed. But, when a man pressured her, the blood in her veins immediately ran hot. The people pulling the strings knew what they were doing when they assigned an older, seemingly frigid, motherly type to be Amanda's supervisor.

"You're not one of those guys, are you? The kind who thinks just because you have money and prestige, you can swoop in and 'take care of your woman?' Exert your macho power? Tell me how to live my life?" she demanded.

Her words sliced through the air, sharp and unrelenting. Tristan sat up straight, his face shifting from surprise to vulnerability in a flash.

"Woah…. no. That's not what I'm saying at all," his voice getting quieter. "I'm sorry if it came across that way. I'm just… trying to find a way to keep you close."

She stopped pacing, her arms crossed tightly. "Well, you might want to rethink how you do that. I'm not some damsel in distress waiting for a knight in shining armor to come fix my life."

Tristan's eyes softened, and he leaned forward, elbows on his knees. He was mindful enough to know that standing would seem more like a confrontation than an invitation.

"I sincerely was not trying to save you from anything, Amanda. I think you've got it all wrong about me. Sure, I've never known a day without luxury, but you know what? None of that matters. Deep down, I'm still just a desperate kid trying to make the world a better place. Money doesn't buy love, and it sure as hell doesn't fix what's broken on the inside."

Amanda came back to her senses, knowing she had a job to do, not a relationship to nurture. His words felt raw and honest, and she could use that to her advantage.

"Maybe," she nodded, returning to the plush outdoor seating. "But I don't know you well enough to believe your money and lifestyle don't matter. And maybe *you* don't know yourself well enough to consider that you may be lying to yourself about it, too."

Tristan blinked, the words hitting harder than he expected. His mouth opened slightly, but no words emerged, just a slow exhale as he tried to grasp a response that wouldn't yet come. His brow furrowed, and for a moment, he looked as if she had yanked the ground out from under him. A weak chuckle escaped, uncertain and hollow. *Did she really think that?* Or worse—*was she right?*

He nodded, his expression resigned. "Fair enough. But don't write me off, please."

"I'm sorry," Amanda said, shaking her head. "That was harsh. I didn't mean it," she regretfully apologized.

"No, it's alright. It's not untrue. I suppose it's possible that I might be lying to myself, but I don't have anything to compare it to—not really. Even after going off on my own and volunteering in South America with the Peace Corps, I had the security of knowing that it was a choice to live that way, not a destiny. I crave purpose—I don't chase the same fame and wealth as the peers in my circle. That's why I love Julius so much. He is unassuming. He never seeks the spotlight."

"Yet anyone who subscribes to the *New York Times* knows who he is... or who people report him to be," Amanda clarified.

"Report falsely, mostly, might I add?" Tristan retorted.

"You may... but how do you know?" Amanda leaned in. "Are you saying it's not true?

"Which part? The affairs? The secret investments? The diamond mines?"

"Sure, all of it," Amanda said. "I mean, can you blame people for thinking he's maybe not a good guy? The diamond thing alone is enough to ask questions. Lab-grown is the way of the future. My generation—and women younger than me—we don't want blood diamonds on our hands. And we buy our own jewelry too," Amanda said with conviction. "And what's up with him refusing to be photographed?! How can he possibly attend an event like the gala last weekend and not be?"

"Are you gonna be the one to break his rule about that?" Tristan's question sounded like a dare.

"Well, no..." she admitted.

"Exactly," Tristan laughed.

"Enjoying the sunset?" They heard Julius's voice approach them from behind.

"Yes, indeed," Tristan said, standing to shake Julius's hand.

"No, no, please. Don't get up. Anton and Clarisse just got here and will be down in a few minutes. I let the chef in, and he's started dinner, so we'll be good to go soon. I know it's a bit late, but you won't regret having to wait. I'll get myself a drink and join you. Or perhaps you'd like the full tour?" Julius offered.

"Oh, I'd love that," Amanda replied enthusiastically before Tristan could say a word. "I love architecture and interior design. I almost majored in it," she lied. She did have impeccable taste and a great eye for design, but Amanda had never considered studying the craft.

"Splendid. Follow me," Julius gestured, walking towards the bar before pouring himself a bit of his nightly bourbon.

The heart of the villa was an expansive, open-air great room, a place where the warm Caribbean breeze drifted lazily through the arching wooden beams and high ceilings. At its center stood a grand, circular bar crafted from polished mahogany, its deep, rich grain catching the flickering glow of candlelight and lanterns hung from iron sconces. Behind it, a wall of glass shelves displayed an array of rums and tropical liqueurs, each bottle gleaming amber and gold in the soft light of the evening. The bar was more than a place for drinks, it was the villa's soul—where stories and secrets unfolded over the clink of ice in crystal tumblers.

Tristan and Amanda followed closely, Tristan daring to clasp Amanda's index finger when they accidentally brushed up against each other. He tugged at her finger until he could interlace each of his fingers through hers, one by one. Amanda lowered her gaze, a telltale flush of color spreading over her skin, giving her away.

"Mmm, to the happy couple." Julius raised his glass to them as Tristan drew Amanda in closer.

"Not so fast, loverboy," she laughed, then turned her gaze to Julius. "Don't encourage this one," she said, thumbing towards Tristan.

"Why not? Young love is tantalizing. Let an old man live vicariously," he said, with a sly twinkle in his eyes, sipping a slow mouthful. "And take my word for it, time passes sooner than you realize. Don't let youth be wasted on the young, as they say. I know people have told you before, and each one of us thinks that we'll be the one exception to the rule when we're young, but rest assured, Miss Hopkins, time is a predator that knows no contentment nor defeat. Age will get you in the end like the rest of us. Live it up while you can."

Amanda's head tilted slightly towards him, accompanied by an amused glint in her eye, acknowledging the remark with quiet appreciation. Julius was beginning to remind her of the Southern grandfatherly types she grew up around.

"I told you you'd love him," Tristan winked.

Amanda's eyes brightened in amusement. "So, what do we get to see first?" she asked, changing the subject without acknowledging that she actually did think about finding love and settling down sometimes. Not that she could admit it.

"Ah, well, yes, the tour. I'll save the best for last, so let's begin with the study. It's where I spend most of my time on the island when I don't have guests, so it's the most disorganized. I don't let the maids touch it," Julius said, sweeping his arm upward. "Right this way."

From the bar's central hub, a series of arched doorways led in every direction, blurring the line between indoors and out. To one side, a lounge spilled into a sunken living area adorned with handwoven rugs and low, cushioned sofas, their fabrics rich with the deep blues and greens of the sea. Gauzy white curtains billowed in the evening breeze, framing the glow of lanterns strung along the villa's outer terraces.

On the other side, wide wooden doors swung open onto a sprawling veranda, where the polished stone floor met the infinity pool's edge. Just beyond, the ocean stretched endlessly, its waves murmuring against the shore. Palm trees leaned over the terrace like lazy sentinels, their fronds rustling in the warm night air.

The hallways led to cool, shaded bedrooms draped in soft linen, their carved wooden doors leading out to private courtyards lush with hibiscus and the scent of frangipani. The villa was a world unto itself—open, fluid, and humming with the rhythm of the island, a place where time slowed.

"Here it is. The study. I would've skipped this room, but I love the layout of the house, and—not to oversell you on it—but this is my favorite piece in the whole place. If you love design, you'll appreciate it." Julius walked over to an antique desk, stroking its edges as if it were a lover.

The desk stood like a relic from another era, its presence commanding yet quietly dignified in the study. More than a century old, it bore the marks of time—subtle indentations on its surface where restless hands had once drummed, and faint ink stains that whispered of letters long forgotten. Crafted from aged teak, the wood had deepened to a warm, honeyed patina, polished smooth by decades of compassionate hands. The grain swirled in mesmerizing patterns, rich and undulating like the tides beyond the villa's stone terraces.

Ornate brass handles adorned its deep drawers, their once-bright sheen now mellowed to an antique gold, dulled by the salt air and the passage of time. Only the owner would know, but one drawer stuck slightly when pulled, as if reluctant to give up its secrets. The writing surface carried the faint scent of parchment and old tobacco—ghosts of a hundred deals still lingering in its grain.

Perhaps once belonging to a merchant who had traced the Caribbean's trade winds, or a scholar who had penned letters by lamplight as the waves whispered just beyond his window, Julius basked in the inspiration the old desk gave him.

"We can leave you two alone if you'd like," Tristan teased.

"She's a beaut, isn't she?" Julius ignored the joke, still running his fingers along her edges.

"She is," Amanda confirmed, walking to the front of the desk and jostling the middle drawer before crouching down to see its underbelly. "Is it in separate pieces? If it's as old as I think it is, these sections should be connected by this beam at the front."

"So, you *do* know design, don't you?" Julius lifted his chin, his instinctive wariness of people kicking in. Before Tristan brought Amanda to the gala, Julius had run a background check and combed through her internet history—nothing concerning had surfaced. Yet, something about her question unsettled him. It wasn't just intrigue; it was distrust. And in Julius's world, trust wasn't given; it was earned.

"I mean, I'm interested," she brushed it off.

"Hmm," Julius didn't expound. He knew that anyone who understood the mechanics of a desk made more than a century ago would have had to be more than marginally interested in design.

"My parents used to take me antiquing," Amanda said, raising her shoulders in a quick, uncertain movement before letting them drop, sensing Julius's incredulity.

That was true, and Amanda had begun to understand the value of truth in a moment like this.

Amanda grew up in a house where survival meant hustle. With three kids and an annual income that barely stretched beyond thirty thousand dollars, her parents had learned to chase opportunity wherever they could find it. There was no shame in scraping by, it was just reality. If there was a way to turn a quick profit, they tried it.

Antiquing had been one of their more ambitious ventures, an unpredictable gamble that promised the thrill of buried treasure but more often delivered dust-covered disappointment. Every weekend, they piled into their aging minivan and drove to estate sales, flea markets, and local auctions, sifting through piles of forgotten belongings in search of something valuable. Amanda remembered the way her parents' eyes would light up at the prospect of a rare find, the hopeful energy in their voices as they debated whether a chipped vase or a faded oil painting might be worth something.

Most of the time, it wasn't.

Still, they kept at it, hauling home wooden chests with broken locks, porcelain figurines missing limbs, and stacks of yellowed books with cracked spines. The house was a revolving door of old furniture and odd trinkets, each item lingering just long enough for her parents to convince themselves they could flip it before eventually giving up and moving on to the next scheme.

It wasn't glamorous, but it was how they survived. Amanda learned early how to spot a desperate seller, how to talk down a price, and how to keep her expectations low. She learned that value was subjective and that one man's junk was another man's payday.

"Yoohoo, hello, my dears," a woman's sing-song voice chirped from the echoing hall.

Tristan stepped to the doorway and beckoned. "Oh, hey, guys, we're in here!"

"Tristan, my dear! How *are* you?" Clarisse's syllables were over-exaggerated and elongated as she spoke. She was old-school French, a woman who loved fashion and luxury, and wasn't afraid to flirt with any man she found attractive. And for most straight women, Tristan fit the bill.

"Kiss me, my love. Let an old woman die happy," she laughed.

"Hello, Clarisse," Tristan greeted her with a peck on the cheek as Anton followed behind his wife, hands extended to greet Tristan with an embrace.

"Tristan, my boy, so lovely to see you!" Anton boomed, taking Tristan's hand in a firm shake before pulling him into a brief, warm embrace. As he released him, Anton's lips curved, letting out a soft laugh at his wife's playful demeanor, his weathered face crinkling with amused affection. Possessing the ease of a man who had long grown accustomed to Clarisse's flirtatious humor, he clapped Tristan heartily on the back, his touch both congenial and paternal, as if welcoming a family member.

"How are you, Mr. Filby?" Tristan received Anton's affection in kind.

"Quite well, quite well, old chap," he said. "Where's that lovely wife of yours?"

The older couple had not yet directed their attention any further than the doorway to glimpse Julius and Amanda standing near the desk. Amanda's face flushed as the word *wife* hurdled towards her ears. *The wife? Had she even thought of that? Had she asked?*

"Erm... ex-wife," Tristan corrected Anton as quickly as he could. "It's been quite the adventure, but we're on the other side of it now."

"Oh, I'm sorry to hear it. But I..." Anton didn't complete his thought as Clarisse stepped fully into the study and Julius approached.

"Julius, darling," she said, embracing her old friend tightly. "If only you were younger, I'd be inclined to flirt with you too. You look fabulous."

"Careful," Anton protested. "I'll separate you two if I must. We may be the best of friends, but I will not allow you to steal my wife." He slapped Julius's back as he moved in for a hug.

Amanda stayed near the desk, studying the room like a seasoned detective hiding behind a mask of casual indifference. Her fingers trailed lightly along the edge, her gaze flitting from the ornate carvings in the wood to the stack of papers beside the lamp, searching for anything out of place. A hidden compartment, a cipher, a clue. Something Julius might be keeping from them.

All the while, her mind spun with the revelation that Tristan had been married. A wife. An ex-wife, but still. She kept her expression neutral, not allowing the slight tightening in her chest to show. It wasn't her business. She was here for a mission, not to actually get her feelings involved. There was no training on how to not have emotions, though.

She let out a soft hum of amusement at Clarisse's antics, feigning interest in the conversation as her sharp eyes scanned the bookshelves. The placement of titles and the gaps between them. Was one a lever? Did they conceal a safe? She took a slow, steady breath, willing herself to focus as her thoughts refused to stop racing. *You are not a jealous woman. You are a professional.*

Amanda leaned against the sturdy desk, one hand resting on a small decorative box. Innocuous at first glance, but something about the way it was placed, just slightly askew compared to the other neatly arranged objects, caught her attention. Surely, that couldn't be the box of information Katherine referred to, but she did mention old-fashioned methods like microdots. *Could there be untold information in this small, unassuming cube?* With everyone distracted by conversation, but still in the room, she resisted the urge to lift the lid immediately, instead drawing her hand away as though she had merely been admiring the craftsmanship.

Clarisse's laughter trilled through the room, masking the faint rustle of paper as Amanda's fingertips brushed the corner of a letter half-tucked beneath a ledger. *Interesting.* She made a mental note of it. Later, when no one was watching, she'd find out what it contained.

For now, she smiled faintly, meeting Tristan's glance with a cool, unreadable expression.

"Clarisse, Anton, I'd like you to meet Amanda," he said, gesturing towards her with an easy smile. "She's a close friend of mine."

Amanda straightened, stepping forward with a polite nod, her veil of calm firmly in place. "It's a pleasure to meet you both," she said, offering her hand.

Clarisse took it first, her grip surprisingly firm for a petite woman who dripped in silk and jewels. "Ah, a close friend, you say?" she purred, eyes gleaming with mischief. "How close, I wonder?"

Tristan only smiled. "Hmm... not going there, Clarisse," he widened his smile and his eyes.

Anton took Amanda's hand next, giving it a warm shake. "Any friend of Tristan's is a friend of ours," he said genially. "And what do you do, Miss Amanda?"

"Oh, I work in hospitality," she said smoothly, keeping her tone light. A familiar half-truth.

"She works as a flight attendant for a luxury flight company," Tristan explained to his sophisticated friends.

"Yes, I work for a fascinating company, Obsydian Aviation Services. We have trained pilots on rotation as luxury attendants in case of emergency," Amanda furthered the lie she fed Lyla, testing its believability. She'd have to tell Katherine that the fictional company that *equips attendants with skills in high-profile client relations, fine dining presentation, and in-flight safety for private jets and luxury airlines* would have to add, *and we provide extra pilots on demand.* It sounded absurd already.

Anton inattentively hummed in approval. "A useful skill."

Tristan's surprise was unhidden from his countenance, but he remained silent, wondering if Amanda was referring to herself as that pilot, unsure if he understood her correctly.

Amanda only smiled, her mind still working behind her composed exterior, regretting the decision to test the waters with her lie—the urge to demand respect for her accomplishments too strong. She had to let the regret go for now and stay on task. There was something in the room, and while she couldn't piece it together just yet, the circumstances of the evening were already enough to have something to report back to Katherine.

The group of old friends and the one outsider headed to the terrace for dinner, and the chef began to present details of their first course as waiters seated them and poured chilled beverages into their glasses. Amanda quickly realized she could use their bond to her advantage, allowing them to dominate the conversation and observe everything. The meal was a lavish affair—seared duck, truffle-infused potatoes, and a rich red wine that Clarisse insisted was the finest in the villa's collection. Their dialogue meandered effortlessly, bouncing between travel, business, and old stories that sent Anton and Julius into deep, nostalgic laughs.

Amanda let Tristan and the others carry most of the conversation, only chiming in when it seemed natural. She was focused on noting everything—Julius's occasional glances towards her, not with affection, but seemingly trying to get a read on her, Anton's cryptic way of speaking about business with an ease that suggested deep connections, the way Clarisse, even through her playful flirtations, seemed to be subtly assessing her too.

Before the dessert was presented, as the others turned their attention to a story Julius was telling about an ill-fated trip to Vienna, Tristan leaned in closer, his voice low enough that only she could hear.

"A pilot?" he murmured, his breath just grazing her ear. "Do you have pilot experience too, or were you referring to others in your company?"

Amanda didn't flinch, she merely took another sip of wine before turning her head slightly towards him, a teasing smile ghosting her lips. "Does it matter?"

Tristan's eyes shone with intrigue, but before he could press further, Clarisse's voice cut through the quiet moment.

"So, Amanda, tell me, where has your work taken you lately?"

Amanda turned to face the table, smoothly deflecting the conversation into safer territory. But even as she spoke, she could feel Tristan's gaze lingering on her, quietly questioning her.

She swallowed the fear threatening to make her squirm. A lie her bestie would buy may not work on someone who had no reason to believe her and no history of trusting her.

"Actually, Tristan and I were recently in Greece." Her voice sounded light and cheery.

"Oh, I adore Greece! And you were smart to go before this month, darlings; it's unbearable in July," she quipped before taking a sip from her glass. "So, this friendship..." she pointed her finger back and forth between the two of them, eyebrows raised with a sly grin. "...it requires travel?"

Amanda kept her expression composed, but inside, she could feel the heat of scrutiny pressing against her. Clarisse was a woman who lived in a world of wealth, charm, and carefully woven social intrigue. She knew how to read between the lines, and Amanda could only hope her performance held up under such sharp observation.

Just as she opened her mouth to craft a response that she hoped would be both vague and charming, Tristan leaned back in his chair and laughed, effortlessly stealing the spotlight.

"Oh, believe me, Clarisse, it's a hell of a story," he said, his voice warm, animated, effortlessly captivating. "You see, I first saw Amanda one night in Chicago—just a passing moment, really. We brushed past each other on the way to the bathroom at a restaurant, and that was it."

Clarisse's playful grin faltered slightly. "That was it?"

"That was it," Tristan confirmed, taking a sip of his wine. "But for four years, I couldn't get her out of my head. I didn't know her name, didn't know a single thing about her, except that she was the most beautiful woman I'd ever seen. And then, completely by chance, I found out we had mutual friends, and that she was *single*." He set his glass down, his eyes flickering briefly towards Amanda. "Fate, right?"

Clarisse gasped, her hand fluttering to her chest in delight. *"Mon Dieu,* a love-at-first-sight story! How utterly romantic!"

Anton tilted his head, a cynical glint skimming his expression. "And here I thought you weren't the sentimental type, Tristan."

Amanda forced a light laugh, tucking a strand of hair behind her ear. "I'm not sure 'love at first sight' is exactly how I'd put it," she teased, trying to downplay the intensity of his confession.

Tristan smirked. "Maybe not for you."

Clarisse all but swooned. "Oh, this is better than the movies," she sighed, thoroughly enchanted. "A man remembering a woman for years before fate brings them back together? Amanda, my dear, you must have made quite the impression."

Amanda's fingers tightened around the stem of her glass. Before she had to find yet another way to deflect, the servers entered, presenting dessert with an elegant flourish. The conversation shifted, and Amanda exhaled slowly, allowing herself a moment of reprieve.

Chapter Eight

"I can't do this anymore," Amanda blurted out. "I'm not cut out for covert operations, Katherine. I can't keep lying to everyone."

Amanda stormed into Katherine's London office, her heart pounding. The sleek, minimalist décor of the room only heightened her frustration with the negligible explanations she had been given. Katherine sat behind the desk, her expression unreadable.

She arched an eyebrow, leaning back in her chair. "You knew what you were signing up for."

"Knew?" Amanda scoffed. "What? No, I didn't!" she snapped. "I was coerced. I signed those papers because of that damn picture. Do you know what I've been through with those people? I let you manipulate me into this, and I am literally scared for my life while pretending to party it up with these snobs. I can't keep doing it! What good was my entire trip? I got nothing. And I don't know how or why or what I'm even looking for. I'm out," she said, her words emphatic and percussive.

Katherine's expression didn't waver. "You know enough. You know what's at stake."

"I'm not afraid anymore," Amanda said, her voice trembling with anger. "Sue me for breaking the nondisclosure. What do I have to lose, anyway? I'm out," she repeated. "Out. Don't call me," she said, placing her spy phone on the desk.

Katherine stood, her calm demeanor finally cracking. "Amanda, if you walk away now, you won't just lose this job. You'll lose any chance of finding out the truth. About Tristan, about Julius, about your past—about everything. Are you really willing to give that up?"

Amanda stared at her, her fists clenched at her sides. The room felt suffocating, and for a moment, she considered walking out without another word.

"What do you know about my past?" Amanda asked through gritted teeth.

Katherine drew a breath through her nose, slowly letting it out in measured precision. "I'm not your enemy," she finally said.

"But I want answers, Katherine. Real ones. No more cryptic bullshit."

Katherine's lips curled into a faint smile. "You'll get them. When the time is right. I promise. I'm not just your handler or supervisor, Amanda. I am your advocate, I promise you that."

"The time is now, Katherine," Amanda calmly demanded. "I will share my side of the story if you help me make sense of it, deal?"

Katherine's eyes searched Amanda's.

"It'll make me a better agent," Amanda said with a convincing tone.

Katherine could relate to the frustration of having her normal life sidelined. But even she didn't know all the details of Amanda's past. Perhaps if she got them, she would be able to help her be a better agent, or ideally, get out altogether.

"All right," Katherine agreed. "Take a seat. It's about time we get to know each other. Start with the photograph. Who is it? And why is it so powerful?"

"Don't you recognize him? You work for the Hansen family, right?" Amanda presumed.

"Our company..." Katherine hesitated, "...is a conglomerate, you could say. My level of security clearance is not top, so there is information that I don't have access to, but I can confirm that, yes, the Hansen family is part of it. Though, I do not know how deeply their ties go."

The thought of recording devices flashed through Amanda's mind. She grabbed the notepad and pen sitting on Katherine's desk and quickly scribbled the words, "We aren't being recorded, are we?"

Katherine shook her head. "No, I do have enough power to demand that my every word isn't archived for the records." She sounded almost sarcastic in a way that endeared Amanda.

"Okay, well, I was sixteen in that picture, almost seventeen. Cooper was eighteen."

Katherine's breath caught. After decades in this business, she wasn't accustomed to being surprised by information. But this was the first time she had heard a secret about one of her bosses—or, to be fair, one of their children.

Amanda placed the photo she always kept close on Katherine's desk.

"It *is* him," Katherine said. "Remarkable. It's stunning how men can look so boyish at that age and how womanly you seem."

"I was becoming a mother," Amanda let a long sigh escape her lips. "We were so in love. Cooper was supposed to leave for college in a couple of months, and I still had a year of high school left, but we were going to make it work," she scoffed. Even Amanda couldn't believe how naïve she'd been.

A tear plummeted down her face as she quickly flicked it away. "Mr. Hansen, Cooper's granddad, showed up one day. We hadn't told anyone—I mean, except for Lyla, and I didn't think they knew. I didn't even show for the first five months.

But somehow... his family got wind of it. They said I was ruining Cooper's life. People think times have changed, but let me just tell you, a man running for office, even just a state representative, they don't even let your kids mess up. Not even today. Anyway, they came storming in one day, demanding to talk to us all... Mr. Hansen is the one who told my parents, I didn't even get to." Amanda had to take a moment. She hadn't said these words aloud in a very long time.

Katherine reached her hand over to touch Amanda's. "That's awful. I'm so sorry."

"Yeah, it was pretty horrible," Amanda agreed. "So, they sent me away. I had the baby in September of that year and started my last year of school only a couple of weeks later than I was supposed to. Cooper's dad eventually became Governor Hansen, and Cooper went off to West Point, even though he had detested the military when we were together. His top choice was Michigan State, but... I guess that never happened."

"And... your parents? They just agreed to send you away?" Katherine asked.

Amanda's face flushed with a mix of regret, heartache, and childhood trauma. "Well, there's something you should know about that too, I guess. I'm kind of the black sheep of my family. My biological mom is my mother's sister. The elusive woman I grew up knowing as Auntie Kate was my actual mother. I have siblings who still don't know. My father, I'm told, is British—I've never met him—so... maybe that's why I hold it against you." They both laughed. Amanda depended on humor to lighten life's otherwise unbearable burdens.

"When my parents found out I was pregnant at the same age my mother had me, they were furious. But it wasn't just anger. It was... convenient. They'd spent my whole life pretending I was theirs, covering up the truth about Aunt Kate being my biological mom. So, my pregnancy gave them an out—an excuse to cast me aside and tell me it was high time I grew up... and, in a way, a chance to erase the lie they'd been living. So they took it." Amanda's shoulders dropped, feeling the heaviness of defeat and betrayal as if it were happening in real time.

"And the baby? Do you know what happened? Or was the nondisclosure thorough?" Katherine asked.

"As thorough as it gets," Amanda replied. "The Hansens think I don't even know the gender, but we went to an ul-trasound before we told anybody, even Lyla. Cooper and I wanted that experience together as we were making our secret plans. So, we knew it was a girl. He was so happy. I was going to finish my GED and move into his apartment once he got settled in Michigan... but... they caught us."

Amanda paused, swallowing hard before continuing.

"The day I gave birth, the doctor cut the cord and walked out with the little bundle that was supposed to be a source of joy. It's a strange type of emptiness, that feeling. Not just absence, but loss. Like a whole person that was there—solid, certain, yours—and then, in an instant, they're gone. Snatched, stolen. And in its place? Nothing. Just a hollow space where they, or the dream of them, used to be—a silence where there should be sounds. It's killed any motherly instinct I ever had, that loss."

She exhaled shakily.

"The Hansens didn't just want Cooper and me apart—they wanted to make sure no one could ever connect us to each other *through her*. If I kept my baby, people who knew us would eventually figure out the truth. The timing, the resemblance... it would have come out. Taking her away wasn't just about control, it was about erasing proof our ties ever existed in his world. They didn't want to risk anyone putting the pieces together.

"And it's not just about the baby being gone at times. It's the *taking* that unsettles you. The violation of it. The sudden, sharp realization that the world isn't as secure as you thought it was. That you aren't as capable of protecting yourself and those you love as you believed.

"At first, there's shock, then the anger comes—hot, sharp, directionless. But the worst of it, the part that lingers, is the emptiness. A kind of echo inside you. A space that shouldn't be there, reminding you of what was, of what *should* still be.

"And the truth is, no matter how much time passes, you never quite stop noticing that space. You just learn to live around it."

Katherine felt the encumbrance of Amanda's plight blanket the room in a cloak of sadness. It was never as evident as this, normally lingering just beneath the agent's skin. Katherine understood Amanda on several levels, but never guessed the breadth of pain such a young woman was carrying.

"What did they threaten you with?" Katherine asked.

"What didn't they?" Amanda huffed. "They threatened to block my entrance to MIT, not that it mattered. I was so depressed that I never went to classes. I just wanted to fly my planes and leave everything. They said they'd keep me out of a job and never threatened my life, but you know how they are. Cryptic messages of accidents happening... you know, I got a clipping from the newspaper once reporting a fatal accident on the highway not far from where I was living. Cooper's dad literally signed the card inside after writing, 'What a tragedy.' Sick, right?"

Katherine nodded in agreement.

"And they told me they monitor his phone so they'd know if I ever contacted Cooper again. They had already scared the shit out of me, I wasn't going to go anywhere near Cooper anyway. So why did they have to take my baby away from me? Seems they just wanted me to suffer. And he clearly didn't know they tracked him because I got a few messages from him trying to meet up to talk after he just let them railroad us, but... I never responded. I couldn't. Anyway, Lyla told me that he's going into politics now, too. What a joke," Amanda rolled her eyes, letting a short breath escape her lips in what sounded more like a laugh than disgust.

She did find it almost comical. "I used to think he was so loving and kind and could never be the type to get wrapped up in crazy government schemes like his dad and grandpa. So much for fighting the system."

"Like you?" Katherine said without a beat.

"Hey..." Amanda wanted to protest. "I'm pouring my heart out here; the last thing I need you to do is throw my own hypocrisy back at me. We all think we're better than our in-stinct to survive. But... I guess not. Cooper did what he had to, and I do what I have to."

"As do I, Amanda," Katherine agreed. "As do we all. And... is that everything?" Katherine asked.

"Why wouldn't it be? Them stealing my baby and making me sign a nondisclosure that I'll never tell anyone I'm her mother, or put my name in an online DNA database, isn't enough to manipulate me? I shouldn't be scared of them enough to say 'how high' when they tell me to jump?"

"I'm not accusing you, Amanda. I'm simply asking," Katherine explained, letting the room fall completely silent, unbothered and patient.

The weight Amanda had been holding up for so long suddenly, without warning, came crashing down. Her breath hitched as she braced her elbows on her knees, fingers curled into fists, nails biting into her palms as she fought to keep control, but it was useless.

Amanda's chest tightened, her breaths coming sharp and uneven—like she'd been running for miles with no end in sight. She pressed a hand over her mouth as if she could physically hold back the sob that threatened to escape, but the dam had already broken. Her shoulders shook. First, small tremors that turned into full-body quakes, and then, finally, she shattered.

Katherine rushed to put a hand on her back, soothing, stroking, but Amanda bristled at her touch, and Katherine pulled back, crouching down in front of her instead. A choked, ragged sound escaped Amanda's mouth, somewhere between a gasp and a sob, and once it started, she couldn't stop. Tears blurred her vision, spilling down her cheeks unchecked as silent cries wracked through her body. She had spent so long keeping it together—so long pretending she was fine—that now, in the quiet, there was nothing left to hold the pieces in place.

Her body curled inward as if she could make herself smaller, disappear entirely. The room felt too big, too quiet, and too suffocating all at once.

"It's all right," Katherine comforted. "Let it out. I'm not going anywhere," she assured.

"No one knows..." Amanda inhaled, trying not to hyperventilate. "I've never told a soul. The NDA is ambiguous, but it's in there, though. When you look for it. They'd kill me—I know they would."

"Amanda, you're safe here," Katherine whispered, extending her hand.

"How can I know that?" Amanda pleaded through her sobs, eventually accepting Katherine's sympathy.

Katherine warmly placed Amanda's hand between both of hers. "Because I have been there—a newbie, scared, and desperate to find my way out from under their thumb. And now... I am healthy. I don't drink heavily like my counterparts. I take care of myself and come from a family with a history of longevity. I am destined to live possibly another ten or fifteen years before they let me resign. And I've already given them twenty. An older woman goes relatively unnoticed and is an invaluable asset to them. So, as I know and understand my lot in life, I will do everything in my power to get you in and out of this game as fast as possible. I am your ally," she said, lowering her voice. "I will not see you with the same fate. *That* is why you can trust me."

Amanda let her guard down for the first time in nearly twenty years.

"We were there," she whispered.

"What? Where?" Katherine didn't follow.

"In the boat," Amanda kept her voice barely audible. "Mr. Bubba... you know, Cooper's grandpa? He had a mistress. Cooper and I were just kids, and the Hansens let us hang out on the big boat with them when they'd take it out on the lake. This was before I got pregnant, of course. The Hansen family didn't approve of Cooper being with a girl of my family's status, but Mr. Bubba and Mr. Jimmy? They knew a thing about indiscretions and let us fade into the background. Mr. Jimmy didn't ever bring a woman on board, but in the drunken talks he had with his daddy, he sure said a lot."

Amanda's girlish Southern speech took over when she talked about the past.

"I always thought that calling a grown man Bubba was a theatrical exaggeration," Katherine lifted an eyebrow.

Amanda laughed. "It's a Southern thing, I guess. They all have the name James, and most of them have their mother's maiden name in the middle. And you can't exactly call them all James, so the oldest of the bunch usually has the name Bubba—you know, for brother—until it skips a generation or two of Jims and Jimmys and goes to the youngest again. Cooper just refused to be called by anything but his middle name by the time he was three, so I'm told. He didn't like Jimmy, Jim, James, *or* Bubba," Amanda remembered with a smirk.

"So, Mr. Bubba, James the first, or whatever number in line he was, had that scandal…" Katherine remembered the international news coverage of James Hansen, a US District Attorney turned celebrity defense lawyer who was suspected of killing his wife and mistress.

Amanda nervously nodded her head in affirmation, putting her fingers to her lips as if trying to will herself not to say more.

"And you… were… *there?*" Katherine asked, sounding incredulous, not because she thought Amanda wasn't telling the truth. But because she knew she *was*, and Katherine was realizing that her own briefing on this assignment was far from complete.

"I…" Amanda tried to stutter out a few more syllables.

"No. Say no more." Katherine waved her hand in front of Amanda, standing to her feet after being face to face with her, intensely gripping her hand. "I don't need to know the details to understand the danger, and you were right to acquiesce to their demands. They could bury you," she affirmed.

"Yeah," Amanda swallowed the harsh truth of her reality. "I mean, Old Mr. Hansen is dead now… but the Governor? He would never be able to run for president if people knew what he did to protect his dad," Amanda contemplated aloud.

"Indeed," Katherine said pensively, attempting to conceal a relentless stream of thoughts churning in her mind and refusing to settle.

"You think there's more? I mean... more that the Governor is hiding?"

"No, no, it's not that," Katherine deflected.

"Buuuut?" Amanda pressed.

Katherine squinted her eyes, blowing a soft whiff through her nose and complying. "There are those of us who find the death of Mr. Hansen... suspicious. He dies just after the story breaks, just after the internet frenzy demanding answers from this generationally controlling family? There's more than what meets the eye here."

"I don't think Mr. Jimmy could've killed him!" Amanda gasped, surprised at herself for defending the man.

"No, no. Neither do I," Katherine wasn't interested in elaborating. She'd already said more than she should.

"You... don't think he's still alive, do you?" Amanda quickly sifted through fragments of the conversation, rearranging them into a picture that hadn't fully formed.

"I do not know. But, what I can say is that twenty years ago, I worked in this office. I sat behind this desk. And when the Hansen family came into our orbit, the wealth they had before the senior Mr. Hansen passed, and what they have today is remarkably different. Either he is a cold-blooded killer who will do anything to fill his coffers, or he has the worst luck in the world. After his mistress drowns, his wife dies in her sleep from carbon monoxide poisoning? Just after he collects millions of dollars in insurance money, he kicks the bucket before a proper investigation can take place? It's fishy at the very least."

"I thought you were in the business of fishy," Amanda smirked.

"Fishing, dear, not fishy." Katherine met Amanda toe-to-toe with her humor.

"Touché," Amanda smiled.

"Well, I'm glad we got that out of the way," Katherine said. "But none of this has anything to do with our current assignment," signaling that she was ready to get back to work.

"Doesn't it, though? I'm here because the Hansens own me," Amanda reminded.

"Yes, of course, I just meant the suspicious death… forget I said anything," Katherine said. "Now, shall we? I wanted to talk about the Filbys and MI5."

"MI5? I thought it was six," Amanda looked confused.

"Oh, it is, in fact, both," Katherine explained. "People often get MI5 and MI6 muddled, but the difference is quite simple. MI5 is concerned with threats *inside* Britain. MI6 deals with threats *outside* Britain.

"MI5 is officially known as the Security Service and is responsible for counter-espionage, counter-terrorism, and protecting national security from internal threats. If there's a foreign agent operating in London, a terrorist plot being hatched in Birmingham, or some group trying to undermine the state from within, MI5 is the one handling it.

"MI6," Katherine continued, "officially known as the Secret Intelligence Service, operates *beyond* British borders. Their focus is gathering intelligence on foreign governments, terrorist organizations, and anyone else who might pose a threat to the UK from abroad. MI6 officers aren't out chasing criminals in the streets of London, they're embedded overseas, recruiting informants, running covert operations, and obtaining intelligence that helps shape British foreign policy.

"If you want a simple way to remember it: MI5 watches our own back; MI6 looks beyond the horizon. Both are essential. Both deal in secrets. And both, more often than not, go unnoticed... unless something goes very wrong."

"Oof!" Amanda exclaimed. "So... Anton... has he been *noticed* by MI5?"

"No. Not Anton. Clarisse," Katherine informed.

"No. Way." Amanda's mouth fell agape. "I would've put my money on him, not her."

"I told you, women make better spies. Not because they are often more intelligent, but because they are the most underestimated, the most invisible. And thus, perfectly under the radar."

"Wow. But... I didn't find anything. The box that Julius literally handed to me after seeing me admire it so much, turned out to be nothing," Amanda scoffed. "She couldn't have been there to look for clues too, right? And does Anton know? Now I have a *million* questions." Amanda let the heaviness of her breakdown melt away, realizing her curious excitement had shifted the mood.

"Well, who would have imagined that this would be both a therapy session and a history lesson?"

Katherine was happy to get down to business. Her harsh exterior wasn't natural, but she was rusty when it came to feeling her feelings. She had worked tirelessly to train herself to be cold and distant, but it had been decades since she let her guard down. Her comfort zone was pragmatism and relentless work.

"Do you know about the Cambridge Five?" she asked, returning to her chair and bringing up a Google search.

"Oh, the Burgess guy, right?"

"Guy Burgess," Katherine corrected in a teacherly cadence, "but, yes. It was the kind of betrayal that shakes a nation, not with the force of an explosion, but with the slow, creeping realization that the damage has already been done," she explained.

"It started in the 1930s at Cambridge, where five bright young men were recruited, not by their own government, but by the Soviets. It didn't appear to be treason, but ideology and conviction. They truly believed that the world was shifting and that communism was the future they wanted. So, they positioned themselves as double agents working for us, but really they were in Russia's pocket.

"Kim Philby was the most famous of them. Clever, well-connected, and utterly without hesitation. He climbed to the highest levels of MI6, all while passing Britain's secrets to Moscow. Then there was Guy Burgess, brilliant but reckless, perhaps the most memorable of them because he hid self-destruction behind his charm. Maclean, steady and deliberate, held a position in the Foreign Office, where his access was invaluable. Anthony Blunt, an art historian of all things, wove himself into the very fabric of the Establishment. And then John Cairncross, quieter than the rest, but no less complicit.

"They weren't amateurs. They embedded themselves so deeply within British intelligence that by the time anyone realized, it was far too late. They compromised wartime operations, fed Moscow everything from nuclear intelligence to diplomatic secrets, and, worst of all, they were trusted. That was their real weapon—privilege, education, class. No one suspected them because they *belonged*."

"Wait," Amanda stopped her. "Are you drawing a comparison? Are we spies for the good side... and Tristan is possibly a Russian asset? Feeding them information about Ukraine and her allies, under the guise of a privileged man disillusioned with the system, but actually believing the wave of the future is Putin's dominance? And I'm supposed to find out if Clarisse is on my side or his? Where does Julius fit in? What is my actual mission here?" Amanda barely took a breath.

Katherine grinned. "There are indeed many moving pieces, and we don't know where they belong. Even the best-placed spies can't outrun suspicion forever, so we're trying to advance before they do."

"Who, though? How do you know you're fighting on the right side? How do you know the Hansens are the good guys? How do I?" Amanda sounded as if she was pleading for mercy, and perhaps she was.

"That is part of your mission. I have worked hand in hand with multiple government agencies since my mid-forties, Amanda," Katherine let out a percussive laugh, remembering her youth with fondness. "Our company is owned by many members, committed to the ideology that no powerful state, government, or entity shall be allowed to make sweeping decisions that affect the entire population without some accountability. And we operate most effectively as covert agents—spies," she said, wagging her head towards Amanda with a sigh. "But we are in a crucial time, and some of the tactics we use are not kind. They are not ethical. And they are dangerous. But I want you to be spared from this life. So I will do what it takes to get to the bottom of this web of men who threaten the planet more now than ever."

"And you'll use me to do it," Amanda said, not meaning it as an accusation.

"Yes," she replied slowly. "Do you know what happened to the Cambridge Five?" Katherine asked.

"No," Amanda replied flatly.

"Burgess and Maclean fled to Moscow in 1951, their sudden disappearance confirmation of what many had feared. Philby held out longer, convincing some that he was innocent until the weight of evidence forced him to defect in 1963. Blunt was unmasked quietly, spared public disgrace for a time, though Margaret Thatcher made sure that didn't last.

"And what did they gain? A life in exile. Moscow welcomed them, but it was never home. Philby drank himself to death, disillusioned. Burgess never fit in. The Soviet Union was not the utopia they had imagined, and they were never quite trusted, not even by the people they had served.

"The story of the Cambridge Five is not a dramatic spectacle, it's colder than that. It's a reminder that betrayal rarely comes from the outside. It comes from those already inside the walls, the ones you think you know. And when you realize it, it's far too late. And what's more... is that we suspect, and have evidence to support the fact, that these double agents recruited their family members, passing the torch generation after generation."

"Wait... Filby? But you said it wasn't Anton," Amanda blurted.

"Coincidence," Katherine dismissed the idea. "One is spelt with an *f* and the other with a *ph*—I can never remember which."

"That's *quite* the coincidence," Amanda pointed out.

"Yes, but it is Clarisse who is believed to be our culprit."

"Okay, so you're saying Clarisse is possibly what? The daughter of one of these guys?"

"Not the five," Katherine said, "the more than *fifty* suspected to have been among the traitors at the time. The man we are after is in politics, and his own daughter just joined the ranks of Parliament with ties to people like..."

"Like Governor Jim Hansen and Julius Babb," Amanda completed the sentence for her.

"Precisely," Katherine confirmed.

"So... it still doesn't make sense. They're the good guys? They're the bad guys? What? You said the Governor is in this no-name company we're working for."

"We are figuring it out. We can never be too careful. We are not above being duped, Amanda. No one is," Katherine said.

"Oh!" Amanda exclaimed, exasperated. "So I'm tasked with finding out *if* Julius Babb and Governor Hansen are working for the Russians? And if they're going to use Tristan's technology to spy on everyone? And if Tristan is in on this..." Amanda considered the possibility. "Good. God. You could've told me," she stuttered. "This is bigger than me witnessing a likely murder."

"Don't ever say those words aloud again," Katherine scolded.

"I won't. I don't think I ever have before," Amanda sputtered. Letting the words escape her body felt like releasing tiny boulders stacked year upon year in the pit of her stomach, finally tumbling out into the abyss. She decided to allow that to be enough, letting a small measure of anguish go that she'd carried for nearly two decades.

"You know, a cop offered me the witness protection program," she continued her spiral of thoughts. "Once Mr. Hansen died, though, they closed the investigation and declared it an accident. I heard the cop was transferred to some other precinct. Anyway... he told me then that someone saw us that night on the boat. I knew the Governor would come after me if I talked, so I denied it—kept my mouth shut all these years. It was that, or lose my identity in witness protection. But I already had so many flight hours... I just couldn't. Oh... and I have something to tell you. I kind of tested a little lie that may not have... landed, no pun intended."

"What do you mean?"

"I kind of told them I'm a pilot... well, that Obsydian offers services with an extra pilot on board," she grimaced.

"You mean, other than the captain and the co-pilot?" Katherine's eyes widened.

"Kind of... *question mark?*" Amanda scrunched her lips together like a three-year-old in trouble.

"Ugh," Katherine sighed. "Try to be more believable, please. Every agent makes mistakes, but perhaps this is a good thing. Truth is easier to build upon than fiction. I'll make sure the website is updated—and we'll come back to that police officer who questioned you. I'll need his files," Katherine said, shaking her head. "I think we've both had about enough for today, wouldn't you say?"

"Oof, yes," Amanda agreed, turning on her heel and leaving the office, her mind racing.

Chapter Nine

The city lights of London glittered beyond the floor-to-ceiling windows, but her reflection on the glass was what held Amanda's attention—an image of someone she knew but barely recognized.

A phone buzzed beside her, breaking the silence. She lifted the screen to see a text from Lyla.

Thinking of you. Call if you need me. Amanda found Lyla's constant use of red heart emojis endearing.

Her stomach twisted. She wanted to call Lyla more than anything, to spill every secret, every doubt, every fear. But the idea of burdening her best friend with the truth felt impossible, and the danger that now loomed was undeniable. How could she explain any of it? Not even Lyla knew the full truth of what she had been through with the Hansen family. She, like the rest of White Pine just assumed them to be rich assholes who always got their way and never cared who got hurt as long as they got ahead.

Even with Cooper... Lyla was a fan at first, helping her best friend and secret teenage lover sneak away for secret meetups and clandestine adventures. But when he ghosted everyone from high school and suddenly became some decorated military dude instead of fighting the establishment like he had always sworn he'd do, she shut the door on him and threw away the key. She was devastated by his choices and fiercely protective of her best friend. Lyla was operating with a fictional account of Amanda's life.

Can't chat. Have to fly. Call tomorrow. Amanda lied. She hadn't yet dealt with the emotions of the day before, still reeling from all of the information she had both shared and received.

Her watch hummed, illuminating the small screen on her wrist. It had been almost two months since Amanda had found herself caught in this *Venus Spy Trap,* as she began referring to it in her head.

Amanda's mind was a world unto itself, a labyrinth of sharp observations, half-formed theories, and private jokes that no one else would ever hear. It had always been that way—her mind didn't just process information; she would rearrange it, categorize it, dress it up in clever disguises, and make it more palatable.

She had a habit of narrating her own life like an unreliable tour guide, assigning people nicknames based on first impressions and cataloging experiences with small euphemisms that softened the edges of reality. A bad situation wasn't a disaster; it was a *learning opportunity.* A close call wasn't terrifying; it was an *unplanned adventure.* A mistake wasn't failure; it was *a plot twist.* It wasn't about denial—it was about keeping herself entertained. If life insisted on throwing chaos her way, she might as well give it a clever tagline.

If she didn't bring her wit into her own private inner workings, the information she was able to store would have been unbearable. Her photographic memory meant that her brain was a library, full of crisp, detailed recollections, but it was also a trickster, organizing them in unexpected ways. She'd recall an address by the way the numbers "felt" together—twenty-one Baker Street was a *friendly pair,* but seven-thirty-nine West Elm was *prickly and impatient.* Dates and names came with built-in associations: April fourteen was *a little too close to taxes for comfort,* and a man named Greg was always mentally filed as *Greg, the guy who may or may not wear a pen behind his ear and constantly apologizes for accidentally touching your arm.*

Even when she was spiraling, when anxiety clawed at her chest or uncertainty made her second-guess everything, her mind still worked in its peculiar, automatic way. A tense situation became a game of chess, each person a piece, their movements predictable if she watched closely enough. The lies she had to tell herself turned into catchy slogans, easy to remember, easier to believe.

It was her secret language, her own private coping mechanism. Because as long as she could keep herself half amused, she could keep herself in control. This was the only thing she could currently control as everything seemed to spiral around her.

She had finally switched her Apple Watch to receive notifications from Katherine, after missing a grand total of four texts for more than twelve hours. For every bit of precision and methodology Amanda brought to the table, her use of technology wasn't impressive. She liked the advancement of life's most convenient apps but hated the overabundance of information at her fingertips. She had enough of that twirling around in her head already.

I'll be at yours in five, the text read. She knew what that meant. Katherine was coming to give her another assignment. She'd be kicked from her little London nest to fly somewhere yet unknown. Until recently, the skies were her biggest comfort, but somehow, the perch in this city had come to give her more comfort than she'd ever had. Still in thought, Amanda moved slowly, standing to get herself a drink as she heard the ding of the elevator.

"A little less than five, wasn't it?" Amanda glanced at her watch.

"Four minutes and twenty-eight seconds, but who's counting?" Katherine quipped. She was a stickler for schedules, always knowing what time it was and the number of hours, minutes, and seconds even the most menial tasks took.

Katherine spread a few papers on the table. "Here. Your next assignment."

"You're joking, right?" Amanda said in disbelief after seeing the location—Tenerife South Airport. "I haven't been invited."

"This is just your flight information to get you on the island. Lucky for us, Julius scheduled a flight with an attendant already on staff, but only one pilot confirmed, so we were able to fill the spot. You'll be on board not as the Captain, but as the co-pilot."

"The term *First Officer* is what we use nowadays," Amanda smirked.

"What is it with your generation needing to reword commonly used terms and phrases to something that is different, but essentially means the exact same thing? As First Officer, are you not still second in command?"

"Sure, but it doesn't sound that way," Amanda chuckled.

Katherine grunted. "Well, whatever you are called, this allows us to have your skill displayed in front of Julius. After your little faux pas, we decided that it could potentially work in our favor. Julius may turn to you for your services if there's a quick flight he needs to schedule for any... quick turnarounds if you will."

"Ha, so it was a good thing—my slip-up, is what you're saying?" Amanda felt vindicated.

"We shall see. Tristan will not be on this flight, and Julius has not yet known you professionally, so if it comes back to bite us that no company has—nor will ever—offer flight attendant services with an emergency third pilot aboard remains to be seen."

Hearing Katherine say it aloud made it much worse. Amanda twisted her face, scrunching her nose and mouth with a sigh.

"Yeah, okay," she conceded.

"But if we can get you in with Julius, we can schedule you more often as a pilot, remove your flight-attendant-emergency-pilot status from our roster, and schedule you as a *captain* or *first officer,*" Katherine smirked.

"Yeah, you could have done that from the beginning." Amanda tilted her head, eyes wide, she arched a brow, lips pressed together as she spread her hands like it was the most obvious thing in the world.

"Hmm, there were certain opinions about you being too intimidating for Tristan Montgomery. We weren't sure if he'd be as likely to pursue a woman who didn't, well, seem a little more needy than you. And the unexpected turn that he had been interested in you already didn't happen until we had you on the flight manifest as the attendant. So, to keep the story, we stuck with it," Katherine explained.

"You know it didn't have to be this way, right? If I would have been approached by someone I knew... if Governor Hansen would have reached out personally, I would've come," Amanda admitted.

"Would you?" Katherine sounded genuinely surprised. "After the man put you through so much?"

"Sure, I fear nothing more in life but the power that man has had over me. But it's more than that. I mean, I wouldn't have agreed to be a spy without your tactics, so kudos to you, but... I can't tell you the number of times I've dreamed of seeing him again. Finding answers. Seeing if I made stuff up in my head or if my recurring nightmares were real. Reconnecting..." she let her voice trail off.

"Amanda." Katherine sensed where this was going. "There is not now—nor will there *ever* be—an invitation for you to reconnect with Cooper. That has been made abundantly clear. He has his own life. His own family."

"His family?" Amanda questioned. "But I thought..."

"He is engaged. Any politician is expected to have an adept partner," she began to explain.

"You mean a trophy wife," Amanda quipped.

"Perhaps," Katherine admitted the reality that the patriarchy was as robust as ever in our modern day. "But, I hear it is quite authentic, this relationship. They seemed to be smitten. So, there is no reason for you to let your mind wander."

"I can assure you that any warm feelings I had for Cooper have turned into deep disappointment," Amanda confessed. "I don't know, I just thought, one day, I'd put the feelings to bed. I half-convinced myself that I was an exaggerative teenager who made the whole thing up."

"It's funny what our minds do to us, isn't it?" Katherine said.

"Yeah," Amanda agreed.

"All right, that's about it for now. I'll have instructions for you once you reach your destination," Katherine began to gather the papers she had brought.

Amanda stared at the collection before watching Katherine place each one back into the folder she had entered with. "What do you do with those after our meetings?"

"Incinerate them," Katherine replied smoothly as if there were no other option that made sense.

"Naturally," Amanda replied sarcastically. She was going to need to walk off some of her angst. "Hold the elevator, I'll come down with you," she told Katherine as she slipped on a pair of sandals, grabbing her crossbody.

Amanda and Katherine rode the elevator down in relative silence, saying a quick goodbye as they walked out of the building. Amanda picked up her pace, walking briskly through the London streets, the city's usual charm lost on her. Her phone buzzed, and she pulled it from her bag to see Lyla's name flashing on the screen.

"Hey," Amanda said, trying to inject some normalcy into her tone. "I was gonna call, promise!"

"Really?" Lyla said with an incredulous sigh. "What's going on with you?"

Amanda hesitated. She had never outright lied to Lyla before Katherine entered her life. But now, every conversation felt like navigating a minefield. "It's just work. Busy season, you know."

"Busy spending all your time with Tristan Montgomery?" Lyla teased, though there was an edge of concern in her voice.

Amanda forced a laugh. "It's not like that."

"Uh-huh. And the sun doesn't rise in the east." Lyla paused. "Listen, I know Tristan's got that whole brooding-genius-billionaire thing going on, but I feel like something's off."

"But you just loved him a couple of months ago," Amanda reminded her.

"I *know*... I've loved him for a long time!" she exclaimed.

"And yet you didn't tell me he was married," Amanda launched the accusation with little grace. She knew part of her disappointment stemmed from the fact that her best friend—the person who knew her better than anyone—had kept a crucial detail from her. Lyla had known that a married man spent years longing for a stranger in a picture, unaware that the woman he dreamed of was Amanda. But when she found out, instead of warning her—instead of telling her that his divorce had been finalized only a short time before they met—her best friend had simply found it romantic.

"I didn't know it was you he was dreaming about... not at first..." Lyla explained, "And they were separated for such a long time, Amanda. It didn't cross my mind because I had known about their unhappy marriage ever since Tristan came back into Kyle's life, honestly."

"Okay," Amanda accepted the explanation, "but I do think I'm alright. I'm not falling for him, truly." She felt a tingling of self-denial on her skin.

"Okay, I'll support you whatever you decide, you know that. But I can feel when things aren't quite right. Call me fickle; it's fine. I was ready to pick out bridesmaids' dresses when I heard of all the ways the universe is throwing you together... you know I'm psychic, right?"

"Yes, I know," Amanda's singsong reply placated her bestie.

Lyla was the kind of person who floated through life as if she were following an invisible current only she could sense. She believed everything and nothing all at once, picking up and discarding philosophies like thrift store finds, one day devoted to the power of manifestation, the next convinced that free will was an illusion. It wasn't indecision, exactly. It was more like an openness to the shifting tides of the universe and a willingness to rewrite her beliefs based on the way the air felt when she woke up in the morning.

She was an artist in every sense of the word, not just in the way she photographed, painted, or sculpted but in the way she existed—her life was a canvas, and she colored outside the lines without hesitation. She read tarot but didn't believe in it, burned sage but rolled her eyes at the idea that the smoke could clear bad energy, and trusted her gut but second-guessed herself immediately after. Yet, for all her contradictions, Lyla had an unnerving way of sensing when something was off.

And something was *definitely* off.

She didn't know what it was, only that it curled around the edges of the conversation like a shadow just out of sight, making the hairs on her arms stand on end. The air felt different, thick with something unspoken, and Lyla didn't need logic or evidence to know that whatever it was, it wasn't good.

"Well, just... be careful, okay? I can't say if it's something with Tristan or if it's with this job change situation, but I don't want you getting sucked into something you can't get out of."

Amanda's stomach churned. "I hear you, but I can handle myself."

"I know you can," Lyla said. "Just promise me you'll keep your guard up."

"I will... and about the job, they have me scheduled as a pilot on my next flight. The company is considering discontinuing the service for attendants who serve as emergency pilots. It was pretty short-lived. Turns out even the rich aren't buying it as much as they thought they would," Amanda said.

"Okay, well, that's good. Maybe it's nothing, maybe it's something. Just keep your eyes peeled," Lyla admonished.

"Will do," Amanda promised, though the words felt hollow.

Hanging up, she pressed her back against the cold glass of a towering skyscraper, blowing out a forced sigh. The city buzzed around her, each unspoken truth heavy bricks against her chest.

Chapter Ten

"Mr. Babb," Amanda greeted with a slight nod, her voice polished and steady. "Welcome aboard."

Julius was stepping onto the sleek, private jet, exuding the kind of effortless confidence that came with obscene wealth. But staring at Amanda caught him off guard, and that was something that *never* happened to him. His glance shifted as he locked eyes with the woman he knew as Tristan's love interest in a first officer's uniform standing at the cockpit door. Amanda was amused that she was the one who had to feign surprise. It was fun to see Julius Babb squirm just a little.

He recovered quickly, but not before she caught the slight hitch in his expression. Amanda smoothed her delight away, standing poised and professional.

"Amanda." His tone held something unreadable. "I wasn't expecting you."

She gestured him inside, her composure unwavering. "I was as surprised to see you on the manifest," she said lightly. "I'll be your first officer for today's flight to Tenerife."

Julius stepped further in, studying her as if she were a puzzle he hadn't quite solved. "And where are you staying on the island?"

Amanda gave a practiced smile. "It's an Airbnb. I'll have to look up the address. Can I let you know when we land?"

"Of course," Julius hummed, eyes still on her, his lips curving as if he found her deflection more interesting than her answer. "A person should always know where they're going," he mused, slipping into his usual habit of threading philosophy through casual conversation. "Then again, some destinations reveal themselves only once you arrive."

"And other times, you never find where you're going," Amanda volleyed the wit back to his side of the court.

"Indeed," Julius smiled.

Amanda stepped aside, motioning towards his seat with the same easy grace she appeared to handle most things. "Make yourself comfortable, Mr. Babb. We'll be departing shortly."

Julius chuckled softly, truly impressed. Knowing her humble background, he had been gripped by watching her keep her composure in an elegant atmosphere with the most elite people on earth, the ease with which she slipped into an intimate social setting, and now her ability to maintain absolute professionalism.

As he settled into his seat, he threw out one more thought, just to see if she'd react. "Funny, isn't it? How the people you least expect to guide your journey always seem to turn up at the helm."

Amanda simply met his eyes with a knowing smile before disappearing into the cockpit.

Game on, she thought.

The flight was uneventful, and Amanda remembered the name of the place she was staying, the *El Mirador*, known for its breathtaking views, so she had the information at the ready for Julius as they both prepared to disembark.

"Here's my number. You'll need it," Julius told her as he handed her a business card, before descending the stairs.

Stepping off the plane, Amanda felt the embrace of summer wrap around her like a living thing—the thick, honeyed warmth of the season settling on her skin after hours in the pressurized cabin. The scent of hot pavement and jet fuel mingled in the air, carried by a breeze that barely stirred but still felt like freedom. She loved stretching her legs after a flight.

Her uniform was crisp despite the long flight, the uniform's navy fabric absorbing the late afternoon heat. For a moment, she simply stood there, letting the heat sink into her bones, feeling the pulse of the airport around her, the distant whir of taxiing planes, the occasional call over the intercom, the organized chaos of arrivals and departures. It was a rhythm she knew well, a constant in the ever-changing nature of her life.

As she wheeled her suitcase through the bustling airport, the rhythmic murmur of Spanish and the distant strumming of a street musician drifted through the air, adding to the island's effortless charm.

Stepping outside, she paused, letting the tawny light settle over her. The jagged peaks of volcanic mountains framed the horizon, a striking contrast to the sapphire-blue sea stretching endlessly beyond the coastline. The air carried a hint of adventure, something untamed, something promising, or maybe it was menacing—she couldn't be sure yet.

This venture had her emotions in a dizzying push and pull—one second, she was soaring, adrenaline pumping, heart pounding with exhilaration; the next, she was free-falling, her stomach lurching, breath catching as terror clawed at her ribs. It felt like standing on the edge of a cliff, arms spread wide, caught between the intoxicating rush you feel when falling in love—or lust—for the first time in a very long time, and the paralyzing knowledge of falling hard.

Amanda's cell service kicked in, and her watch buzzed with a welcome text. She was happy to be on the island and flicked through her notifications to find the address for the little house—with promises of stunning views—she was renting for the week. If she didn't get an invite to join Julius on the island, she'd have to rely on Tristan. He was set to arrive the next day for the big birthday bash Julius was throwing himself.

She walked to the edge of the lane where passenger pickup signs with Spanish words and universal pictures indicated directions.

"Get in," she heard a familiar voice call from a black sedan. The door swung open by the man sitting in the backseat.

"Oh, Julius," Amanda responded," I..."

"I'll take you to your place," he interrupted. "My driver knows where it is. If you'd like, I can give you the tour of my estate on this island as well," he smiled alluringly. "You can do a comparison of the two."

Amanda's throat tightened. She didn't want to turn him down. Saying no to a man like Julius Babb wasn't impossible, but it wasn't wise, either. He was the kind of person who never demanded; he simply expected. His power wasn't about his wealth as much as it was about his influence. People leaned in when he spoke; doors opened before he even reached for the handle.

So when he invited her to tour this place when it was just the two of them, she hesitated. Not because she wasn't curious about this enigmatic man tangled in whispers of accusations that never quite stuck, but because she knew that stepping deeper into his world without backup was risky.

"Come," he said smoothly, a faint smile playing on his lips. "I'll have my driver take you to your place afterward."

The way he said it, so casual, as if she'd already agreed, made her stomach churn. She knew better than to trust him. But she also knew better than to say no.

Amanda felt the brush of her compact pistol, slim and matte black, secured in a garter holster designed for seamless concealment. She had spent every afternoon in London at shooting practice, learning the art of a quick draw, the signs of lingering danger that go unnoticed by most. She had slipped into the bathroom after going through security, taking a moment to strap the weapon to her body.

The holster pressed against her skin, reassuring but unobtrusive, allowing her to move freely without revealing the secret fastened to her leg. If necessary, a quick shift of her stance, a subtle tug at the hem, and the weapon would be in her palm in a second, silent, unnoticed, and ready. She may not have had backup, but she could rely on the training she'd had.

"Of course," Amanda replied, pulling her suitcase towards the car as the driver walked to the trunk, took the bag, and gestured for her to get in. "I appreciate the kindness."

"No trouble at all," Julius smiled, scooting himself back to the opposite side of the car as Amanda slid in. "This one's my favorite, I think you'll love it."

"Your favorite home?" Amanda was used to saying goodbye to her passengers on a tarmac and rarely—if ever—seeing them again. To sit and chat with one of them about which was their favorite villa seemed absurd.

"No, honey, my favorite island… but, actually, it might be my favorite house too. We built this one, so it doesn't have the history of the other one, but I do love it," Julius smiled.

"*We?*" Amanda pointed out his pronoun usage.

"Yes, my wife and I," he explained.

"Wife?" Amanda was truly shocked, eyes agape, unable to hide her surprise.

"It's what we call her here, anyway," Julius grinned. "Her family is very… Catholic… and with the age difference, their approval comes by offering them gifts and telling people we're official. So, we try to keep them happy. You should come by and meet her tomorrow. She'll be flying in for the party. She lives in Barcelona most of the year while I travel, so we only see each other when I'm here, but we make that time count!"

Amanda imagined a sultry, twenty-something beauty with expensive taste and a well-rehearsed pout. The type who draped herself in designer clothes and diamonds he'd carelessly gifted her, delicate fingers scrolling through luxury travel itineraries, a bored sigh escaping glossy lips as she waited for Julius to return from meetings with men who ran the world.

"Oh," she bumbled as Julius turned his phone screen towards her, showing her a picture of the lovely couple nuzzled close in each other's arms. She looked younger, yes, but not mismatched.

The photo captured Julius and Esmé at an exclusive garden party, the kind where laughter was measured and champagne was not. Julius, appearing a decade younger than his actual age, stood with effortless confidence, his tailored suit crisp against the lush greenery of the estate. His silver-streaked hair was impeccably combed back, his tanned skin smooth and nearly unaged—proof of what money, discipline, and perhaps a few well-kept secrets could do for a man. His alert green eyes, still keen and knowing, hinted at the power he wielded, even in repose.

Esmé, poised at his side, rested a manicured hand on his arm, her fingers adorned with discreet but unmistakable jewels. Her ivory silk dress draped elegantly over her frame, looking like liquid that would shift with each subtle movement of her body. She smiled, the kind of smile that had learned to hold its shape through decades of scrutiny, and yet, the moment captured in pixels seemed genuine. They were a striking pair, not because of their age gap—which was not scandalous in their circles—but because they were a testament to how carefully curated lives could defy time.

"You thought when I said age difference, I meant cradle robber, huh?" Julius smiled. "She's an architect. She's got beautiful work, you'll see. She was a model when she was younger, and I think her family wanted her to have kids and settle down instead of working so hard, but she's the go-getter type," Julius spoke fondly, causing Amanda to be more perplexed by him than ever. She didn't think he had a soft side.

"I can relate to that," she shared honestly.

"Oh, honey, you have time," Julius sounded almost comforting.

"Tell that to my family," she quipped.

"Don't let them scare you. Life is what you make it. I've never been a father, despite what those pesky reporters say, but I have lived exactly the life I wanted. No regrets. And I'm turning seventy this week," he laughed.

Amanda would have guessed sixty, and it made her wonder how old Esmé really was. "Wow," she remarked. "But I thought you didn't take pictures," Amanda dared to say.

"I make exceptions when I own the image myself," he smiled. "Come to my party. I thought about inviting you sooner, but I wasn't sure where you stand with Tristan in your... friendship," he winked.

"Oh, I don't want to impose," Amanda lied, thrilled that she had already secured her way into the estate and now his world.

"Nonsense. It's a multi-day affair—change your plans if you have to," he said as if it wasn't an order.

"Wow, okay," Amanda said, unsure of how to react.

"Look, this is where the drive gets spectacular," Julius pointed through the window, rolling it down to feel the island air on his skin.

The road to the villa twisted and climbed, hugging the rugged coastline as the car ascended towards the cliffs. The island sprawled around them in layers of striated earth and deep green vegetation, the Atlantic stretching endlessly to their left, glowing beneath the afternoon sun. Amanda followed suit, lowering her window, the scent of salt and warm stone drifting through the openness, carrying a breeze that made Amanda's loose strands of hair dance against her face.

"You'll notice the difference soon enough," Julius said, his voice calm over the drone of the engine.

Amanda had already noticed. The drive to his other island home had been a journey into untamed wilderness, roads lined with dense jungle, the air thick with humidity, and the chatter of unseen creatures. This? It was a world away. The only audible sound was the wind rushing through their car—the terrain drier, harsher, volcanic rock formations rising like ancient sentinels against the sky. The homes were fewer, tucked into the landscape with an intentional privacy, built for those who sought seclusion rather than spectacle.

As they rounded the final curve, the villa came into view, an architectural marvel of clean lines and glass perched atop the cliffs like it had grown from the rock itself. The driveway was long and smooth, leading up to a minimalist entrance where the modern structure blended seamlessly into the surrounding nature. No extravagant gates, no ostentatious displays of wealth, just quiet luxury, a whisper rather than a shout.

The driver pulled the car to a stop, cutting the engine. For a moment, there was only silence, save for the breeze and a distant crash of waves against the cliffs below.

Julius turned to Amanda, a facetious smirk on his lips. "Welcome to the quiet side of my life."

"This is... I don't have a word for it. Enchanting? Mystical? It... doesn't seem real," she said as she stepped out of the car.

Julius's delight in watching people's reactions to this place never waned. "This way," he gestured, leading Amanda through the open-air corridor as the driver hurried with the luggage.

"This house is a little less... wild than the other," he remarked, glancing at her as he stepped into the expansive living area. Floor-to-ceiling windows framed an uninterrupted view of the Atlantic, the water stretching endlessly beneath a sky that seemed too blue to be real. "Just clean lines, open space, and a damn good view."

Amanda took it in, the modernity of it, the carefully curated minimalism that somehow still felt lived-in. The walls were a soft white, letting sunlight flood every corner. The furniture was sleek but comfortable, all earth tones and natural textures that kept the place from feeling cold. There were subtle hints of warmth—an abstract painting here, a carefully chosen sculpture there—but everything was intentional.

Julius walked ahead, gesturing as he spoke. "This place was designed for quiet. For thinking. The other house? That one thrives on noise and chaos." He glanced back at her, relishing every reaction.

He led Amanda past the open-concept kitchen, the marble counters gleaming under pendant lights. "I won't pretend I actually use this," he said with a grin. "But my chef is one of the most well-known in Europe, and my wine selection is top-tier. Don't tell the Spanish, but my true love is Italian wine." He winked, looking more animated and spritely than Amanda imagined he could be.

Down the hall, Julius pushed open a set of double doors, revealing a bedroom that spilled out onto a private terrace. The bed was massive, dressed in crisp white and striking blues. Beyond it, the terrace held an infinity pool twice the size of the one at the other place, blending seamlessly with the horizon.

"You see the difference now?" he asked, leaning casually against the doorframe. "One home is meant to be lived in. This one is meant to be... escaped to."

Amanda stepped onto the terrace and took her shoes off, the warm tiles grounding her as she looked out at the unfath-omable vastness. One home had been alive, breathing—unpredictable. This one was measured—controlled. It felt like a sanctuary built for someone who knew how quickly life could spiral.

She turned back to Julius, her gaze thoughtful. "So which one is more, *you?*" Her curiosity was something that peeked its head too often, some might say.

His grin was slow, enigmatic. "That depends on who I'm trying to be. Why don't you let my driver bring your stuff in? There are plenty of rooms here. You can get out of that uniform and join me for an evening swim," Julius spoke kindly. His voice carried a warmth Amanda wasn't accustomed to, a richness that felt almost out of character. It was as if the colors of the island—the golden light, the vibrant blues and greens—had seeped into his personality, softening his usual edge.

"I... can't." Amanda sincerely did not intend to accept. She may have been fishing for an invitation to his house and party, but she had no desire to be on a secluded island mountainside with this man, no matter how much of his soft side she witnessed.

"Of course, you can," he insisted before being interrupted by one of his staff.

"Your bags, sir? Would you like them in here?" a young man rolling two large suitcases asked.

"Yes, yes," Julius waved him in, directing him to the opposite side of the room. "You can take Miss Hopkins' things to an open suite. Our other guests arrive tomorrow. I'm sure there's room," he said.

"Yes, of course, right away," he replied, dragging the bags behind him towards the walk-in closet.

Amanda sighed, practically unable to utter a word. "Uh..."

Sensing her unease, Julius let a faint, knowing grin tug at his lips. "Three of the staff are live-in—we won't be alone up here," he assured.

Amanda's face flushed, embarrassed by the keen accuracy of Julius's intuition. Perhaps a man like him didn't rely solely on power and money; perhaps he saw more than most. She had never encountered a man with such precise intuition, and the realization was a bit unsettling.

"Thank you, that's so... generous," she let out a short laugh.

"I guess we're spending the night together," he chirped.

Amanda shook her head. "Let's not give those pesky reporters anything to write home about, okay?" Something about Julius's ability to disarm her with wit and banter felt strangely comforting.

The young man emerged from the dressing area, presumably to get more from the trunk of the car when Julius stopped him. "Leave the rest of my things for later. Show Miss Hopkins to her room first so she can change. I can't imagine those clothes are comfortable."

"Not at all," Amanda agreed.

"Perfect, dinner will be at seven-thirty, and we'll take it on the terrace," Julius instructed—he rarely let a moment pass without giving orders.

"Sounds good," Amanda complied, picking up the shoes she'd kicked off, refusing to put them back on her feet, and followed the young man to her suite.

"Here you are, ma'am."

"Thank you," she said, taking in the understated luxury, designed with the same effortless elegance that defined the rest of the villa. Despite its openness—another terrace to enjoy with floor-to-ceiling windows—the suite provided a sense of privacy, a place where she could be alone with her thoughts, though Amanda could never be sure if that was a gift or a curse.

She quickly entered the en-suite bathroom, its own little spacious retreat, with a rainfall shower and a deep soaking tub positioned beneath a window that framed the endless Atlantic. Her bags were delivered while Amanda was still in the shower, and as she stepped out, she wrapped herself in the plush bathrobe hanging from an open hook. She was happy that she had packed a few flowing dresses, knowing that the small holster would be less detectable on her thigh than trying to conceal it through her straight-lined uniform trousers.

Scooping up the pile of clothes on the floor, she quickly hid her weapon between the layers before walking into the bedroom. She placed the bundle on the bed and walked to the edge of the room, standing at the spacious windows. Amanda noticed Julius in the pool that seemed to stretch from one end of the palatial estate to the other. Suddenly, the glass she was leaning on gave way. The windows were actually massive bifold doors that opened her room to the sprawling terrace. She nudged then pushed until the wall opened, the crisp air of the trade winds sweeping down from the mountains, offering a fleeting coolness against the heat.

"Join me!" Julius called as Amanda stepped onto the terrace.

"I'll have to grab my suit. I was just admiring the open doors. This place is incredible, Julius. I've never had my breath taken away quite like this." Amanda was close to tears. She wasn't overly sentimental or what people would call the most *in tune* with nature, but she felt the essence of the island in every inhale, on the wind that tussled her hair, in the languid rhythm of an endless summer.

"Yeah, come on out, the water's perfect," Julius said, as a woman stacked towels on a wooden shelf near the outdoor bar.

He wasn't kidding about a live-in staff, she thought.

"Oh, and I talked to Esmé; her flight gets in early in the morning. Sleep as long as you like, and Crisel will make you breakfast if you have to leave by the time we get back, okay?"

"Sure, but I'll be okay," Amanda assured.

"I know you will. I'll make sure of it," Julius grinned. "Now, get your suit. Laps before dinner is great for digestion; take it from an old man."

"Okay, I'll be right back." Amanda hurried with quick strides from the terrace to her room to change into her swimsuit. She never could have imagined that enjoying an evening with a man she had only read about before this summer would ever be part of her job description.

Chapter Eleven

Amanda woke to the soft glow of an August morning filtering through sheer linen curtains, the light casting patterns across the crisp sheets. The air was warm but not stifling, carrying the scent of salt and sun-baked earth through the slightly open terrace doors, beyond which the infinity pool mirrored the cloudless sky. The crash of waves against the cliffs below was a constant hum, grounding her in the present before she had even opened her eyes.

She stretched beneath the lightweight duvet, her limbs slow to wake, her body reluctant to leave the cool comfort of the bed. The villa was silent, save for the distant call of seabirds riding the early breeze.

The sun climbed higher, warming the air inch by inch, the day just waiting for her to step into it when she suddenly remembered her check-in with Katherine. Amanda bounced out of bed, looking for her phone. She hadn't thought to text or call the night before when she had been hypnotized by Julius—his effortless charm, the way he commanded every room without raising his voice, his unshakable power that made everyone rotate around his axis.

Amanda fumbled through the sheets, standing to check the floor, the nightstand, and the chair, before finally finding her phone. The screen was black. She tapped on it. It was completely dead.

Cursing under her breath, she grabbed the charging cable and jammed it into the port, but even as the screen flickered to life, she saw no bars of service. Her stomach tightened. Katherine would be expecting a message by now, and Amanda knew better than to assume silence wouldn't raise alarms. She typed out a quick text.

Got caught up. Everything fine. Will check in ASAP, but the moment she hit send, the dreaded *Message Failed to Send* notification flashed back at her.

Throwing off the silk robe she had draped over her the night before, she grabbed a sundress from the chair and pulled it on in a hurry. Barefoot, she dashed across the cool marble floors and out into the hallway. She hadn't exactly memorized the estate's layout, but she remembered passing staff near the main atrium the day before.

If anyone could get her online, it was them. She wanted to see if she had the chance to call Katherine, not just send a text. Julius was getting Esmé from the airport, and he probably wasn't driving there himself, so there were very few people around. It was the perfect time for Amanda to let Katherine know that she'd already made her way in.

She moved quickly through the airy hall, passing sunlit archways that framed breathtaking views of the island, but she had no time to admire them—she needed Wi-Fi. As she moved through the house, she caught the savory scent of eggs, butter, and a hint of peppers.

Following the smell, Amanda found a woman standing by the stove. She was petite, somewhere in her late forties, with dark hair pulled into a loose bun and a floral apron with the embroidered name *Crisel* tied neatly around her waist. She turned as Amanda entered, her face lighting up in a warm, expectant smile.

"Buenos días, señorita. ¿Omeleta?"

Amanda blinked. "Oh... I... um..." She gestured towards her phone, flustered. "I actually need Wi-Fi. Do you know...?"

The woman tilted her head, clearly not understanding. She motioned towards the pan in front of her, lifting a spatula in one hand. "Huevos. Con queso. Con jamón. Sí?"

Amanda exhaled, pressing her lips together. Of course. She was a guest, and Crisel was here to make breakfast, not troubleshoot her lack of internet access. Still, she tried again, slower this time. "Do you know... Wi-Fi?" She held up her phone, mimicking typing.

Crisel beamed, nodding enthusiastically. Amanda felt a flash of relief until the woman reached for a plate and placed a perfectly folded omelet in front of her.

Amanda ran a hand through her hair, sighing. She had no idea where the router was, no way of explaining what she needed, and, apparently, no choice but to accept that breakfast was now happening whether she liked it or not.

She glanced down at the omelet, fluffy yellow pores steaming upward. Her stomach, the traitorous fiend, growled at her. Maybe she could afford one bite. Then she'd figure out how the hell to get online.

"Gracias," Amanda said, putting a forkful to her lips. "Mmmm, this is incredible... delicioso," she nodded in delight, muttering through a perfect balance of salt and cream.

"De nada," Crisel said with a casual wave of her hand. Then, remembering something, she quickly spouted a string of Spanish sentences that put Amanda in a tailspin. Crisel didn't take a breath, as if expecting her to fully understand, mimicking the actions she was describing as she spoke.

Amanda blinked, her fork hovering in midair. Her mind scrambled to piece together the Spanish she had been lackadaisical about learning in high school. Ropa... clothes. Lavar... wash. Did she say towels... maybe? A slow realization crept over her, tightening in her chest.

She forced herself not to react. *Her clothes? The gun. Where had she put the gun?* She kept a steady grin, noticing an outlet near her, and took a moment to plug the cord in so she could at least use the time to charge her phone.

The screen illuminated, showing the time was already seven forty-five. Amanda tried to remember how long the drive had taken the day before. Enjoying the views so much kept her from bothering to monitor the passage of time. She was great at some aspects of the job, but becoming as fastidious as Katherine about tracking the clock would take patience and practice.

Crisel placed a clear glass of freshly brewed coffee distinctly layered with golds, browns, and creams next to Amanda's plate. She thanked her before lifting it to her lips and taking a big, coffee-hungry gulp. "Oh, that's sweet!" Amanda exclaimed before letting out a slight cough. "And spiked!" she laughed.

"I see you've tasted tradition here already," Julius's voice boomed from behind them.

The lasting flavors of the barraquito still tingled in Amanda's mouth. "Yeah, it's delicious, but I was totally unprepared!" She kept her cool completely. "What's in it?"

"It's a Canarian specialty—strong espresso, sweet condensed milk, a splash of *Licor 43* for a hint of vanilla and citrus, steamed milk, and a dusting of cinnamon, finished with a twist of lemon peel." He tapped the side of the glass lightly. "You can drink it as-is, enjoying the layers, or stir it up if you prefer everything blended.

"They say it started as a simple way to serve coffee with a kick, but the locals perfected it, turning it into something both elegant and comforting. I always insist that my guests are served a barraquito during breakfasts here. Bring it with you. Esmé went straight to the bathroom when we came in, but she should be finished now. I'll give you a proper introduction."

Amanda didn't pick up the drink again, preferring to stay clear-headed in this potential mess. She slid off the chair to follow Julius. "Gracias," she thanked Crisel with a smile before Julius instructed her—in perfect Spanish—that he and Esmé would take their breakfast on the terrace.

Julius beckoned Amanda through the villa's open-air corridors, the scent of jasmine catching flight on the morning air. It still carried the crispness of the early hours of the day, though the sun was quickly warming the house, and staff were opening the large windows and doors of the home to let a breeze blow through until it was absolutely necessary to turn on the air conditioning.

Julius glanced over his shoulder at Amanda as she followed, a hint of amusement playing at his lips.

"She's going to love you," he said, his tone excited and seemingly sincere.

Amanda shrugged her shoulders awkwardly, still taken aback by this overly warm side of Julius, curiosity permeating her distracted mind. As they reached the entryway, the wide glass doors were already open, framing the sunlight spilling onto the driveway as staff unloaded luggage from the car. To their left, a door swung open as Esmé stepped into the room with effortless poise.

She moved with the practiced grace of someone who belonged everywhere yet owed nothing to any place. Her deep brown curls were swept back into an elegant bun, and a pair of sunglasses perched atop her head, waiting to be called into action when the sun became too much. Even after a flight, she looked impeccable—soft linen pants with a fitted blouse in a shade of blue that made Amanda think of the sea at dusk.

Julius stepped forward with his usual, unhurried confidence. "Esmé," he said, his voice carrying more fondness than a casual relationship would demand, "meet Amanda."

Esmé was a quiet but commanding presence who exuded mastery in the art of influence without saying a word. Her face, flawless, had once graced the pages of high-fashion magazines. She was elegance personified, favoring flowing satins and tailored couture over fleeting trends, her wardrobe a collection of silks and crisp linens in muted, sophisticated hues.

But beneath the polished exterior, there was an edge—something sharp and knowing in the way she observed a room.

"So lovely to meet you," Esmé radiated. "I am so happy you get to celebrate with us. I've heard so much about you already," she said as she moved directly in, cheek-to-cheek with Amanda.

"Me?" Amanda couldn't hide her surprise. "I... uh..." she stuttered.

"Oh, don't be modest. You made quite an impression on our Tristan. And the photos of you two at the ball," she purred.

"Charity gala, my dear," Julius corrected.

"Ah, yes, ritziness for a cause," she smirked. Amanda let out a short laugh. She could see why Julius thought the two of them would get along.

Esmé linked Amanda's arm to hers and began walking towards the terrace. "I can smell Crisel's breakfast already. I've been up for hours. I'm famished."

Amanda was envious of the ease with which these people of the world glided from one language to the next with mastery. Esmé came from a distinguished Catalonian family whose wealth was rooted in the high-end ceramics and glassmaking industry. Her ancestors had founded one of Spain's most prestigious artisan glassworks in the late nineteenth century, crafting bespoke pieces for royal families, luxury hotels, and architectural landmarks across Europe. A powerhouse of design, they produced everything from hand-blown glass chandeliers to the custom tile work adorning Barcelona's most famous buildings. Though Esmé never officially joined the company, she carried its legacy in the refined aesthetic and effortless sophistication she brought to every building she designed.

Her parents had been adamant about giving her a world-class education, enrolling her in elite English-speaking schools from the age of six. Throughout the years, she was taught by a rotating collection of instructors from across the English-speaking world—Miss Harper from London, Mr. Donnelly from Belfast, Ms. Liu from Toronto, and the particularly spirited Mr. Henderson from Wellington, who instilled in her a love for debate and a sharp wit. By adulthood, Esmé's accent was impossible to place, a smooth blend of global influences that made her sound like she belonged anywhere and everywhere.

"Sit," Esmé instructed Amanda when they reached the terrace. It was no wonder that she and Julius were a compatible couple. Esmé was as direct and demanding as he was, except her soft femininity and allure rendered the strongest of individuals defenseless. Few would have considered her demands as anything other than insistent hospitality.

"So, before the others arrive, you must tell me everything," Esmé continued, excitedly. "I have yearned to live vicariously through a fresh love story for too long!" She said as Crisel and Marco—the young man whose name she'd now heard them use—set fresh fruit, croissants, and piping hot omelets in front of them.

"Don't give this one too much info," Julius nodded towards Esmé playfully and sat down with the women for the meal. He lifted a pat of butter and began slathering it on a thick piece of oven-baked bread. "Tristan will ditch you for spying on him."

Amanda flinched at the word, trying to pass it off as needing to shift in her seat to grab a pastry.

"Tristan would *never*," Esmé argued, "he and I are the best of friends for life. How do you say it in America? *BFFs*, yes?" She let out a charming, fragmented laugh, somewhere between a giggle and a scoff.

"Oh, I didn't think... I didn't know you two were close," Amanda admitted. "There's probably not much to tell from my end. He likes to exaggerate, I think." Amanda grinned. "Speaking of which, when did you say the other guests arrive? I haven't had a working phone since I got in, so I haven't spoken with Tristan at all. I'm sure he'll be surprised that I'm here."

Esmé clapped her hands together before Julius could answer. "What a lovely surprise it will be! Oh, Julius, he doesn't know? You're playing Cupid now?" she raised her tone in delight. "How did you arrange it?"

"I didn't," he said, lifting his own cup of barraquito to his lips, layers of liquid swaying with the motion. "That's all on her," he grinned.

"Oh... well... no. I didn't exactly *mean* to be here. I was working on Julius's flight," she said, tumbling through her words.

"She was the *pilot,*" Julius emphasized.

"The first officer, actually," Amanda said. "I... had no idea he'd be on board," she blurted.

"Until you saw the manifest," Julius reminded her, but intonated it more like a question, raising an eyebrow.

"Yes, of course," Amanda nodded. "Small world, am I right?" She deflected, smothering a rush of fear threatening to overtake her.

"*So* small," Esmé agreed. "And it seems like this man knows everyone in it, she smiled, turning to Julius.

"And that's why I come up here. Too *many* people." Julius spoke between bites. "No service. No internet. Just us and nature as God intended it."

Amanda felt her stifled panic gaining momentum. *And no check-in for me,* she thought.

"Yes, thank God for the masterpiece he created with this villa," Esmé winked, raising her cup to drink, unbothered by the liquor in the morning. "But do tell us, darling, when *do* the others arrive?" she asked. "I'll have to freshen up before anyone else comes. Damn planes are a cesspool." The complaint sounded more like positive feedback than criticism coming from her mouth. "Not all of us fly private."

"You could have flown in with Anton and Clarisse later today," Julius pointed out.

Amanda swallowed. When she heard the couple's names, her mind began to search for details, hoping there weren't things she'd forgotten about during their time in the Caribbean. Amanda prided herself on her photographic memory, it was what made her so good at slipping into different roles, remembering the smallest details of a forged identity, and keeping track of conversations and timelines with precision. But fear had a way of making even the sharpest mind unravel.

Her mind was gripped by one unlucky circumstance: *Did Crisel take the gun? Where in the world did I put it? And there is literally no WiFi in this place?*

Her stomach tightened. If Crisel had found the gun, then Amanda could try to get to her before anyone else. She had to excuse herself and check her room one last time before finding a quiet moment to approach Crisel.

"My family thinks you're too extravagant, dear. It's easy to find a first-class fare that brings me here without any trouble," Esmé explained.

"Well, twelve—no, thirteen with Tristan—arrive this afternoon," Julius finally divulged. "The rest are meeting us on the ship tomorrow for the real celebration. I hope you've come ready to party it up, Amanda. I don't plan on living long enough to make a raucous like this again!" he chortled.

"My dear, you mustn't say things like that," Esmé scolded. "I plan on doing this every year for the next twenty," she joked.

"Nonsense, next year we may be throwing the most elaborate wedding you can imagine. Wouldn't this be a lovely place for it, Amanda?" Julius poked.

"Oh, um... I don't know about that." She swallowed a sip of water before standing. "Excuse me, I need to use the restroom," she said, pushing back her chair with an ease that belied the urgency rattling through her. She kept her pace measured as she left, but the moment she turned the corner, she all but sprinted down the hallway, her breath coming faster, her heartbeat throbbing in her ears.

The door to her room swayed behind her from the force of her push, and she immediately tore through her surroundings. The closet—her uniform hung neatly inside, pressed and pristine, her white blouse freshly laundered. She raked her fingers through the pants pockets and patted down the fabric. *Nothing.*

The bed was made perfectly in her absence, every sheet tucked with crisp precision. Yanking back the covers, she felt along the mattress underneath the pillows, and swung her head to peek under the bed. Still nothing.

She rushed into the bathroom, eyes darting over the spotless countertop and the neatly folded towels Crisel had left behind. Her pulse pounded harder as she crouched, flinging open cabinet doors and rifling through drawers.

Her hands braced against the ensuite vanity, gripping the edge as she tried to think—tried to remember exactly where she had put it before collapsing into sleep the night before. But the only thing her mind kept whispering was, *It's gone.*

She walked helplessly back into the bedroom, sensing a presence that sent a chill curling down her spine. She turned sharply towards the door, and there he was, leaning against the frame as if he were a fixture there. Julius said nothing, only lifting his hand, letting the small holster dangle from his fingers, the gun still strapped inside.

Amanda's breath caught in her throat.

"Quite the thing to misplace," Julius murmured, his tone unreadable, his sharp gaze locked onto her.

"Oh, thank goodness, you found it. I was panicking," she said quickly, knowing she hadn't masked her distress. "I carry this when I travel. A girl can't be too careful," she shrugged, walking towards Julius and taking the strap from his finger.

"Only feds are allowed to fly on planes with a gun on their person. I mean, at least it wasn't loaded," Julius said incredulously.

"No, of course not. It's effective as a scare tactic with or without bullets," Amanda explained, more successfully regulating her breaths as she developed her story. "And I didn't have it on me during the flight. I only put it on after I get my bags when I travel," she said.

"Alright then. Crisel told me she found it when she was hanging up your uniform and gathering your wash this morning. She wanted me to be safe in my own home… is what she said. So… Amanda," he paused, "am I safe with you?" Julius asked. His voice was low, almost casual, but his eyes betrayed him. His expression simmered with suspicion. The air between them felt thin as Julius took another step forward.

"I'd like to believe I am," he added, his tone softening slightly with an underlying subtext of letting Amanda know exactly who was in charge.

"Of course," Amanda said a little too emphatically. "Yes, of course, you're safe with me."

"Alright. Well, you tell Katherine I can spot one of her trainees from a mile away. She's gettin' sloppy. I'll disable the WiFi blocker this evening. Too many guests to keep it off for the whole weekend," he winked.

Amanda had no time for a reaction; she stood frozen, watching as Julius turned on his heel and made his way down the hallway. She remained immobilized, gripping the holster as the tiny pistol pendulated. The room pulsated with anxiety, a force pressing down on her as if gravity had inverted. She tried and failed to process what Julius had just said, his words a direct shot. *One of Katherine's trainees.*

An icy dread spread through her chest, warring with the sheer audacity of Julius's calculated warmth. Amanda was a mouse trapped in the luxurious estate of the king cat.

Chapter Twelve

"Excuse me, señorita?" Marco tapped on the door, pushing it slightly ajar.

Amanda stayed in her room trying to focus on reading a book she had stared at for hours, unable to find the courage to face Julius and Esmé who had mentioned she wanted a nap before the afternoon arrival of the birthday celebration entourage.

"I have been asked to guide you to the terrace," Marco called.

"Oh, thank you," she replied, putting the book upside down on the bed. "Come in."

Marco stepped inside and waited for Amanda to get off the bed before speaking further. "I am to accompany you to the terrace. They are serving drinks and showing the new guests to their rooms, ma'am."

"Of course," Amanda said, slipping her feet into the sandals by the bed.

Marco caught a glance of the book title as he stood, hands clasped behind his back. "Oh, I love to read spy novels," the young man said.

Marco had worked in commercial hotels, resorts, and cruise ships before being hired at Julius's estate. In other venues, he was lively and conversational, serving drinks and swapping stories with the spirited tourists that changed every four to ten days.

He hadn't been trained in luxury hospitality. Crisel's best friend, Beatriz, was Marco's mom and had been suddenly taken by cancer a year prior. The Santana family needed Marco on the island more than they needed his salary from abroad. So, at twenty-seven, after burying his mother, he returned to his roots after Crisel recommended him to Mr. Babb. Julius didn't need another full-timer, but couldn't stand the thought of refusing a favor to Crisel, so Marco hopped from one task to the next under the direction of the house butler.

Marco brought a brightness to the home—a vibrant and magnetic inquisitivity—loved by all, but there were times he overstepped, and was scolded by the live-in boss who ran the entire estate, Señor Arocha.

"Oh, I'm sorry. I didn't mean to pry," he apologized.

"It's okay," Amanda smiled. "This one's even better than a novel. It's real life," she said smiling, picking up the book and handing it to him.

She had hopelessly checked her phone for a signal or WiFi icon to pop up and had finally just decided to read a book—it was an obscure historical non-fiction from the nineties that she had found on Katherine's bookshelf, *The Spy Who Saved the World: How a Soviet Colonel Changed the Course of the Cold War.*

"Take it—it's a book that'll make you question reality, though. Don't say I didn't warn you," she grinned.

"No, I couldn't," he replied.

"Sure you can. I doubt I'll have time to get in much reading now that other people are here," Amanda said flippantly.

"No, Miss, you don't understand. You can't let Mr. Julius catch *you* with this, either. He hates the Russians. If it's not a novel, he'll think... well, I can't say," Marco hesitated. "Just keep it in your bag, Crisel picks up everything. You can't leave nothing lying around," he warned.

"Oh, trust me, I know," Amanda said. "Fair enough, I'll stick it in my bag." She walked to the closet and put it in her carry-on. "Now, time to party, I guess," she smiled.

"Yes, ma'am," Marco said, then lowered his voice. "I like you—you're not like most people who come here."

"Rich?" Amanda scoffed.

"No, *rude!*" he exclaimed, as they both laughed, Marco throwing his hand over his mouth as if he couldn't help himself.

"It's okay. You're safe with me," Amanda stated, recalling her last exchange with Julius. She took a deep breath.

"Everything okay?" Marco asked.

"Yes, of course," she answered, hearing the sounds of arriving guests echoing through the halls.

The estate buzzed with the arrival of houseguests, the grand foyer filling with warm embraces, laughter, and the subtle clink of glasses served to them as they walked up the terrace and into the main house. Couple after couple stepped through the wide entryway, their voices rising in excited chatter as they exchanged greetings—some old friends reuniting, others meeting for the first time in this lavish setting. The marble floors reflected the glow of the chandelier overhead, adding a dreamlike sheen to the excitement.

Anton and Clarisse were among the first to spot Amanda, their expressions lighting up as they approached.

"My dear, look at you," Clarisse cooed, pressing both of Amanda's hands in hers. "You seem to be finding yourself in all the most fascinating places, don't you," she winked. "Tristan rode up with us, I'm sure he'll be elated. If he had known you'd be here, I'm sure we'd have heard nothing else along the drive."

Anton gave her a good-natured nod, stepping in for a hug. "What a surprise to see you here."

Before Amanda could answer, movement near the entrance caught her attention. Tristan had just stepped inside, his gaze sweeping across the room before landing on her. His expression darted from shock to bewilderment, then unabashed joy.

"Well, well," he mused, making his way towards her. "Didn't expect to see you here."

"Neither did I," Amanda admitted with a slight grin.

Julius, ever the host, appeared at Tristan's side with an exuberant smile. "She was on my flight," he explained, as if fate had simply decided it. "And, I thought, why not invite her to stay for the celebration?"

Tristan's brows lifted, clearly intrigued, but before he could respond, chatter from three staff members in a huddle drew Julius's attention. One of the members approached, looking a touch uneasy.

"Sir," the young woman said in a hushed tone, "it appears we may have miscalculated the room assignments. We're one bedroom short."

Julius waved a dismissive hand, the matter a mere inconvenience. "I'm sure we can figure something out."

Amanda exhaled slowly, glancing at Julius. It wasn't a miscalculation. He was too precise for that. No, this had been entirely intentional. And she had a feeling she knew exactly where this was heading.

"You two lovebirds don't mind sharing a room, do you?" Julius winked.

"Oh, Julius, I wouldn't presume," Tristan began to object, but was cut off.

"It's okay," Amanda replied nonchalantly. "There's a king-sized bed, and I don't take up too much space," she smiled demurely, sending a little quiver down Tristan's spine as his eyes lit up.

"Perfect, I knew you were a good sport," Julius gave Amanda the kind of atta-boy look that coaches give in high school. She hated sports. And she made sure Julius could read it all over her face.

She was going to figure out what kind of game he was playing and, more importantly, where Katherine fit into it before she found herself trapped in the lifelong game of cat and mouse that had ensnared her handler.

"C'mon," Amanda took Tristan's arm cheerfully, defying her fear, and now aggravation, with Julius. "I'll show you the room."

Tristan smiled, accepting her affection with delight, raising his eyebrows to give Julius a silent *thank-you* look.

They entered the bedroom as the door clicked shut behind them, sealing them inside the suite, and for a long moment, neither of them moved.

"Oh, sorry. I slept in it last night," Amanda finally said, straightening the duvet at the edge of the bed.

One corner did not match the otherwise untouched luxury of the smooth and taut linens. There, a faint indentation in the mattress marked where she had curled up for the night and much of the morning.

"You must be a deep sleeper then. This place doesn't look touched," Tristan said.

"That's more Crisel than me. That woman must clean and straighten things in her sleep. Word to the wise," Amanda pointed towards him, "Crisel picks things up and puts them away at all hours of the day. If there's anything you don't want to be disturbed, keep it under lock and key," she laughed.

"Noted," Tristan said, inching closer towards her. "So... Do you want to tell me what you're really doing here?"

"What do you mean? It's true, I worked on Julius's plane. They were short a pilot last minute so I... was the first officer," she explained truthfully.

"Oh, okay, cool. So you *were* messing with me?" he smirked. "You are one of the pilots?"

"Maybe," she had to keep up the flirtation now.

"So, I guess it's nice to be in the cockpit, right?" Tristan looked at her fondly. He could imagine that having the skill to fly and not using it would be annoying.

"Yeah, Obsydian was trying out a new service with the pilot-flight-attendant thing. Doesn't look like it's going to stay on the list of services," she said, hoping to God that her face did not resemble the facepalm emoji.

"Yeah, I'm surprised they even tried that one," Tristan said, shaking his head. "It's, like, if you want to burn money, burn money, be my guest, but don't charge me for it," he scoffed.

"Right?" Amanda huffed, arms hovering slightly at her sides before settling, she glanced away, the corners of her mouth twitching in hesitation. In that instant, she promised herself that she'd lie as little as possible for the rest of her life. She fully understood why Katherine told her to use truth whenever she could, and hoped she was finally free from the initial cover story.

Tristan let out a slow breath, rubbing the back of his neck as he glanced around. "Well... this is... lovely."

Amanda laughed, shifting her weight from one foot to the other. "Miscalculation, my ass."

Tristan smirked, leaning against the doorframe, watching her with an easy confidence. "Julius does like his games." His gaze flickered to the bed, then back to her. "I can sleep on that couch."

Amanda tilted her head. "That's not a couch. That's an accent chair." His six-foot frame would not have been able to handle as much as a few hours in the elongated chaise.

"Well," he smirked, "I had to at least *try* to be a gentleman."

"You're incorrigible," Amanda let a slow, breathy exhale slip past her lips like a secret.

Tristan walked to the undisturbed side of the bed, dropping himself onto it and slipping off his shoes before stretching his legs downward and his arms up to cradle his head. "Yeah, this will do," he grinned.

Without saying a word, Amanda knelt on the opposite side of the bed, taking the abundant display of pillows at the top, and began arranging them down the middle between the two of them.

Tristan's mouth arched upward. "What are you doing?"

Amanda lifted a brow. "Just setting boundaries," she flicked her head in a short, playful motion.

Tristan rolled himself onto his belly, placing his chin on one of the pillows she had commandeered to section off his territory, and smiled. "I'm not a color-inside-the-lines kinda guy," he said, not quite a protest, but definitely declaring something.

"Are you the kinda guy who respects women?" Amanda shot back without a breath, still busy with the task of lining the bed from top to bottom.

"Absolutely," he replied, unmoved from his position, his face framed by the striking blues and whites of the plush decor.

Amanda placed the last pillow and turned around to see Tristan roll onto his side, placing one hand to his head for support and extending his other, offering a clear invitation. "You know a thing about crossing borders, right?"

His eyes sparkled in the brightness of the room, the sun casting its afternoon glow through the windows. Amanda's breath hitched. She couldn't speak. She could not remember a time when a man took her breath away. She accepted his hand and his soft tug pulled her effortlessly into him, crossing the perimeter meant to separate them. The warmth of his skin pressed into her as he wordlessly ran his fingers down her back, enfolding her with his arms, keeping his gaze fixed on her eyes.

Amanda wished she could read his mind. A man so forward with his words, obsessive with his thoughts, and slow with his hands was an enigma to her. It sounded cliché, but she had never met anyone like him. And it wasn't just his class, intelligence, money, or looks, though none of that hurt—it was *him*. The paradox that was Tristan Montgomery.

He, finally, haltingly, pressed his lips against her skin. First, just below her ear on the space between the face and neck, sending a chill directly down her spine. Then, her cheek, and at the last moment, just as she felt tempted to beg him to kiss her, he moved his face just inches from hers. He peered into her eyes once more, before cradling her cheek in his hand, tipping her chin up, and pressing his lips against hers.

A sharp knock at the door caused Amanda to leap in one motion, finding herself on her feet next to the bed, surprising even herself. She pressed her hands to her abdomen, letting out a slight cough.

"Um… I'll get it," she swiped her palms over her hair to smooth everything, her body feeling as if she'd had a full-on romp in the hay, heart pounding.

Tristan moved intentionally and methodically, making Amanda more nervous about spending the night in the same bed with him. She wasn't about to get into another relationship where he wasn't as into her as she was into him. She flicked the thought away as quickly as it came. *This was a job, not a relationship.*

"Señor, I have your bags," Marco said, holding the handle of two oversized suitcases with a boxy leather duffle perched on top of one.

"Light packer," Amanda said sarcastically, eyes darting to Tristan.

"Hey, you can't look this good without a little prep," Tristan quipped, waving his hand from head to torso in a quick motion.

Amanda laughed out loud, "Of course not. Here, Marco, you can put his stuff on the left side of the closet, mine's on the right."

"Certainly," Marco said, arranging the bags in the space before asking, "Would you like me to unpack for you, sir?"

"No, no, that's fine. I'll take care of it," Tristan said briskly, wanting to rush Marco out of the room and regain privacy.

"Yes, sir. And ma'am, this is for you." Marco handed Amanda a folded note. "I'll be your concierge for the weekend. If you need anything at all, please let me know. I'll be nearby. And... sorry about the room mixup," he said, reaching for the door handle.

"Mmhmm," Amanda smirked, "the mixup," she repeated, wide-eyed.

Marco pinched his lips together as if forcing himself not to laugh before shutting the door behind him.

Amanda unfolded the note and read: *Join me in my room when you can. I want you to look through my closet so we can find fitting attire for you this weekend. I know you packed light and didn't have time to prepare. Kisses, my dear. ~ Esmé*

"Well, I guess I won't make fun of you again for overpacking. I'm invited to Esmé's closet for a dress-up party," Amanda said, lifting the note, "This should be fun," she said, handing the paper to Tristan.

"I had other ideas of fun in mind," he smiled, snatching the note carelessly and wrapping his arms around her.

"Did you?" she grinned, slightly recovering from the self-doubt she felt creeping in. "Well, you need to unpack and I need to change, apparently. What exactly are the plans for this whole thing?"

"Oh, I kept the invitation and itinerary. I'll show you," Tristan said, rifling through the pockets of the duffle bag. "Here," he extended the papers towards Amanda. "You should have seen the little box it came in. Julius doesn't do anything without class, that's for sure."

Amanda took the invitation—a work of art—thick, cream-colored cardstock with Julius Babb's name embossed in gold script, shimmering under the light. The edges were trimmed with a subtle filigree design, a nod to old-world elegance, and the itinerary inside promised extravagance.

The celebration would begin with a garden party on the lower terrace of the Tenerife estate, where guests could sip vintage champagne—a list of hand-selected sparkling assortments included. A celebrated Michelin-starred chef would provide a spread of Iberian delicacies, and live musicians would set the mood with a mix of Spanish guitar and jazz.

Day two marked the start of a two-day cruise aboard a private ship. It was more than a yacht, or superyacht. It was a small cruise ship that slept thirty-two, where guests would be whisked along the Canary Islands' most breathtaking coastlines. Luxurious staterooms awaited those staying overnight, while the days promised deep-sea diving excursions, helicopter tours over Mount Teide, and exclusive shopping stops at hidden gem boutiques you needed a reservation to access. The advertised onboard entertainment boasted a private performance from an internationally renowned artist—unnamed on the invite for the ultimate surprise—and a high-stakes poker tournament in the ship's opulent casino lounge.

The grand finale would be a decadent candlelight dinner beneath the stars, with a resplendent fireworks display illuminating the Atlantic, all synchronized to a live performance by a world-class symphony orchestra.

At the bottom of the invitation, in Julius's signature bold script, was a simple line: *"Come celebrate the years, the legacy, and the moments that truly matter."*

Amanda was a little weary of being stupefied by the lifestyles of the rich and famous—or infamous—and tried to hide being awestruck.

"Oh, it's okay," Tristan said as if reading her thoughts, "This shit's crazy. No one lives like this," he snorted.

"Yeah, I'm gonna need a different dress," Amanda finally managed. "Phew! Are you sure you brought the right girl to this soireé?"

"I am," Tristan smiled, brushing her arm with his fingers before taking her hand to his lips, and offering a quick peck. "Go get a gown. I'll start taking my suits out of these bags since I sent our concierge away," he said, rolling his eyes.

Chapter Thirteen

Amanda stepped onto the capacious lower tier of the home's multiple terraces wearing a flowing, satin gown in sapphire blue, draped effortlessly over her figure, catching the evening light with every movement. The fabric was impossibly soft, with a subtle shimmer hinting at wealth without screaming for attention. Its delicate spaghetti straps framed her shoulders, leading down to a deep but tasteful V-neckline.

The back dipped into a graceful low scoop, exposing just enough, cinched subtly at the waist before cascading into a gentle, asymmetrical hem that flirted with her ankles. The breeze revealed glimpses of her toned calves and the gold-strapped heels Esmé had insisted she wear.

Just a whisper of Esmé's signature perfume—amber and white florals—lingered in the fabric, making Amanda feel as though she had momentarily stepped into the other woman's world, wrapped in an elegance she had not dared fathom.

Tristan had already joined Julius and a few other guests in the garden as waiters circled with champagne, serving punctual participants, while others took full advantage of stylists and makeup artists before joining the party fashionably late. They entered, in pairs or trios, as if on cue, completing the intimate gathering of invitees. Fifteen people were staying at the house, and at least another twenty were staffed for the event.

Amanda spotted Tristan near the stone balustrade, a glass of something dark and expensive in his hand, his posture relaxed yet unmistakably self-assured. The evening light accentuated the crisp lines of his charcoal linen suit, perfectly tailored to his broad shoulders. Unlike the more traditional black tie attire of some of the older guests, Tristan's choice was effortlessly modern—a jacket left unbuttoned, a deep navy silk shirt underneath, collar open just enough to hint at nonchalance. Amanda smiled, they almost looked like they had tried to match each other for a photo shoot.

Tristan's sleeves were pushed up just slightly, revealing the hint of a tanned forearm—on his wrist, a timepiece that anyone in this crowd would not just appreciate, but expect.

Amanda swallowed. It was undeniable how well he fit into this world of power and privilege—not just as a guest, but as a fixture. And when he spotted her, his smile shattered any perilous insecurities that were taunting her.

He walked towards her, his sexy signature gait threatening to unnerve her. She twisted her mouth in a side grin.

"Hey, handsome," she bantered, "got a date?"

"Only the prettiest woman I've ever seen," he slipped his arm around her waist, something she'd begun to crave. "Have you met everyone yet?"

"No," Amanda replied. "I've met Eduardo and Richard," she started listing the couples, "Anton and Clarisse, of course—Clarisse and I got our hair done at the same time—did you know that Esmé has four stylists and make-up artists here? They are apparently staying in the back-house—did you know there was a backhouse? And they'll be on the boat with us all weekend too," Amanda kept her voice low, hoping that Tristan wouldn't judge her for being enamored with the events, but assuming everyone else would.

"It doesn't surprise me," he smiled.

"Anyway, the only other couple I've met are the two over there," she pointed subtly, "Justin and Jessica."

"You're so good with names," Tristan remarked.

"Two *J* names—easy to remember," she shrugged. Amanda was already feeling loose and free after a cocktail during the primping and preening.

"Well, let me introduce you to the rest of the group. Tomorrow, I think another six or more are going to join us. So, there will be a quiz in the morning."

"Not after this much champagne," she laughed, raising the glass she had taken from the waiter's tray offered to her upon entrance.

The striking couple meandered through the garden party with effortless grace, turning heads without even trying. Amanda kept her arm hooked in Tristan's—no longer out of uncertainty, but with a quiet confidence, her fingers casually twiddling the fine fabric of his sleeve. An unspoken rhythm of easy smiles and hushed words pulsed between them, as they navigated the party like diplomats.

The long banquet tables beneath a canopy of garden lamps were lined with crystal and fresh-cut roses, each place setting customized with an engraved gold keepsake. They found their names embossed on place cards that resembled the event invitations. Amanda, seeing her name next to Tristan's, shook her head in appreciation of every last—and last-minute—detail being covered.

While discreet staff glided through the small crowd, offering caviar and gold-leaf-topped canapés, Amanda withdrew her arm from Tristan's. "I'm going to get another drink," she said, motioning towards the bar at the end of the luscious green yard.

Amanda had seen Julius leaning against the bar in conversation and she wanted to make her presence known. She didn't know how she was going to handle the situation, except to play it cool. It was all she knew how to do after the trauma she'd attempted to mask for years. Stepping lightly through the grass, trying to avoid dirtying Esme's heels, she approached the bar.

"Can I give you this champagne glass and get one with Chardonnay?" Amanda asked.

"Certainly," the bartender replied as Julius turned to see her.

"Miss Hopkins, are you enjoying the evening?" he smiled cordially, with an unreadable tone.

"I am, thank you." Amanda kept pace with his cadence.

"Glad to hear it... and you enjoyed your morning... resting up?" Julius was clearly trying to get a rise out of her.

Amanda let a harsh breath escape through her nose, "I did. I caught up on some reading, actually," she nodded.

"Lovely, I always enjoy a good book. What are you reading?"

Amanda's heart jumped. "Um... it's an older book about history. The Cold War."

"Oh, I love studying history," Julius exclaimed, his words loose and easy, the telltale warmth of a few drinks already settling in.

"So, what part of the Cold War? That thing lasted from the end of World War II until the USSR came crashing down in ninety-one, and if you listen to some, it's still going on." Julius was no stranger to facts.

"Yeah, it's... about a spy actually," Amanda said. *Truth is better than lies,* she repeated to herself, going against Marco's warning.

"Ah, my favorite," Julius's smile widened.

"Your favorite what?" Tristan asked, approaching the pair as they both scooted to make room.

"We're talking books here," Julius explained. "I think you have a girl with brains and beauty, son."

Tristan didn't realize it consciously, but his heart swelled when Julius warmly used the term *son* with him.

"I think I do," Tristan agreed, pulling Amanda into his side.

"What you *have*," Amanda emphasized, "is your own brains and beauty, and I have mine," she insisted, watching the evening light play in Tristan's eyes.

Tristan tilted his head downward in playful concession as Julius let a wide grin spread across his face.

"So," Julius pivoted back to the subject at hand. "Which spy?"

"Oh," Amanda swallowed. "Oleg Penkovsky." She had started with a truth, so she may as well run with it.

"Nice," Julius replied. "That's a great story."

"You know it?" she asked, genuinely curious.

"Of course—one of the greats," Julius said.

"Yeah, I'm not even halfway through..." Amanda explained, "...but it's so interesting. Practically unbelievable. You would think the movies aren't like real life, but this guy? Goodness, he seems kinda crazy."

"Absolutely," Julius agreed, sharing no detail.

"That's it?" Tristan said, "But now I'm interested. You gotta give me more than that," he laughed.

"Alright, here's the deal with Oleg Penkovsky," Julius said, leaning on the balustrade and tapping his fingers idly on its concrete surface. "He was a Soviet military officer—a colonel in the GRU, their military intelligence—who basically decided that the USSR was a sinking ship and started feeding intel to the West."

Tristan raised a brow. "Just like that?"

"Not exactly. He was disillusioned. Saw the cracks in the system. In 1960, he reaches out—first to the International Trade Administration through a couple of business contacts, but nothing happens. Then MI6 and the CIA catch wind of him, and they start working together. Over the next two years, he hands over thousands of documents—and when I say thousands, I mean more than any agent had ever seen. So much that they didn't believe the guy was for real at first. They suspected him of making up excess information just so he could be seen as the greatest spy of all time—like he was on an ego trip. Anyway, they start checking his facts, and he's giving them secrets hand-over-fist. Real, hard, verifiable intel. Soviet missile capabilities, military strategy, how fast they could actually mobilize if things went south—all of it."

Tristan leaned forward. "And this was around the Cuban Missile Crisis, right?"

Julius nodded. "Exactly. When things got tense with the Soviet nukes in Cuba, Penkovsky's intel was the key to knowing what we were actually up against. The U.S. wasn't just guessing—his information gave them the confidence to push back without triggering an all-out war."

Amanda chimed in. "Yeah, this book I'm reading is literally called *The Spy Who Saved the World.*"

Tristan shook his head. "Wow. And what then? What happened to him?"

Julius took a breath. "Unfortunately the Soviets caught on. The KGB was already suspicious of him—too much information was leaking. So, in 1962, they arrest him, put him on trial in '63, and then..." he paused for dramatic effect, "they, execute him."

Tristan remained wide-eyed. "Brutal."

"No kidding. But his intel changed everything—*everything,*" Julius reiterated.

"Okay, spoiler!" Amanda stood, mouth wide in shock. "I haven't finished the book," she said, mind still reeling. A spy executed. Just. Like. That.

"Honey, if I have to give you a spoiler alert for something that happened in 1963, then consider this a blanket warning: I will give you the facts of history without apology or abandon," Julius lifted his glass towards her with a wide grin.

Amanda's laugh came out light and dry like she was humoring a joke she hadn't quite decided was funny. "Fair," she met his toast with a clink of her glass. She wasn't sure if that was another test, another way for Julius to let her know that he was onto her, but his directness did give her an odd sense of ease.

A sea breeze curled around Amanda and Tristan as the evening went on, carrying the lingering scent of expensive cigars and night-blooming florals. Tristan regularly leaned in throughout the night, offering remarks that had Amanda arching a brow before silently smiling in response. It was a dance of words, a symphony of unrequited lust.

Amanda wasn't sure how she was going to survive the entire trip without succumbing to her desires. She put a hand to her neck, trying to ground herself and brush away the passions rising within her when she suddenly remembered Julius's words—the WiFi would be on for the party. *What was she doing?*

She had been so distracted by the day's events—one after the other—that she hadn't thought to check her phone again. The one thing Katherine instructed her to have on her *at all times.* Since the guests had arrived, she hadn't had a moment alone.

"I'm going to head inside," she leaned into Tristan's ear, hovering her lips just above his skin. "The WiFi wasn't working earlier, and I forgot to check in with home." *Lies wrapped in truth.*

"Sure, go ahead. This thing has to end at some point," Tristan said, lifting his Rolex, showing the clock had already passed 11 p.m. "I'm not leaving without this guy's dessert, though," he smirked, enjoying every bit of the three-hour spectacle of this celebrity chef-catered meal.

"Save my spot?" Amanda smiled as Tristan gave her a quick wink.

She made her way inside, the cool air of the house a sharp contrast to the warm, fragrant night outside. Amanda had managed to slip away unnoticed, but the nagging pressure in her chest only grew as she navigated the dimly lit hallways. Her phone was still nestled in her bag, untouched since she'd taken it from the charger that morning. She had to see if the WiFi was actually on.

She made it to her bedroom and fished her phone out of her purse, quickly connecting to the open guest network of the estate. The phone buzzed to life in her hand, her fingers shaking slightly as she typed her message to Katherine, trying to keep her thoughts focused.

I'm fine. Made my way in. Will check in later.

Her thumb hovered over the screen, and for a brief second, she thought of adding more. She hesitated, unsure if she should tell Katherine about Julius's remarks—or masked threats. She didn't know where any of them fit into this game, and she was embroiled in the counterplot more quickly than she could have imagined possible.

She hit *send,* feeling the weight of the message hang in the air. It wasn't much, but it was enough. Katherine would assume Amanda was still playing her part, and Amanda could buy a little more time for business, and possibly pleasure.

She returned to her place next to Tristan as the synchronized wait staff arrived with the meal's crescendo. They presented each guest with a gleaming gold-dusted chocolate sphere and retreated without breaking formation. Delighted whispers rippled through the tables, the guests debating if they could possibly break something so beautiful in order to taste the decadence within.

Then, in a perfectly timed showcase, the waiters returned, each carrying a small copper pot of vanilla bean sauce. The warm liquid cascaded over the spheres, melting the chocolate shell and revealing the treasure inside—a core of rich caramel and tart raspberry coulis, swirling together in a mesmerizing display, and one edible diamond extending from the middle.

Gasps of approval spread among the guests as Clarisse began a delicate applause that every guest mimicked. "You've outdone yourself, darling," she announced, *"incroyable,"* she sputtered in French, *"incroyable."*

The guests dipped their spoons into the indulgent dessert, and most didn't stop until they polished it off. Laughter mixed with the distant chords of a string quartet, ending the evening on a perfect note.

"Now, off with the lot of you," Julius stood with the announcement, swinging his arm in a sweeping wave. "Let an old man get some rest. There's partying to be done tomorrow!" his voice getting louder with each declaration. "We sail at noon!" he chirred.

As the guests sauntered away, Tristan and Amanda were practically euphoric. This had been their only *this-is-not-a-date* encounter that felt like an actual consensual and eagerly anticipated outing. They walked to their room side by side, their steps slow and unhurried.

Tristan pushed open the door, flicking on the light. Amanda stepped inside, her eyes immediately landing on the singular, sprawling bed in the center of the room.

She turned towards him as the familiar sound of the door clicked shut behind them. He followed her gaze and let out a low chuckle. "Well, you want to use the bathroom first?"

Amanda smiled, feeling the room spin slightly. The evening was long, and she had coupled her wine with equal amounts of water, but her vulnerability to the mind-altering substance was showing. "I..." she leaned herself into him, digging her nails into the folds of his shirt at the collarbone.

Tristan placed both hands on her hips, nudging her backward. "I don't want to mess this up," he said, "and I want to be fully lucid for every moment of my first time with you." He gathered a handful of her dress, drawing her closer until she was pressed against his chest again. He brushed his lips lightly over hers. "I want to make it worth the wait."

Amanda felt her knees buckle as she fully lost her balance, shocked at the way she actually swooned in his arms.

Chapter Fourteen

Morning crept high over the horizon as most of the house slept off their sumptuous evening. Amanda's eyes, sensitive to the radiant light slipping through the curtains, began to twitch open. Turning away from the intrusion, her form sunk deeper into the mattress, before the awareness of where she was—and who was with her—pulled her completely from her sleep.

She blinked against the haze of slumber, and there he was—bare-chested, his breathing steady, one arm resting above his head. The night before, she had been the one blurring the line, testing boundaries he had somehow upheld. A gentleman, even when she hadn't wanted him to be.

Her fingers ached to trace the contours of his torso, to feel the warmth of his skin beneath her touch. Last night had been a blur of indulgence and restraint, and now, in the quiet morning, her temptation was even stronger.

She sucked in a long breath, forcing herself to shift away, exhaling deeply to clear her head. Her phone was nearby, tucked under the pillow where she had hidden it before she had returned to the party. She hadn't gotten a text back from Katherine, so now she had to call.

Amanda held a breath, reaching for the device, but her gaze drifted back to Tristan. He was still asleep, his lashes dark against his cheekbones, the faintest trace of a smirk lingering on his lips. As if even unconscious, he knew exactly what kind of effect he had on her.

She allowed herself one more enduring glance before slipping out of bed and walking towards the ensuite. The towering archway into the bathroom prohibited a closeable door, but the toilet itself was cocooned in a private space. She texted as she walked.

Can chat now. I don't know how much time I have. She hit the send button, closing the door behind her.

She perched herself on the lid of the commode, her arms wrapped tightly around her legs, knees drawn up to her chest. Her fingers curled over her shins, gripping just enough to still the restless energy thrumming beneath her skin. Her phone buzzed.

Are you alone? Katherine's text read.

Kind of. Long story. I'm holed up in the bathroom. Tristan's in the bedroom. Amanda replied.

Too risky. Thanks for the sign of life. Record what you can. Report back when you're alone.

"Record?" Amanda whispered, "What? How am I supposed to do *that?*"

"Chatting with someone?" she heard a tap on the door, causing her to spring to her feet and flush the toilet, instinctively covering her tracks.

"Ha, caught me—just talking to myself," Amanda said, opening the slatted wooden door that separated them. "Sorry, I didn't mean to wake you," she apologized.

"Oh, you didn't. Nature calls," Tristan said, stepping around her and closing the door behind him.

"Got it," Amanda said, walking to the sink and washing her hands, forcing herself not to think about Tristan's shirtless body only two feet away from her.

"Phew," he said, exiting the bathroom, "what time is it?"

Amanda, still holding her phone, looked down. "Oh, it's eight-thirty," she tilted the screen towards him to show the numbers, glowing atop an image of her and Lyla.

"How are they?" Tristan asked, referencing the photo.

"Oh, Lyla and Kyle? They're great," she shrugged.

She loved having her new phone, the one that integrated both her old number and her new line seamlessly. This device, though it looked exactly like her old one, had been customized for her, equipped to run separate identities without switching any settings. No more juggling between her real phone and the burner. Now, one SIM held her personal number—the one tied to the life she was *supposed* to be living. Another was a direct line to Katherine. A third carried an optional alias—one Katherine insisted she have active.

A single swipe could toggle between them, her truth and her deception. She could openly take photos, share social media posts on occasion, and generally be normal with her phone around her assigned marks. But using it as a recording device? She was not sure she'd be able to do that undetected.

"You should tell me more about you and Lyla when you were teenagers. I get such a kick out of hearing her stories about you guys. I was close to Kyle when we were in school, but we only reconnected a few years ago... when I... you know, Elise and I weren't in a good place. And Kyle was really there for me," he said, leaning his hands on the front of the sink, the sprawling mirrors behind him revealing every arc and bulge of his muscles.

Amanda tried to focus. "Yeah, it's funny, Lyla never mentioned to me that you were married when we talked," she raised an eyebrow, trying to be as elusive as possible.

"Well, I *wasn't* married when I finally met you," he pointed out.

"Fair, you weren't," she accepted, feeling heat rise up the back of her neck.

Tristan grinned, "Am I... distracting you?" he winked, feeling the mutual desire rising between them, turning to face her and drawing his palms upward to lift himself onto the wide counter of the double sink. He moved his legs to each side, gesturing for her to step between them, hands outstretched to take hers.

She complied, placing her palms on his as he pulled her close. "I thought... you weren't wanting to rush anything," Amanda whispered.

"You're right. I don't want to rush anything. I plan on taking this *incredibly* slow," he said, sweeping his lips across her neck.

A ship glided into Julius's private dock with effortless grace, its sleek, gleaming hull reflecting the afternoon sun. At nearly four hundred feet long, it was a floating palace—its multi-tiered decks lined with tinted windows and polished railings. The low hum of its engines softened as it settled into position, the crew moving like clockwork to secure it.

From the cliffside above, the guests watched the ship dock, its presence alone commanding attention. A private cable car station was perched at the edge of the estate property, its glass-walled cabin waiting to carry the guests to the aquatic escapade below. One by one, the guests stepped inside, and a soft whir of the mechanism kicked to life, as the car began its descent over emerald waters.

The beeline ride down the cliffs showcased the vast, endless blue of the bay, the sun casting a glowing path across the waves. As they neared the dock, the ship's name came into view, inscribed in silver lettering along the stern—*Esmé*.

A few crew members and some of the familiar house staff stood at the ready in crisp uniforms, prepared to welcome them aboard.

The doors of the cable car slid open, and a warm sea breeze met them as they stepped onto the dock. Customary champagne flutes waited on silver trays as the gangway extended to bridge them into limitless luxury.

The guests had dressed for the occasion, an effortless blend of elegance and nonchalance that only the truly wealthy seemed to master. Flowing linen dresses in soft pastels and crisp whites, and designer sunglasses perched on top of artfully tousled hair. Men in lightweight trousers and tailored shirts, some leaving the top buttons undone, the sea breeze dictating their level of formality. Gold flashed at wrists and throats, understated yet deliberate. Sandals were sleek and minimal—no one here needed to prove anything. Esmé was generous enough to help Amanda pack an entire suitcase with options for their various activities. The only items belonging to her were her purse, phone, undergarments, and toiletries. Everything else was Esmé's.

From Esme's closet, Amanda had chosen an airy, wide-legged silk trouser in a deep champagne hue, paired with a fitted white halter top that left her shoulders and upper back bare. The outfit clung just enough to highlight her waist before flowing freely down her legs, catching the wind as she moved.

A gold chain belt sat low on her hips, subtle but intentional, glinting under the afternoon sun. On her feet, she wore delicate, lace-up sandals in soft tan leather, the thin straps winding elegantly around her ankles. Her accessories were minimal—a single gold cuff on her wrist, and a pair of oversized, tortoise-shell sunglasses that could hide her expression as needed. Her hair was swept into a sleek, low ponytail, ensuring not a single strand would stick to her skin in the heat.

Tristan, the textbook on relaxed sophistication, had opted for beige linen trousers and a blue button-down, the sleeves casually rolled to his forearms. His shirt was unbuttoned just enough to hint at his sculpted collarbone, a leather watch strapped to his wrist. His hair was naturally tousled, and the faintest trace of stubble only added to his appeal.

As the guests emerged onto the dock, the scent of salt and wild dill daisies mingled in the air, the aquamarine depths feet away. Amanda adjusted her sunglasses, catching a glimpse of Tristan's stare.

"Try not to fall in," he whispered to her in jest.

She smiled, slow and deliberate. "I never do."

"That's not what I witnessed this morning," he lowered his brow, giving her a subtle grin.

"Shhh. Someone will hear you," she giggled, reminding him to stay well-behaved among his fancy entourage.

"Oh, trust me, these people are *dying* to hear all about it," he gibed.

Before she had time to react, they heard Julius greeting everyone.

The last two people to embark, Tristan and Amanda approached Julius Babb, waiting at the top of the entrance stairs, a glass in hand, his blazer crisp against his tanned skin and salt-and-pepper hair, like he had been born on a yacht. A smile played at his lips as he spread his arms in welcome.

"At last," Julius drawled, his voice as smooth as the whiskey in his glass. "My two favorite stragglers."

Amanda smiled, slipping her sunglasses down just enough to meet his gaze. "We won't shy from making an entrance."

Julius chuckled, stepping forward to kiss both her cheeks, the faint scent of expensive cologne clinging to him. When he turned to Tristan, the handshake was firm but warm, an exchange between men who understood each other in ways neither needed to say aloud.

"Welcome aboard, darlings," Esmé said, gesturing grandly towards the open deck, where guests lounged with drinks. "We should have our first toast of the day. Champagne?"

Amanda accepted the glass handed to her, the chilled stem cooling her fingers. She glanced at Tristan, who had already taken a sip of his, amusement flickering in his honey-gold eyes.

"To Julius," Esmé declared, raising her glass with a bright, loving smile. "A man who never does anything in halves—especially not his parties." A ripple of laughter moved through the crowd. "To the man who brings us together, who reminds us that life is meant to be tasted, savored," she paused, tilting her glass towards him with a smirk, "and occasionally drowned in champagne."

Another laugh, a few scattered cheers, and the first unison sip of the afternoon. Julius inclined his head slightly in acknowledgment, his grin deepening as he watched them all drink to him.

"Now, let me introduce you to the rest of the guests we have this weekend, Amanda." Julius returned his attention to his favorite couple. "And Tristan, I don't think you know the Tennessee governor, do you?" he asked, turning to eye the man approaching from behind.

"Julius," Governor Jim Hansen said, his southern drawl unmistakable. "You've outdone yourself. Again. But I suppose I shouldn't be surprised."

Amanda felt her breath lodge in her throat as Hansen greeted Julius warmly, clapping the billionaire on the back like an old friend.

Julius laughed, shaking his head. "Oh, stop. You flatter me. And you, Governor, have been a godsend to our whole operation. We wouldn't be where we are without your, shall we say, gentle encouragement." Gesturing towards Tristan, he continued. "This is my number-one man for tech—he's changing the world," Julius beamed. "Tristan Montgomery."

Tristan extended his hand, "A pleasure, Governor. This is my... friend," the subtle hesitation barely noticeable, "Amanda Hopkins." Tristan's arm glided around her back, touching her bare skin before landing on her waist, a now familiar comfort that steadied her. "She's from Tennessee, but we won't make you answer to a constituent while off duty," Tristan charmed.

The Governor's microexpressions betrayed him momentarily, but thankfully, not many people are skilled at detecting a liar based on the subtle movements of a face.

Amanda's heart nearly stopped. Governor Hansen's gaze fixated on her, his smile unwavering but his eyes narrowing slightly, assessing her.

"Miss Hopkins," he said, extending his hand. "Pleasure to meet you."

"Likewise," Amanda said, managing a polite smile as she placed her hand in his. His grip was deliberate, his stare uncomfortably knowing.

"Tristan's a lucky man," Hansen added, releasing her hand.

"Very lucky," Tristan chimed in, instinctively tightening his arm around Amanda, oblivious to the storm building inside her.

Chapter Fifteen

"Here we are, señorita." Amanda followed Marco down the hallway towards the cabin she and Tristan would share for the two nights onboard.

"You can download the ship's app on the welcome card inside. I'll be just a call or text away. Let me know if you need anything," Marco said with a kind smile, sensing there was a reason she had stepped away from the others.

"Thanks, Marco," she said in farewell. Inside the room, she discovered her bags had already been unpacked with care—the gowns, blouses, and slacks hanging neatly in the small closet, each piece perfectly in place.

The cabin was a masterpiece of compact luxury, where elegance met efficiency. Rich mahogany paneling and soft, ambient lighting gave the space a warm, intimate glow, while plush cream-colored linens draped over a king-sized bed that threatened to stretch wall-to-wall. A sleek glass-topped vanity and a polished wooden nightstand framed the room, their surfaces gleaming under golden sconces.

Floor-to-ceiling windows led to a private balcony, doors slightly open, where sheer curtains swayed lightly in the ocean breeze, framing a view of glistening waves. Despite the indulgence, the room's modest size made every detail noticeable: the faint hum of the air conditioning, the gentle creak of the ship's hull.

Amanda sank onto the bed, drawing in a slow, measured breath as she let her gaze drift across the room. The neatly placed welcome card on the vanity caught her eye; its crisp edges and elegant lettering—this design also a nod to the invitation—practically demanded her attention. With a quiet exhale, she reached for her phone and scanned the QR code, watching as the app loaded in seconds. A sleek interface unfolded before her—an itinerary button neatly organizing the ship's schedule, times, and locations laid out with precision, an interactive map, curated menus, and even a direct line to call or text a personal concierge. She let out a soft, incredulous laugh, shaking her head. Julius Babb had to be the most fastidious man on the planet.

Setting her phone down to guarantee uninterrupted solitude, Amanda stepped onto the balcony, the hush of the open sea stretching endlessly before her. The breeze curled around her like a whispered secret, lifting the loose strands of hair that had escaped her sleek ponytail. She pressed her hands against the cool metal railing, grounding herself to counter the yacht's gentle sway. She had to think. To make sense of what was happening.

Katherine had acted like Julius Babb was some unknown character that she had to investigate, and now? Turns out Julius knows her? And Hansen is not just connected in some way, he's on the actual trip they had sent her here to infiltrate? She sifted through a few scenarios.

Theory one: Hansen wasn't directly tied to her mission, and his presence was a coincidence. But no, Katherine would've gone over the guest list with a fine-tooth comb.

Theory two: In cahoots, Hansen and Katherine wanted to intimidate her, and knew sending Hansen in the flesh would more than do the job. But why do it so publicly, with Tristan and Julius so close by? That seemed reckless.

Theory three: Tristan wasn't the target—Julius was. But if that were true, what role did Julius really play?

Each theory unraveled almost as soon as she formed it. Hansen's presence didn't make sense, and Katherine's stories didn't add up either. So much for cloaking things in truth.

She tilted her face towards the sun-soaked sky, letting the briny air fill her lungs, willing it to slow the rush of thoughts tumbling inside her. The party thrummed on in the distance. Her fingers tightened around the railing. Tristan. Julius. Katherine. They bounced around her head like racquetballs flying off walls.

Theory four: Katherine and Julius were playing her—good guy/bad guy game. But could Katherine and Hansen be the ones working with Russia, and Julius the good guy?

The wind swept around her again, clipping against her skin, as if urging her to let go. She exhaled slowly, rolling her shoulders back, and closing her eyes against the pull of exhaustion.

Behind her, the door creaked softly, footsteps barely audible over the sound of the waves. She didn't turn. Not yet.

"Hey, you disappeared," Tristan said, enveloping Amanda in his arms from behind, her bare back pressing into him.

She turned slowly to face him, wrapping her arms around his neck—her mind still reeling, begging herself to keep him at a distance emotionally, but incapable of refusing his touch. She couldn't share her secrets, so she'd have to figure out a way to get him to share his. But those eyes. Hints of honey pooled around his pupils, bleeding outward into a halo of mossy green, as if the forest and the fire had struck a quiet truce within his gaze. In the dim light, they darkened, rich and mysterious, but when the sun hit them just right, they came alive, impossible to look away from.

Amanda felt a tear fall from her face.

"Hey, what's going on?" Tristan asked. "Did something happen?"

"I just... don't know what I'm doing here," Amanda admitted.

"What do you mean? You're my date—my plus-one—you're with *me,*" he charmed her more with every word.

Amanda let out a soft sigh.

"Don't let anyone make you feel like you don't belong. I've got you," Tristan said, gripping her like an anchor, steady and unyielding against the tide.

"Thanks," Amanda whispered, longing to break her facade and trust him. She leaned her head onto his shoulder as he wrapped her in an unfaltering embrace.

Amanda had read enough to know that some of history's most skilled spies had not been undone by faulty intel or a wrong step in enemy territory—it was love that ruined them. Emotions blurred judgment, desire compromised discretion, and in the end, their hearts betrayed them long before their enemies did. Time and again, agents who had trained to be ghosts left traces of themselves where they shouldn't, not because they were careless, but because they couldn't separate duty from longing. And that was always the beginning of the end.

"Thanks," she repeated with a long exhale. "Sorry, this has just been a whirlwind," she said, lifting her head again to meet his eyes.

"You can let me into that world of yours, you know." Tristan didn't let go. "I feel like I've just begun to scratch the surface with you, Amanda. One minute I feel like we've known each other since that day in Chicago, and the next…"

"Like we've only known each other a month?" Amanda said, tilting her head with a dry smile, her words dripping with sarcasm in an attempt to shake off her unease.

"Hey, it's been almost three," Tristan corrected her.

"Has it?" she smiled.

"Yes, in fact, three months tomorrow," he informed.

"Oh! Three whole months. Are you marking off a big red X on your calendar each day?"

Tristan exhaled a sharp laugh. "No, I just happened to notice the date," he lifted his shoulders in a glib shrug. "Your birthday… that was three months ago tomorrow."

"Hm, okay," she chimed. "Longer than many of my past relationships," she poked fun, letting it slip through her lips before she could think. Immediate regret made her face flush.

Tristan stepped back, his hands landing gently on her hips. "Oh, so this *is* a relationship?" His voice was more playful than ever.

Amanda silently moved forward, fully placing her body into his arms again, meeting his lips in a slow, lingering touch, warmth spreading between them like a secret shared without words. Soft but electric breaths mingled in the dissolving space between them as a quiet intensity built. Time stretched, wrapped in the hush of their closeness, each second carrying the weight of unspoken emotions.

Taking a step back again, as decidedly and intentionally as she had begun the moment, she looked at him with a smile.

"I'll take that as a yes." The gleam from Tristan's eyes spread across his face. He kept one of her hands in his, leading her from the room's small balcony back into the quiet of the cabin and motioning to the bed. "Sit. I have something for you," he said before going to his bag.

Amanda lowered herself to the bed, curiously watching him. Tristan reached for something just out of view, and a shiver of expectation pulsed through her. Amanda hated surprises. Surprises in her past were not gifts but blows.

"Here. I didn't have time to get you more of a birthday gift, so, I wanted you to have this," he said, handing her an elongated jewelry box, gold-foiled and tied with a matching satin ribbon.

He pulled a chair to the edge of the bed and faced her knee-to-knee in anticipation. Tristan, for one, loved surprises.

Nestled in the velvet-lined box, a whisper of a bracelet lay against the dark fabric. Each delicate gold link caught the light with an understated shimmer. No elaborate embellishments—just quiet elegance, refined and intentional. In the corner of the box, a small eighteen-carat gold tag gleamed, a testament to its worth, though the true value wasn't in the metal alone. It was in the simplicity, in the thought behind it, in the way it seemed crafted especially for the one who would wear it.

"Tristan, this is so lovely," Amanda gasped. "When did you...?"

"I got it in Rome," he smiled, taking it into his hands to help Amanda with the tiny clasp.

Amanda turned her wrist, watching the bracelet settle smoothly against her skin. No adjustments needed, no links to remove—a perfect fit.

"I wanted it for when I..." a lump formed in Tristan's throat. He was not a shy man, nor did he lack confidence when it came to women, but after a relationship that lasted more than a decade and ended in him facing his childhood trauma and questioning his ability to love someone well, he felt more vulnerable than ever. "...for when I ask you to be my girlfriend."

A quiet sense of inevitability settled in Amanda's chest, warming her from the inside out. She wasn't used to things falling into place, to someone knowing her well enough to choose something that unquestionably belonged with her. Her fingers traced the delicate chain for a moment before she looked up at Tristan, something unspoken passing between them. Acceptance. Maybe something deeper. She hadn't planned for this—for these feelings—but like the bracelet, things seemed to fit. Perfectly.

She let a forceful breath escape her lips. She was not without her own baggage; whether this was going to be a real relationship or her deepest cover, she didn't know. But she was truly enjoying mixing business with pleasure. She just had to keep her wits about her.

"Yes," she said softly with a nod as they both stood. Their mouths met in a slow, unhurried press, Tristan's touch a quiet promise on her skin.

The flash of meeting Hansen on this very boat rushed through Amanda's thoughts. She blinked her eyes open, cutting through the romance like a shard of glass slicing through flesh. It would take time to exercise the muscle of leaning into him, yet not *giving in* to him. In that moment, she made a promise to herself. She'd never close her eyes in Tristan's arms again. Not until she found answers. Regardless of the soft brush of his skin, the faint catch of his breath, or the way time hesitated in his arms, she could never allow herself to surrender entirely.

Tristan released his grasp and smiled affectionately at her. "Feeling better?"

"Much," she said—without the hint of a lie.

Her phone screen flickered and pinged, a notification glowing for a moment. A good excuse to shake off the intensity she was feeling, Amanda rose from the bed, reaching for it, and as she read the message, her eyes widened. "Oh! Look at this—it's the app. My glam appointment is in an hour," she murmured, surprise evident in her voice.

"Glam?" Tristan smirked.

"Yeah, I could get used to this treatment," she smiled.

"Well, tonight's as fancy as it gets—black tie. You looking forward to seeing me in a tux?" he teased, letting the flirtation build again.

"Can't wait," she lifted herself onto her toes, reaching to give him a quick peck on the cheek.

Tristan smiled and stepped to the perimeter of the room where a built-in minibar was seamlessly tucked beneath the sleek marble-topped counter near the vanity. Inside, chilled bottles of water rested neatly alongside a selection of premium refreshments.

He handed her a drink. "So, are you gonna play or watch?"

"Poker? With these guys? I'm pretty sure they are way outta my league. What's the minimum?"

"Twenty-K," Tristan replied without hesitation.

"Yeah, I'm good," Amanda said, nearly spitting the cool sip of water from her mouth. "I can be—like—your Bond girl tonight," she said, not even trying to be ironic. "My dress is definitely glitzy enough." She opened the door of the closet, revealing their clothes side by side as the lights caught the sequins of her couture gown.

The strapless bodice was structured yet elegant, while delicate ruching along the waistline previewed the way it would sculpt her body. Against the neatly arranged blouses and slacks, the dress promised mystery, allure, and flamboyantly fitting of any 007 expectations.

"Oh, yes," Tristan's eyes shone in approval. "It's perfect. Now, let's go enjoy the views on deck before your *glam* appointment." He said the word as if he wasn't used to being groomed and spruced himself. "The scenery is breathtaking."

Chapter Sixteen

The *Esmé's* main casino lounge, a masterpiece of art deco elegance, gleamed with polished mahogany, gilded accents, and the interplay between candlelight and chandeliers. A velvet-lined wall on one side muted the gentle lull of the ocean beyond, while panoramic windows that extended into an outdoor deck curved around the other side, revealing an endless expanse of midnight blue dotted with silver starlight.

Amanda glided into the casino on Tristan's arm, her coruscating gown echoing the opulence of the room, the thigh-high slit revealing a whisper of skin with every step. The rich fabric clung to her frame, while her hair cascaded along one side of her neck in soft 1920s-style finger waves. At her side, Tristan exuded power in a perfectly tailored black tuxedo, the sharp lines and crisp bow tie accentuating his commanding presence.

Heads turned as they moved through the lavish space, the buzz of conversation faltering for just a beat. Billionaires and elite guests, draped in designer gowns and bespoke suits, took notice—the kind of attention reserved for those who didn't just belong in luxury but defined it.

The gaming floor was alive with movement; dealers in smart tuxedos flipped cards and spun roulette wheels with smooth precision, their expressions unreadable. The scent of aged whiskey and fresh orchids drifted through the air as waitstaff weaved between small clusters of guests, offering champagne, delectable bites, and rare spirits. Laughter blended with murmured conversations and the delicate chime of ice swirling in cut-crystal glasses. The occasional cheer or groan of shifting fortunes punctuated the air.

For those who sought more than just cards and dice, the yacht offered endless indulgences—a secluded lounge where the finest cigars were paired with exquisite cognacs, a midnight buffet brimming with caviar and truffle-infused delicacies, and a lantern-lit rooftop deck where the soft glow of lanterns illuminated intimate seating areas, perfect for whispered deals and secret rendezvous.

Just beyond the casino floor, a grand piano set the tone with sultry jazz melodies that wound through the room like smoke. A familiar voice crooned through the atmosphere.

Amanda froze midstep, tugging on Tristan's arm, "Is that... *Michael Bublé...* like the *real-life* singer?" she gasped.

"I believe it is," Tristan squinted under the dim glow of the evening lights. "Well played, Julius."

Tristan led Amanda deeper into the room, his grip on her possessive yet poised, his confidence after she accepted his invitation to be his girlfriend radiating across his face. He smiled and greeted each familiar friend, basking in the admiring stares. He was there to play. Tristan had spent so much of his time trying to figure out the workings of the world, solve problems, and create lasting solutions. It had brought him no enduring solace, no peace, and oftentimes, no hope. The more he tried to deny his privilege, his upbringing, and his lifestyle, the more it haunted him.

The ocean held its breath on this night when reputations were gambled as easily as fortunes. And Tristan Montgomery was about to lean in fully.

Across the casino floor, Julius caught sight of the couple and lifted a hand in an easy wave, exposing the gold cufflinks peeking from his tailored jacket. He leaned back in his chair at the poker table with the relaxed authority of a man who had played—and won—more than his fair share of games. He tilted his head towards the empty seats beside him, a silent invitation. Esmé hovered to his right, her eyes settling on Amanda with a grin.

"Oh, my dear, you look stunning," Esmé gushed. "The gown looks like it was meant for you, not me!" she exclaimed, twirling her around with one hand.

Amanda tried not to blush. "Thank you, it's so elegant. Truly, this night is unreal... magical."

"Tristan, come. Sit." Julius patted the seat next to him as the women greeted each other behind him. He cast a glance over his shoulder. "Amanda, you had better bring luck to this guy tonight. He's always been too chicken to play with the big boys," Julius teased. "It's about time you manned up."

Tristan shook his head. "Okay, some of us roll our money into a business to make it work," he said, raising an eyebrow.

"Well... you have to when you don't have more money than God like Julius!" The table burst into laughter as Hansen's voice boomed, sending a chill down Amanda's spine. She breathed in sharply before turning to view the players.

To Tristan's right, Julius leaned back in his chair, twirling a single poker chip between his fingers, his smirk betraying the fact that, win or lose, he was here for the wine, the celebration, and the entertainment. He didn't even flinch at the notion that he was the wealthiest guy any of them knew. Across from them, Hansen slapped the table in amusement, but he didn't let his poker face slip. He wasn't one to bluff often, but when he did, it was devastating.

Sitting beside Hansen, Clarisse smiled with the detached merriment of someone who has never known want. Her fingers, adorned with heirloom rings, tapped against her stack of chips as she cast delighted glances around the table. Anton, known to be reckless at times and always chasing the next big win, sat next to her—having lost too much once to ever play again without Clarisse there to reign him in.

At the far end, Lucien Beaumont, a French venture capitalist known for his charming facade and cutthroat instincts, swirled a glass of cognac as he studied the table. He had been rumored to bankrupt men with a single hand, his bluffs so smooth they felt like truth until it was too late.

Finally, rounding out the group was Vivian Cross, a stunning and enigmatic hedge fund manager. She sat with an amused glint in her eye. She had an uncanny ability to make her opponents second-guess themselves, her lips curving ever so slightly whenever someone hesitated too long before calling a bet.

Just as the dealer prepared to deal the first hand, a man stepped forward, ambition sharp in his eyes. "Room for one more?" he asked smoothly, his gaze sweeping the table as if he already belonged there.

Julius barely glanced up from his stack of chips, smirking. "Table's closed," he said, flicking a card between his fingers. "Everyone's already paid the minimum."

"Too bad. Guess I'll just have to watch, then," he said, but there was no mistaking the frustration behind his polished demeanor.

"Come, get a drink with me, dear," Esmé murmured, tugging on Amanda's arm.

"I thought you'd never ask," Amanda chuckled, happily accompanying Esmé to the bar. "Who is that guy?" she asked as they walked out of earshot. "I haven't met everyone on board yet."

Esmé's nose crinkled, and her lips curled slightly in distaste. "Russell Drake," she said bitterly.

"That bad, huh?" Amanda raised her eyebrows. "He seemed pretty put out."

"Yeah, everyone knows he can't afford the buy-in. He just likes to come at the last minute and act like we're mistreating him. Same old story. He's one of Julius's earliest business partners, and Julius is nothing if not loyal—vodka tonic, please—" she ordered without skipping a beat, "so Mr. Drake will forever be a thorn in my flesh."

Amanda smiled, unsure of how to process the character assessment Esmé attributed to Drake. "Just sparkling water for me—quarter of a lime with the carcass in, please," she said.

"No drinks for you tonight?" Esmé probed.

"Oof, I've had more drinks in the past few weeks than I normally have in a year," Amanda explained. "My system is begging for a break."

"Don't let Julius know. He insists on indulgence for these things." Esmé sounded serious. "Make sure you put hers in a crystal glass, yes?" She turned to the bartender.

"Of course," he said, placing a crystal tumbler on the bar.

"And a couple drops of orange bitters for a little flavor and color?" she said, as if waiting for approval from Amanda.

"Yes, that's fine," Amanda nodded.

"Perfect. I like you. I will not have Julius's grumpy reactions chasing off one more person... unless it's Russel Drake," she laughed, raising her glass as Amanda picked up the bubbling water.

Amanda caught her infectious chuckle, raising her glass to Esmé's with a clink. The music swelled as the two women walked to the edge of the casino, closer to where the grand piano stood, and Bublé himself was belting out a tune, surrounded by admiring ears. They found a seat on a plush sofa just big enough for two.

Amanda looked towards the small stage, barely six inches from the floor. "That's really him," she said in nearly a whisper, still unable to grasp that she was in the same room with *the* Michael Bublé and fewer than fifty people total. The only other time she had come this close was for a stadium concert she attended while he was on tour. She had a friend who sang backup for him in one of the cities on his schedule, and she got to tag along, with a seat right in front of the stage. It was a night she'd never forget.

"Yes, that's his wife over there," Esmé pointed to a petite woman sitting in a champagne-colored gown with someone who looked like a friend, reveling in the evening sounds as if she wasn't used to them.

"Their kids are staying with a nanny on Gran Canaria, the island we'll do some shopping on tomorrow," Esmé continued. "He travels with them often. He's a real family man. They love the islands here," she explained.

"Who wouldn't?" Amanda murmured, swept up in the moment.

"Indeed," Esmé agreed, clinking their drinks again. "It's mesmerizing, isn't it? Have you ever heard him sing live before?" she asked.

"I have, yes," Amanda admitted. "Just at one of his stadium concerts. A friend of mine was one of the backup singers. In fact, her boss got to sing with him too—it was kind of incredible."

"Nice. You hang out with singers and musicians then? I find them such an interesting lot," Esmé stated.

"Oh, not much anymore, but in high school—and even a little in college—I was really into all the arts," Amanda reminisced. "I used to sing on stage myself. Me—can you believe it?" she laughed.

"Fascinating!" Esmé exclaimed, her eyes lighting up. "Brains, beauty, *and* talent? You're the whole package!" Her melodic laugh rang out, drawing the attention of nearby guests, their curious smiles lingering as they took in the moment. "You're what we would call a triple threat!"

Amanda felt heat rush to her cheeks, a flush of embarrassment at the sudden attention. She forced a small smile, but the praise sat uneasily in her chest. Beneath the flattery, a gnawing sense of dread coiled in her stomach. She wasn't tasked with becoming Esmé's friend, she was supposed to be spying on her lover. Amanda shook her head as if to swat the thoughts away like an unwanted bug.

"Excuse me," she said, "I need to use the ladies' room."

"I'll join you," Esmé replied, rising gracefully to follow Amanda and, as if it were second nature already, linking an arm through hers. "Then we can try our hand at roulette, shall we? Or should I let you mingle with the others?" She laughed, a light, effortless sound. "It's probably best that I don't monopolize all your time here," she added, almost as if scolding herself, though the amused glint in her eyes suggested she rarely worried about such things.

As Amanda and Esmé strolled arm in arm through the casino lounge, they weaved through clusters of gambling guests. The warble of conversations and bursts of laughter that had accompanied them all evening began to slow, and the women paused as they registered the strange shift in the atmosphere.

A murmur rippled through the crowd. Near the center of the room, a sharp, desperate sound—part cough, part strangled wheeze—cut through the air.

Russell Drake stood, clutching at his throat, his face contorted in agony, his movements spasmodic and panicked. A glass slipped from his fingers, rolling against the carpeted floor as he staggered backward. Guests instinctively stepped aside, a widening circle forming around him as the elegant gathering teetered on the edge of chaos.

Amanda took in a sharp breath as she watched him drop to his knees, his eyes bulging, veins straining against the skin of his neck. His lips parted to cry for help, but no words came, only silent gasps. He collapsed with a sickening thud at Governor Jim Hansen's feet.

People were shouting and cursing. Clarisse let out a barely stifled scream.

Then, in a rush of movement, a man knelt beside Russell, pressing two fingers to his neck before starting chest compressions. "Call for the ship's medic! Now!" he barked, his voice snapping some of the frozen onlookers into action.

Amanda felt Esmé's grip on her arm tighten, her nails digging in slightly.

Russell's body jerked violently beneath the man's hands, his back arching off the floor as a horrific convulsion wracked through him. Foam bubbled at the corners of his mouth, his limbs writhing in wild, uncontrollable tremors. Some people gasped. Others whispered a prayer.

Amanda's breath came in short, panicked bursts. Her pulse pounded in her ears, drowning out the frantic voices, the CPR, and the dismayed onlookers. Russell's convulsing body and frothing mouth were seared into her vision. Her stomach twisted violently.

While Esmé was transfixed by the scene, her grip on Amanda loosened, as she slipped away undetected, her steps light as she skirted around the gathering crowd.

Amanda's heartbeat thundered as she exited through a side corridor that led to the guest cabins. The polished walls seemed to narrow around her as she half-walked, half-ran, forcing down the bile rising in her throat.

By the time she reached her door, her hands were shaking. She fumbled with the keycard, cursing under her breath before finally forcing it into the slot. The lock clicked, and she shoved her way inside, barely making it to the ensuite before the nausea overwhelmed her.

She collapsed to her knees, gripping the cold porcelain. Juxtaposed against the luxurious fixtures and neatly folded towels, Amanda unleashed the contents of her stomach.

She knew that scene. She had played it a thousand times in her head.

The violent tremors, the helpless gasping, the foam at the mouth—it was all too familiar. It had haunted her nightmares, whispered in her waking thoughts. Cooper's grandmother was poisoned the same way.

Amanda squeezed her eyes shut, gripping the edges of the sink as another wave of nausea rolled through her. She had been younger then, just an observer in the background, watching as the once-powerful matriarch of the Hansen dynasty withered before their eyes. It had started slowly—fatigue, nausea, weakness—until the sickness had consumed her completely.

When news broke of the woman's death, it wasn't the headlines that stuck with Amanda. It wasn't the interviews or the speculation. It was the description. The detail that made her blood run cold. A heart-stopping fall, followed by foaming at the mouth. Just like Russell Drake.

This couldn't be random or some kind of coincidence. Amanda forced herself to stand, relying on the sink to steady her shaking legs. She stared at her reflection in the mirror—eyes wide, face sweaty, expression panicked. *What the hell was she going to do?*

Chapter Seventeen

"Hey, there you are," Tristan approached the outer deck of the ship from the dining room, bending to kiss Amanda's cheek. "You disappeared last night... and again this morning, apparently."

Amanda had sat alone, nibbling on breakfast at a deck table, the sun casting a majestic sheen over the endless Atlantic. She sipped on freshly squeezed blood orange juice, its tang a perfect contrast to her buttery croissant.

Though the Canary Islands were relatively close to each other, the captain had charted a leisurely and scenic course, one that would keep them on the water for a full two days before reaching Gran Canaria. The yacht would sail along La Gomera's dramatic cliffs, glide past the untouched shores of El Hierro, and linger near the crystal-clear coves of La Palma, allowing for brief stops to swim in secluded waters, or simply drift beneath the August sun as time unraveled.

The islands unfolded around Amanda in a shifting panorama, as the verdant coastline of Gran Canaria loomed ahead, delicately veiled in a morning haze. The impossibly blue water was broken only by the occasional ripple of a passing dolphin.

Amanda leaned back, begging the sway of the waves to lull her into a rare moment of tranquility.

"Yeah, sorry," she took Tristan's hand. "I... had a hard time seeing that. Old memories."

"Wanna talk about it?" Tristan sat across from her, still clutching her hand.

"No, I'll be okay. Just trying to shake it off. Did he... make it?" she asked.

"No, he didn't," Tristan shook his head. "You missed everything. The coast guard arrived and took Drake to shore last night along with Julius and a few guests. They had to bring them all in for questioning, I guess. I don't know how it all works when someone dies at sea."

"No, me either," she took a long breath in. "Geez, that's awful," Amanda said. "Are they changing the schedule?"

"Not that I know of. The captain came out and said getting their statements and writing reports would only take a few hours, and there was nothing more we could do. The Coast Guard will just bring them right back to us," Tristan explained. "I didn't notice you had already gone back to the room until... well... until I came and found you asleep. You looked like you were fully resting, so I didn't wake you."

Amanda sat motionless, breath shallow, and fingers curled tightly in her lap. The silence stretched for a moment before she finally spoke again. "I... got a little sick. It took a lot out of me, so I popped a sleeping pill. That always helps—sleeping it off. Anyway, sorry I didn't say anything."

"It's okay, but you know I'm here, right? You don't have to keep it all in—that's what *boyfriends* are for." The way he elongated the word—like they were middle schoolers from the valley—made Amanda laugh.

"Thanks," she said, allowing a tear to trickle from her eye. She knew she couldn't tell him about the ties she shared with Hansen. There was a reason that he was just as calculated about concealing their connection as she was, but her past was heavier than her current entanglement with him.

"I was with my grandmother when she died," Amanda finally blurted. "I held her head."

"Oh, Amanda." Tristan took both of her hands into his.

"I came home from school that day, and everything felt... *off*. I can't even explain why. It was just this weird feeling... like the house wasn't breathing the same way it always did. You know how some places feel alive because of the people in them? That day, it was like something had already shifted before I even walked inside. The house had always been small, the kind where every creaky floorboard carried the sound of life through thin walls. It smelled of cinnamon, old books, and the lavender lotion Nellie kept on the nightstand.

"She was in her chair by the window—her favorite spot—where she watched everything. I used to joke that she knew more about our neighbors' lives than they did. But when I saw her sitting there, too still, too quiet, I just... I knew.

"I said her name. Once. Twice. I touched her arm, and..." Amanda swallowed, blinking hard, the weight of the memory still pressing down on her chest.

It wasn't what had made her vomit last night, but it had happened to her, and it was a truth she was allowed to tell. "She was still warm. She was breathing... and then she wasn't."

Amanda exhaled slowly, shaking her head. "I just held her. I don't even know how long. I should've called someone right away, but I couldn't move. I kept thinking if I just held on tight enough, she wouldn't go. That maybe she was just resting, that maybe she'd open her eyes and laugh at me for being so dramatic. But she didn't.

"She was gone. And that was it."

Amanda glanced away, her fingers tightening Tristan's. "I grew up thinking my aunt was my mother. Everyone did. My real mom, Kate—she got pregnant with me in high school and disappeared for a while. And by the time she came back, they had already made the decision for her. My aunt, Genevieve, was married, stable, the *respectable* one, so they passed me off as hers. Just like that. A little family secret, wrapped up in polite smiles and whispered warnings not to ask too many questions.

"I didn't know the truth until I was older, but I *felt* it before then. The way Genevieve looked at me—like I was an obligation she hadn't signed up for. And then my real mother, my *actual* mother, treated me like a distant cousin she barely remembered. I was just this... shadow of a mistake no one wanted to talk about. The only person who ever treated me like I mattered—like I was truly loved—was my grandma Nellie.

"She'd slip me money when she could and tell me stories about my mother before everything fell apart. But she kept the secret, too. Because that's what our family did—hide the truth, no matter how much it hurt. But still... she was the only person in the world who ever really loved me. I mean, *fully*. No conditions, no expectations. Just love. And I lost her in one afternoon—in a single breath."

Amanda let out a quiet, humorless laugh. "That's the thing they don't tell you about loss. It doesn't always come in big, dramatic moments. Sometimes, it just sneaks in on an ordinary day, when you least expect it, and suddenly, everything changes."

Tristan was the one wiping tears away now as Amanda's eyes seemed to gloss over. "I don't know what to say," he admitted, flicking a tear away.

"It's okay, you don't have to say anything. Listening helps. Thank you." her voice was low and measured. "Are you going to go on the dive today?" she asked, needing to change the subject.

After giving Tristan a real-life reason to understand her impulsive reactions the previous night, Amanda was ready to move on. Dwelling on it wouldn't change anything. She needed her focus elsewhere—on Hansen's involvement with Julius, on the shocking death she witnessed. Like the ocean, Amanda would be deceptively calm on the surface, despite the chaos churning in her depths.

She shook her head reactively as if the movement could quell her own inner ocean.

"Oh, um..." Tristan stammered, running a hand through his hair. His brows pulled together, and he exhaled sharply. He needed a second to regroup, to find his footing after everything she'd just dropped on him. "I guess... I don't know—what about you? Did you plan to dive?"

"No, I'm not certified," she said, shifting her weight from one foot to the other. She lifted her chin slightly, letting the breeze cool her flushed skin. "I do love to snorkel, though. I just thought maybe I'd hover on the surface and observe." She flashed him a grin, trying to lighten the mood.

Tristan's lips curved into a tiny smile, his shoulders relaxing just a little. "Yeah, that sounds nice. I haven't gone on a dive in a while, so I may be out of practice. I'm sure I could freshen my skills… but maybe I'll follow your lead. Snorkeling sounds perfect."

"I agree," Amanda smirked, leaning slightly towards him as if sharing a secret. "Don't tell Esmé, but I'd choose snorkeling over shopping any day."

Tristan chuckled, but his eyes remained on her, searching. Assessing.

"And… you don't have to babysit me," she added, a familiar defiance feathering her voice. "I'm okay, really."

"Is that what you think I'm doing?" His expression shifted—not offended, but curious.

"I don't know…" She exhaled, her fingers absentmindedly fiddling with the delicate bracelet around her wrist, tracing the shape of each link. "This whole thing is… new."

"Well," Tristan stood, taking her hands as she joined him and he wrapped his arms around her waist. "Let me tell you a thing or two about how this relationship is going to progress," he said, pressing his lips to hers before pausing for air. "I'm going to want to be with you every second I can."

The deck buzzed with anticipation as guests slipped into wetsuits, adjusted masks, and checked their gear. A few crew members moved efficiently among them, offering assistance and double-checking oxygen tanks, their voices calm and practiced. Amid the preparation, an undercurrent of hushed gossip swirled through the group.

"I still can't believe it," a woman murmured as she tightened the strap of her snorkel mask. "He was *fine* one moment, then on the floor convulsing the next?"

"Foaming at the mouth," another added in a low voice, shaking his head. "I heard Hansen looked sick to his stomach."

"I heard he *barely* reacted."

Amanda knelt, pretending to check the fit of her fins as she listened, absorbing every word while keeping her expression neutral. The shock of Russel Drake's death clung to the guests like a damp chill, making their voices sharper and their gestures more animated.

Someone chuckled darkly. "A man like that makes enemies. Maybe he finally pissed off the wrong person." Uneasy murmurs followed.

Amanda's stomach clenched. She forced herself to breathe slowly, nodding vaguely at Tristan when he handed her a snorkel.

"Here, this should fit you," he said, watching her closely.

She mustered an easy smile. "Thanks."

"Still okay?" he winked.

"Still okay," she affirmed, leaning over to give him a quick peck.

"I'm not sure that was convincing," he smiled.

She couldn't afford to let the pull of attraction cloud her focus. But her mind was spinning, trying to piece together how she needed to fit the puzzle of last night's events together.

As she stood, pulling her mask into place, she focused on the rush of the wind and the warmth of the sun against her skin. *Stay present. Stay sharp.* She could sift through the details later.

Tristan nudged her lightly with his elbow. "Ready?"

She nodded, swallowing the unease pressing at her ribs. "Yeah. Let's go."

They joined the others, slipping into the water with a splash.

The waves and people moved in perfect harmony, the sea welcoming them with open arms. Golden ribbons of sunlight glistened across the coral below. Divers glided through the water, their movements like birds soaring on unseen currents. Some plunged deeper, disappearing into the cerulean abyss, while others hovered at the azure surface, taking in the underwater world from above.

Amanda dipped her head under the water, watching schools of fish filtering past her in synchronized billows, weaving through the vibrant coral as if performing for their visitors. Laughter bubbled up from the snorkelers as they playfully splashed, pointing out the creatures hiding in the reef. This universe was untouched by the mayhem of the world above. Amanda kept her breathing steady in the embrace of the sea, focusing on the pulsating sound of air rushing through her snorkel. Below her, Tristan immersed his mask and tube, swimming lower and lower, but still above the descending divers.

No doubt, Esmé, Clarisse, and the others were reveling in the extravagance of upscale boutiques, gushing over exclusive finds and the thrill of being pampered. But for Amanda, no luxury could compare to this, drifting buoyantly in the endless blue, surrounded by the whir of an ancient and untamed ocean. The water didn't care about status or wealth; it welcomed every soul the same. And she wouldn't trade that communion with nature for anything. Tristan bobbed in and out of the seawater, diving deeper each time. He turned to see her face, floating backwards, taking a moment to wave at her with a smile.

Suddenly, a muffled, distorted thrashing echoed through the waves between them, and three or four divers plunged at once, obscuring Amanda's view of Tristan.

Lifting her head above the surface, she ripped her mask and snorkel off to draw a full breath before placing it on her head again and submerging her face into the water.

One of the divers flailed wildly, body twisting as they clutched at their oxygen regulator, erratic bubbles erupting around them. One of the lunging dive masters reached for the gear, while another gestured sharply towards the surface.

Amanda's heart pounded. She could hear nothing but the rush of her own breath, see nothing but the frantic struggle below. It was Vivian Cross, her form coming into view as the disturbed waters settled. Vivian's body jolted as if an invisible force were dragging her down, her limbs losing their coordination. Her tank had malfunctioned and the air supply was blocked.

A sharp pull on Amanda's arm jolted her out of the trance. Tristan. His eyes locked onto hers, and with a quick motion, he pointed up. *Go. Now.*

She snapped her head again above the surface just as chaos erupted around the dive boat. Amanda yanked her flippers off and swam to the ladder as fast as she could. Crew members shouted instructions and tugged at ropes reaching into the water. A moment later, Vivian was hauled onto the deck, limp and gasping, her face pale against the mid-morning sun.

"Breathe, Vivian! Just breathe!" someone urged, slamming the oxygen mask over her face. Her chest heaved as she choked on ragged gulps of air, water spilling from her lips. She did not draw another breath.

Amanda clambered onto the boat, her legs shaking beneath her. Around her, guests looked on in stunned silence, some still dripping as they emerged from the sea, disbelieving their eyes.

"What the hell went wrong?" Tristan's voice pierced the air, sharp and shrill as he panted through short breaths.

One of the crew members inspected Vivian's tank, his expression darkening. "The regulator malfunctioned. She wasn't getting any air."

Amanda swallowed hard, watching someone pump air into Vivian's lifeless body, her fingers still clutching her chest as if she could force air back into her lungs.

For the second time in twenty-four hours, someone was dead.

CHAPTER EIGHTEEN

THE ONCE LIVELY, CAREFREE group returned to the yacht in somber silence, a stark contrast to the way they had set out that morning. Even after the apparent heart attack of one passenger, they went on with life as usual because everyone understood what it was like for the world to keep spinning on its axis even after loss—for plans to carry on as if nothing happened. But now? Gone was the excitement, the easy laughter, the warmth of the sun on their skin. As they stepped onto the deck, dripping with seawater and weighed down by horror, a stillness settled over them. Crew members whispered among themselves, their expressions tight with concern, while others discreetly ushered shaken guests towards fresh towels and quiet spaces to gather their thoughts.

Amanda caught glimpses of Esmé and Clarisse as they arrived back from the island, shopping bags in hand, their smiles fading as they took in the grim faces surrounding them. Whatever lighthearted indulgence they'd been enjoying evaporated in an instant.

But the tragedy was far from over. The death of Russel Drake had already raised questions, and now, with Vivian's drowning, scrutiny was inevitable.

Legally, a death at sea was no simple matter. Maritime law dictated that the ship's captain report the incident to the proper authorities, which typically meant notifying the nearest port state's law enforcement. A formal declaration would need to be made—again—and in international waters, jurisdiction became murky. Local authorities, the flag state of the yacht, and even the victim's home country could all have claims to *both* investigations.

The yacht's staff was making calls, likely reaching out to the Coast Guard or the nearest legal authority. If foul play was suspected, forensic experts might need to board the ship. Guests could be interviewed, their statements taken, and their movements scrutinized. If Russel's death had been deemed natural, a second tragedy onboard could change everything.

Tristan exhaled sharply beside her, running a hand through his damp hair. "This is going to get messy," he muttered.

Amanda nodded, her stomach twisting. "Messy is an understatement."

"I'm gonna go talk to Esmé—you can go. Get yourself dried off—take a Xanax?" His eyes widened in appraisal of his girlfriend's mental state.

Amanda gave him a no-thank-you look, one brow lifting in silent refusal. Not her thing. Instead, she just shrugged, wringing some water from the ends of her hair. "I think I'll just stick to a towel and maybe a strong coffee. See you back at the room?"

"Okay," he leaned in to kiss her, lingering for half a second longer than Amanda expected.

"It'll be okay," she assured him, lying to herself, too.

As Amanda turned away from Tristan, she began to make her way towards their room, the sun now heavier with the weight of death. She wanted to dry off, to change, to find some way to recover from the lingering chill that had nothing to do with the water.

As she neared the hallway leading to the guest suites, a different thought occurred to her. No one had seen Julius that morning, and Hansen didn't participate in the day's activities either. They were probably still detained from the night before, and Russel Drake's cabin was likely empty. No one had mentioned what would happen to his belongings yet, and with the investigation still in its early stages, it was possible—presumable, even—that his room had been left untouched.

She didn't know what she was hoping to find. But if she went to her room now, she'd sit there spiraling, replaying the scene of Drake collapsing at Hansen's feet. The only thing that had ever stopped her from overthinking was action.

Amanda arrived at her cabin door, inserted her key to open it, and pulled out her phone, her fingers hesitating for only a second before tapping out a message to Marco.

I need your help.

She stared at the screen, watching the three little dots appear, then vanish, then appear again. The longer she waited, the harder her pulse pounded in her ears.

She assumed Marco would be game for a little investigation, but his respect—and fear—for Julius might override his curiosity. But if anyone could help her navigate this without raising suspicion, it was him.

Finally, his response popped up. *Where do you need me?*
Come to the room. Need towels.

She didn't want to put anything more in writing.

Marco appeared within ninety seconds, holding two neatly folded towels in his hands, immediately knowing there was no need for them.

"How can I help, señorita?" he smiled, handing over the towels.

Amanda exhaled, keeping her voice low as she motioned for him to step into the room. "I need to get into Russel Drake's cabin," she said, watching for any glimpse of reaction. Marco didn't blink, didn't ask why, only tilted his head slightly, waiting for more. The crew had been just as shaken up by the events that had transpired.

"I just…" she hesitated, weighing her words. "Something isn't sitting right with me. First Russel, now Vivian. That's not a coincidence. I need to see if there's anything in his room—something people aren't looking for."

Marco studied her for a moment, then let out a slow breath, scanning the hallway as if already working through the logistics. He wasn't going to let a chance to solve a real-life mystery pass him by. "You know, if we get caught, I'll have to act like I had no idea what you were doing."

Amanda gave him a tight-lipped smile. "I'd expect nothing less."

"Alright," he murmured. "Let's make this quick."

Marco moved in stride, strolling casually down the hallway before stopping near the corner, leaning against the wall like he had all the time in the world. His posture was effortless, but Amanda could see the way his gaze flicked towards every doorway, every shadow. He was watching.

He placed a key card in front of the door as it clicked open. No one had thought to secure it yet, and why would they?

Marco leaned back against the wall and motioned for Amanda to enter. She pushed the door open just enough to slide inside, then shut it behind her with a soft click. The room was exactly what she expected. A mostly empty glass sat on the bedside table, condensation still clinging to its surface. Drake's suitcase lay open near the dresser, clothes haphazardly tossed inside like he had eschewed unpacking assistance from crew members.

Amanda's pulse hammered as she moved deeper into the space. She didn't have much time. She scanned the room quickly—desk, bed, closet, bathroom. What kind of clue was she looking for? Where would he have kept something important?

There was nothing that stood out—nothing that screamed: *this man was murdered.* The bedside table held only a wallet, a keycard, and a crumpled napkin.

Then, she realized the drink may have been laced with something before he even came to the casino. She grabbed a hand towel from the bathroom and snatched the glass in her hand, wrapping it carefully in the fabric, hoping to protect any trace of chemical that may be able to be tested.

A sharp knock sounded against the door. Marco's signal. Someone was coming.

Amanda moved rapidly back towards the door, glass in hand. She barely had time to take one last look at the room before slipping out into the hallway, following Marco.

"You get lost?" Amanda heard Julius say to her as Marco continued to advance down the hall. She was so relieved that he kept his cool... and his distance. The last thing she wanted to do was get him involved.

Amanda forced herself to turn casually, smoothing her expression before meeting Julius's eyes. He stood with his hands in his pockets, watching her with a look that seemed slightly amused.

"Lost?" she echoed, tilting her head as if the question was ridiculous. "No, just taking the long way back."

Julius hummed, stepping closer, his polished shoes silent against the plush carpet. "That so?" His gaze flicked towards the door she'd just left.

A pulse of heat surged through her chest, but she kept her shoulders relaxed, shifting the towel-wrapped glass in her arms. "I was curious," she admitted, keeping her voice light—like she was discussing a piece of gossip rather than her own breaking and entering. "About what really happened to Russel." Her tone was glib.

She figured the jig was up. Julius knew she was sent by Katherine, so why not try her hand here? She was caught red-handed, and the truth was supposed to serve her, right? And maybe... maybe this was another opportunity to let truth dominate behind a conspiratorial shroud.

Julius studied her for a beat, then exhaled a low chuckle. "Curiosity can be dangerous."

"You've warned me before," she shifted her jaw dramatically, hoping her charm would be appreciated.

His dark eyes narrowed, imagining what she'd say next. "You don't think it was an accident?"

Amanda tightened her grip on the secret she held between her fingers, her pulse ticking faster. "No," she said simply. "I don't."

A slow smile crept onto Julius's lips, one that sent a chill dancing down her spine. Not because it was threatening—because it wasn't. He seemed intrigued.

"Well," he murmured, rocking back on his heels. "That makes two of us."

Amanda blinked, thrown off by the admission. "You?"

"Come on, Amanda," he said smoothly, leaning in just enough to lower his voice. "People like Russel Drake don't just keel over in the middle of a party without a little... *help*, right?"

Her breath caught. He knew something. Or at least suspected. But was he warning her to back off or inviting her in?

Julius's stare flicked deliberately to the towel in her arms before he took a slow step back. "Be careful where you poke around," he advised before turning and walking towards the room she had just exited. "The investigators will be here momentarily," he said, leaving Amanda standing there, heart thumping.

He entered the cabin himself, turning to wink at her before disappearing completely behind its door. Amanda clutched the glass, steadily holding its contents as she hurried back to her room. Marco was waiting at the end of her hallway when she arrived. She motioned for him to join her with a soft flick of her head.

They entered the room without a word.

"What is it?" he asked breathlessly.

"I don't know if it's anything. But this is the glass he must have had before he came to the casino after dinner…" Amanda hesitated. "Or maybe he had something at dinner? I don't know, I thought we could have it tested…" she gulped.

"Tested? For poison? But where? How could we do that?" Marco peppered her with questions.

"I… don't know…" she suddenly felt foolish.

"But what did you say to Mr. Julius?"

"I… oh, God. I told him I thought something was off about Russel Drake's death—and he agreed. He said the investigators were on their way. They're probably already there by now. And here I am, feeling ridiculous. I grabbed this stupid cup, thinking… what was I even thinking? The police have the resources to test for stuff, not me. I read too many mystery novels, and now… look at me."

She let out a breathy laugh, shaking her head. Amanda felt like an inept amateur detective way out of her depth, but more than that, she wanted to downplay her actions to prevent Marco from getting tangled in this madness.

"Maybe we can take it back?" she shrugged, searching her mind for what to do next, half hoping he'd have an answer.

"Oh, Miss Amanda, you can't go there now. They will overlook a small thing like a glass. No one will test it. You did a good thing. Now, let's turn it in to Mr. Julius. If he told you he agreed, he will thank you. He is a man of his word."

"I... I can't go back there now," she protested. "Tell him I had a whiskey glass in my hand, holding on for dear life like I'm Sherlock Holmes."

"Okay, then I will. I will be... cautious," Marco promised. "You leave it to me."

Amanda hesitated for only a moment before nodding, pressing the bundled towel into Marco's hands. "Okay," she said quietly. "Be careful."

Marco gave her a reassuring nod, tucking the evidence under his arm. "You don't worry about me, Miss Amanda. Get cleaned up, and take a breath. I'll handle this."

With that, he slipped out the door, leaving her standing there, the weight of the day pressing down on her shoulders. She exhaled slowly, running a hand over her damp hair before heading to the bathroom. Turning the tap, she let the cool water rush over her fingers before splashing it onto her face. The reflection staring back at her was paler than usual, eyes sharp with adrenaline, her expression tight with thoughts she couldn't quite unravel.

Amanda forced a deep breath, peeling off her damp clothes and changing into a clean sundress that didn't carry the scent of saltwater and nerves. She felt overdressed. Even the most casual thing from Esmé's closet felt elegant.

She heard the door move as she peeked her head from the bathroom to see Tristan.

"Well," he said, rubbing the back of his neck as he shut the door behind him. "That was a hell of a day."

Amanda offered a weak smile, walking to perch herself on the edge of the bed. "No kidding."

He took a few steps forward, hands on his hips, eyes assessing her. "They've adjusted the evening schedule. The formal dinner is off. Instead, they're putting out a buffet on the deck. Drinks, food—whatever anyone needs. I guess they figure it's better to keep people together and let them talk it out rather than sit alone and spiral."

Amanda nodded. "That makes sense. How's everyone taking it?"

Tristan let out a low whistle, sinking into the chair across from her. "Esmé's got her own theories already, something about business rivalries and secret enemies. Hansen's been playing the part of the concerned politician, reassuring everyone that things are under control. Clarisse and Anton are shaken but keeping up appearances. And the rest? They're whispering in corners, horrified but also spinning their own versions of events."

Amanda swallowed. She wasn't a complete cynic, but this didn't help to change her worldview at all. The rich and powerful didn't just react to tragedy, they shaped the narrative to suit them.

Tristan leaned forward, studying her. "You okay?"

She forced a smile. "Yeah. Just... processing."

He watched her for a beat longer, then nodded. "I'm gonna shower, then we can go up to the deck. Eat something. It'll help."

Amanda wasn't so sure. But there was nothing else to do. And nowhere else to go.

Chapter Nineteen

An eerie silence hovered as the ship glided into the dock, heavy under the weight of tragedy. The usual fanfare of disembarkation was replaced with a quiet, subdued efficiency. No champagne toasts, just the hushed murmurs of guests eager to step onto solid ground, their excitement long since drained away. The long extravaganza had been cut short, the aftereffect of catastrophe clinging to everyone like an unwelcome shadow.

Crew members handled luggage, directed guests, and did their best to maintain a sense of order. Some travelers were making frantic arrangements to leave the island early, while others whispered in tense clusters, debating their next steps.

A line of sleek black cars waited at the dock, doors swinging open to accommodate those returning to the villa. The estate had once promised a luxurious end to their lavish trip, but now it felt like a holding place, a limbo between chaos and their everyday lives.

Distress sat heavy in Amanda's chest. Everyone was recalibrating their plans to arrive safely outside of this nightmare, in the arms of their loved ones. But there was no one waiting for her—no one who both knew her secrets and could be trusted.

She barely communicated with Katherine since arriving on the island. The feeling that she had been sent in blind was overwhelming now. Katherine and Amanda's training instructors had warned her to stay calm if there was a loss of communication, but they hadn't told her what to do if she was ghosted, literally left adrift on an open sea. More than ever, she wanted to run. To go home and forget any of this had ever happened. But now? She was an eyewitness to the deadly power of another Hansen.

"Hey," Tristan approached from the back of the sedan after helping their driver with the bags. "The cable car can't carry us and luggage at the same time, so they'll drive us up... or if you want to get there faster... you can ride with some of the others. I think Eduardo and Richard are planning to take the cable with Clarisse and Esmé."

"No thanks, I'll ride with you. It'll give us a few extra minutes of peace and quiet together," Amanda said.

Tristan reached down to open the door, taking her hand as she slipped into the backseat. As they began the ascent, Amanda laid her head on Tristan's shoulder, positioning her head to watch the stunning terrain tick by.

As the road hugged the cliffs, weaving between lush greenery and plunging rock faces, they both remained silent—speechless as the haunting beauty of the island taunted them. When they entered the property, the usual flurry of staff was absent. Instead, a few workers moved about quietly, dismantling remnants of a celebration that would never happen.

The terrace, meant to be the grand stage for the final night's festivities, was grimly empty. No string lights twinkled; no laughter echoed across the marble floors. The extravagant fireworks display would remain boxed away, never to illuminate the sea.

"I'll help with our bags," Tristan said, stepping out of the car. "You go ahead and get settled."

"Oh, I can take mine," Amanda insisted. "Or at least a couple of the small ones."

"Alright," Tristan agreed as the driver helped get their luggage from the back.

The handful of guests still present at Julius' estate were communicating with each other minimally, and Tristan and Amanda were no exception. As they arrived back at their room, they moved around mindlessly, making half-hearted attempts to arrange their things.

"Oh, the big one is Esmé's. I'll need to return it to her."

"Do you want to get anything out of it first?" Tristan asked, lifting it onto the bed.

"Yeah, probably... let me check." Amanda took the few items that were hers and zipped the luggage shut. She let out a sigh. "I think I'm going to take a walk. The sun will go down soon, and I haven't even had time to explore the property yet. It'll do me some good to clear my mind."

"Of course," Tristan said. "I'm going to hop in the shower. I can take the stuff to Esmé if you want. I should check on her anyway—I don't know if Julius will be back anytime soon." The guest of honor at their lavish celebration had been missing for over twenty-four hours.

"That would be great, thanks," she smiled, truly grateful for his calming presence.

Amanda wandered through the villa's sprawling grounds, her steps slow, unhurried, aimless. The sinking sun stretched long across the terraced property, casting warm hues over the manicured gardens and weathered stone pathways. She inhaled the scent of the sea and the floral scents from the hedgerows, elements that remained constant no matter how tumultuous the circumstances.

She traced her fingers along the rough stone wall as she descended to the lowest tier of the terrace, where the groomed met the wild, and the neatly trimmed grass gave way to the rugged landscape colliding with the cliffs overlooking the ocean. A few solar-powered lanterns had switched on, their faint glow contrasting with the last rays of daylight.

She wasn't sure how long she had been walking, lost in motion, her mind a tangled mess of questions when a movement caught her eye—Julius stood just beyond the pathway, the dark silhouette of his frame outlined against the deepening sky. It was as if he was expecting her, his gaze fixed and purposeful.

Without hesitation, he started towards her.

"What?" Amanda stammered. "I... I didn't think you were home yet."

"Come with me," Julius instructed, leading Amanda through a break in the hedges to a secluded alcove tucked away from the main pathways. Two stone benches sat opposite each other beneath the sprawling branches of a jacaranda tree, its violet blossoms scattered across the ground like remnants of the forgotten celebration. The spot was perfectly placed, offering an unobstructed view of the horizon where the sun melted into the sea each evening. Julius gestured towards one of the benches, taking the other for himself.

A knot tightened in Amanda's chest as she sat there. She was supposed to be here for answers, to uncover whatever Julius was hiding. But now, after all the chaos they'd been through in the past two days, sitting across from him in the fading light, it was starkly apparent how little she knew—about him, about the people who had sent her, about Katherine. The lines between ally and enemy blurred.

Her eyes burned, but she refused to let the tears fall. She clenched her hands in her lap, willing herself to stay composed. "Who *are* you?" she asked.

Julius lounged against the back of the bench, one arm draped lazily along its edge, the other hand resting on his knee. He was the picture of composure. None of this mayhem had fazed him in the slightest. Two people had died. The entire trip had unraveled into tragedy. And yet, he sat there as if he had expected every twist, every revelation.

His dark eyes held a knowing glint, not cruel or amused, but certain and unshaken. He absorbed the silence between them like it was a luxury as if he could take his time because he already had all the answers.

Something was infuriating about his ease—like he was merely watching the pieces fall into place rather than scrambling to put them together. He smiled coolly.

"I bet Katherine told you she was MI6," he murmured.

"What?" Amanda was caught off guard. Sure, he told her he knew Katherine, and that he had been playing weird games with her mind, but this was unexpected. "Um... not exactly. But I didn't ask who she was, I asked who you are."

"Fair enough. I'm CIA. The oldest in the business, really."

"What?" Amanda let out an incredulous laugh. "You have got to be kidding me," she said to the universe more than to Julius.

Julius remained stoic, unflustered.

"So... you are telling me that all of this," Amanda gestured wildly around her, "...the government just pays for you to have a billionaire reputation? That's... kind of unbelievable. And you're just outing yourself. To me?" Amanda started to stand, exasperated from being a pawn in this game she couldn't figure out.

"Wait. Amanda." Julius's tone was familiar—demanding yet gentle. "I can explain, and I know you want answers. You deserve them."

She took a seat again as he continued. "I'm sorry to burst your bubble, but power—fame—control—the whole world is nothing but bought and sold. You have to be able to recognize that. To spend our government's money, all they have to do is print some for me. So... for a few decades, as oligarchs and billionaires have bargained and schemed, opulence has been my way in."

"That's crazy," she gasped. "But what does any of this have to do with *me?*" she nearly pleaded.

Julius grinned. "Well, we need you because of Hansen. This was all... a test. And you passed." He sounded truly congratulatory.

"And with flying colors, I might add," a familiar voice approached from beyond the hedges. Katherine stepped forward, appearing as if out of nowhere.

Amanda jumped to her feet, flinging her hands to her head in disbelief. "What the actual...?" she gasped for breath, unable to utter another syllable. "Don't touch me," she protested as Katherine approached.

"Please, dear, have a seat," Katherine motioned.

"A seat?" she let out a nervous snort, teetering on the edge of looking insane. "You want me to have a *seat?*" Amanda's words cut through the air like a spear, sharp and unrelenting. Each syllable was honed to a point, slicing through pretense, her tone unforgiving. "Yeah. Great, let me take a seat for our casual conversation!" she shouted while mimicking Katherine's gesture. "How about I don't, and I leave you two crazy people to manipulate someone else?" She spun on her heel and walked away, her pulse pounding in her ears.

"They have nukes, Amanda. Everyone does. You know that. Cities go up in smoke in minutes, whole populations wiped out, and the world destroyed within an hour. And at this point in history, who can say if we've learned anything from our past? We're closer now to seeing that kind of destruction than ever," Julius said, desperate to convey the life-or-death stakes to her.

Amanda turned slowly to face them. "And I'm supposed to help stop that? Do you know how ridiculous that sounds?"

"A glamorous woman with wealth, and love, and her very *life* to lose? Sounds like a great cover for secret missions to me," Katherine responded.

Amanda slowly lumbered back to the bench, lowering her body and clutching the seat's edge to steady herself. "And I'm supposed to believe you, Katherine? Now? Everything you've told me has been a lie."

"Katherine is what you call a double agent," Julius interjected. "You're familiar with the concept?"

Amanda nodded.

"Okay, well, Katherine has worked with many agencies through the years and has been able to remain... discreet," he said smoothly, his expression unreadable, stating a fact rather than revealing a tangled web. He leaned back slightly, watching her reaction with an air of calm detachment before continuing. "So, when Hansen's cohort approached her, we knew we were in the deepest ring we've ever been part of. His network stretches across continents—a tangled web of power brokers, shell companies, and covert alliances that make his operation the most far-reaching circle we've ever infiltrated."

"But why me?" she demanded, her voice tight. "They blackmailed me years ago. I have nothing more on them. Did you think that I was loyal to them just because I haven't exposed them after all these years?" She stared at Julius, searching his face for any sign that this was some cruel trick.

"We couldn't be sure. We had to test you," Julius said evenly, his gaze unwavering. "Hansen believes Katherine's front company—the same one that *quote-unquote* 'hired you'—is a private investigator firm that can help him protect his affairs. I knew that if you felt any real loyalty to Katherine—or even the

Hansens—you wouldn't have been so quick to point out that Russel Drake didn't just die. The only one that you could be suspicious of was the Governor... so, I knew."

The realization made her skin prickle.

"You thought I could be working with... Hansen?" His name tasted disgusting in her mouth, like something rancid she wanted to spit out.

"As a double agent," Katherine nodded, her expression unreadable.

"Like you," Amanda all but sneered, her words dripping with accusation.

Silence stretched for a beat before Amanda forced herself to ask the question that suddenly lodged itself in her throat. "And Tristan?" Her voice trembled, betraying the fear she had tried to keep at bay.

"I've been keeping Tristan close for years. His technology is truly revolutionary. We believe it can protect us all from an almost certain nuclear disaster," Julius explained. "But Hansen and other partners from all around the world have been courting him too—wanting to outbid us for his intellectual property. And I need to see how involved he is. How close he is to selling, and who's involved in the buy."

"And you want me to help you do that? Be around the Hansens again? Get you documentation?" Amanda shook her head. "I may be a scrappy girl from Tennessee who had to claw her way up to where I am, but I have limits. You have the wrong girl."

"We don't," Katherine said abruptly. "It's in your blood."

"What?" Amanda quipped, unable to access the feelings of warmth she developed for Katherine. "What do you know about my family other than what I told you when I literally poured out my heart and soul to you?"

"I know your father," Katherine said without a pause.

Amanda's pulse roared in her ears. The world tilted beneath her, the edges of reality smudging as if she'd stepped into a dream. Every instinct screamed at her to run, to shove them both aside and get the hell out of there. But her body wouldn't move. She was rooted to the bench, clutching its side like a lifeline.

Her breath came in sharp bursts, her chest tight—stomach a tangled knot of disbelief and fury. She had spent years searching for stability, clawing her way towards something real, something she could control. And now? Now, she was being told that she was nothing more than a piece on a chessboard, maneuvered and manipulated without her even knowing.

And Katherine—Katherine, who she had trusted and confided in—sat there so casually, as if she hadn't just detonated Amanda's entire sense of self.

She felt Katherine's admission, deep in her bones, in the marrow of her past, in the empty spaces she had long since given up trying to fill.

She blinked, barely registering Julius's ever-cool demeanor beside her. Her father. A ghost. A question mark. A missing page in a book she had never been allowed to read.

Amanda swallowed hard, willing herself to keep her voice steady, but the question came out as a whisper. "What do you mean, you know my father?"

Katherine held her gaze, her lips pressed together, as she watched Amanda wrestle with the weight of her words.

"Your father," she said, her voice quiet but firm, "comes from a long line of people like us. Like you."

Amanda shook her head, the denial automatic. "No. No, that's not possible. My father..." She stopped herself. What did she really know about him? A name, a handful of vague stories, an absence that had carved its way into every empty crevasse of her life.

"Remember how we spoke of different agents? Histories of espionage, the Cambridge members, and others? Some of them vanished into history, yes, their identities were never confirmed. But they didn't disappear, Amanda. Their craft passed down," Katherine continued. "Through bloodlines. Through families with a legacy of espionage."

"So... you're saying..." The wheels in Amanda's head were whirring at double speed, "It's not Tristan, Anton, or Clarisse you were suspicious of... it was... *me?*"

Katherine nodded. "Your father was born into one of those families. And whether you realize it or not, that means you were too."

Amanda's flesh curled, her mind scrambling for some logical way to make it all go away. "You're saying spying is... *hereditary?*" she scoffed, but there was no humor in her voice.

"Call it what you want," Julius inserted smoothly. "A tradition. An instinct. A responsibility. But it's in you, Amanda. The way you think, the way you notice things other people miss—it's not just luck. It's an intuition passed down without you even knowing it."

Amanda felt the ground shift beneath her. All the times she had been able to read people too well, to sense when something was off, to move through the world with exceptional awareness—it had always felt like a lucky personality quirk.

"Your father is one of the best," Katherine added, her voice softer now. "And if you let yourself see the truth, you'll understand that you were never just some ordinary girl from Tennessee. You were born for this."

"Born for this? And you claimed you wanted to protect me from this life," Amanda glowered.

Katherine lowered her head. "There's always a chance, a way to escape... when the time is right."

Amanda swallowed hard, gripping the bench like it was the only thing tethering her to reality. She had spent her whole life searching for answers. Now that she had them, she wasn't sure she wanted to know more.

Julius let the air settle, watching Amanda process everything with a quiet intensity. He could see a battle waging in her eyes—disbelief, anger, fear, and beneath it all, the undeniable pull of the truth.

"You don't have to decide now," he said finally, his voice even. "This isn't a trick, and we're not forcing your hand. But you've seen how swiftly Hansen can strike. You saw it with Russel. With Vivian. Right under our noses."

Amanda clenched her jaw, her pulse ringing in her ears. She hated that he was right. Detested the fact that she had been dragged into something so much bigger than herself. But most of all, she hated the part of herself that wasn't sure she could walk away.

"You know the risks now," Katherine added, her tone measured. "The danger. The gravity of what's at stake. And you know that if you step into this world, there's no half-measure. You're either in... or you're out," she spoke slowly, a hint of compassion on her lips.

Amanda exhaled slowly. "And if I say no?"

Julius's expression didn't change. "Then you go back to your life. We won't come knocking again. But we won't have the power to protect you from Hansen. He thinks he has you under his thumb, remember."

She studied him, searching for any sign of deception, but found none.

"And if I say yes?" she asked, her voice quieter.

Julius gave her a small, knowing smile. "Then the next stop is Tokyo."

Amanda's mind raced. The world around her suddenly felt smaller, as if the walls of the villa, the impenetrable barrier of the cliffs, and the infinite expanse of the ocean itself were all closing in, suffocating her. She had spent years trying to outrun her past, trying to leave behind the parts of herself she didn't want to understand. And now? Now, she had to choose between the pain of knowing and the continued pain of unknowing.

She wasn't ready to make that choice. But as she sat there, she knew one thing for certain. Amanda Hopkins couldn't pretend her life was the same anymore.

Not after this.

About The Author

Shelly Snow Pordea is a storyteller at heart, known for her exciting novels that connect, heal, and spark meaningful conversations. She first captured readers' imaginations with *Tracing Time*, a time-travel romance series that remains a fan favorite in its category. In 2021, Shelly and her brother placed in a top screenwriting contest for a co-written family drama based on their experience growing up in a cult—an exciting step into the world of film storytelling.

Her 2024 novel, *The Cheating Wife*, was inspired by a real incident of public shaming—a woman's property vandalized with the words "cheating wife" scrawled in graffiti. "After witnessing graffiti on a woman's property, blatantly accusing her of being a 'cheating wife,' I knew I was going to write a story about how far we've come—or haven't—from the days of public shaming and scarlet-letter-wearing," Shelly says. "The patriarchy is alive and well, and this book is my attempt to remind us all to take a look at our part in it."

Shelly is also the author of the *Flight Risk Spy Series*, which follows a high-flying heroine who stumbles into the world of espionage. She has based the travels of her protagonist, Amanda, on locations she's been lucky enough to visit. She and her family maintain a residence both in Brașov, Romania and St. Louis, Missouri.

Beyond her professional pursuits, Shelly is a dedicated mother to three incredible adults, loving wife to her favorite guy, George, for nearly three decades, and Buni (boo-nee) to one enchanting, magical granddaughter. She invites you to join her journey on social media, where she shares her insights and creative endeavors. Follow her @shellysnowpordea for a glimpse into the world of a multifaceted storyteller and advocate.

Also by

Shelly Snow Pordea

★ ★ ★ ★ ★

"A fun, engaging travel adventure with a female James Bond vibe that keeps you turning the page."

Books in *The Flight Risk Spy* Series:

The Night We Met – One encounter changes Amanda's life forever. March 2025

The Last Flight from Tokyo – Amanda's hunt turns deadly as she races against a ticking clock in Japan. June 2025

The Flowers of May – Back on American soil, Amanda discovers betrayal blooms closer to home than she thought. September 2025

Unfollowed – When everything goes offline, Amanda's past is sure to catch up with her. December 2025

From chance encounters to near-deadly escapes, this high-stakes series takes Amanda across continents, through smoky backrooms, and in a race against time. Each book peels back a layer of deception as Amanda learns that flying under the radar might just be the hardest thing of all.

Fasten your seatbelt! This spy series is a trip you won't want to miss.

"So original, imaginative, and captivating."

Book 1 in the *Tracing Time Trilogy,* Anna Wright grapples with the effects of her depression while living a secluded life with her young family abroad. When her husband disappears, she is faced with accepting the assumption of his death or uncovering the truth behind his work.

Anna returns to the only thing she knows, her Midwest family, but life on the farm isn't like what it was growing up.

Times and people have changed, and her quest to find herself again turns into a burning desire to know the truth. Her husband's colleague, Christopher, and the distinguished Professor Trinkton reveal secrets behind their studies, leaving Anna with the impossible choice to either join their efforts or lose David forever.

While she is an involved and loving mother, she does the unthinkable, choosing to travel through space and time without her children, justifying to herself that she's on a mission to help save the planet and return her husband safely to his family. Her tenacity and determination lead her to successfully embark on an unfathomable journey. And what she finds is unthinkable: her husband, stuck in a time period in which he was unable to access the technology needed to return, has been betrothed to another.

The Victorian British era in which David had been trapped for nearly eight years left him all but hopeless until Anna arrives. Overcoming the epic trials their true love story must face, along with a mystical guide, together they make a way to return. But things aren't simple when toying with the fabric of time.

Book 2 in the *Tracing Time Trilogy*. Fourteen years after the disappearance of David and Anna, Christopher Mack is imprisoned for their murders. Maggie Sturgeon, the young daughter who was left behind had been raised by her mother's brother and Turkish-born auntie, Ami.

Now an adult, Maggie finds that Trinkton, who she knew to be the lawyer involved in the murder case, was actually her parents' former Professor at UCLA. Following in her father's footsteps and being accepted into their science program, she too finds herself uncovering secrets she was never meant to know.

Connecting with a fellow student, and son of a prominent professor himself, Maggie and Rowan join forces to unearth every mystery about the past. What they didn't expect was to be entangled far more than they could have imagined. Rowan finds that his parents were also participants in the infamous time travel program as they uncover a convoluted string of events that led them to become deeply involved in a network of people in *The Program*.

Arriving in 1970s England, they reunite with their parents only to be plunged into a world from which they only wished they could escape. Maggie and Rowan ultimately believe they can make a difference by trying to thwart the growing effects of climate change, but their compromise is being fully controlled by *The Company.*

The family drama an absentee parent must face with their adult children takes on new meaning once Maggie confronts her parents as their paths cross in a time period none of them were meant to experience.

Book 3 in *The Tracing Time Trilogy.* After years in *The Program,* two generations of parents who had struggled to make sense of the lives they built were forced to reveal secrets to yet another generation. Young Maisy had a peaceful life growing up in England as the daughter of expats in the 1990s, but her stoic personality and stunning looks always drew attention. Thinking it was her weirdness that made her feel like she never quite fit in and determined to find herself, she set off on a backpacking adventure that would change her life.

Antonio was unlike anyone she'd ever met. Dropping her a secret note in an airport lounge, he leads Maisy to a startling discovery of who she really was, no spiritual self-revelation involved. Coming to terms with the fact that she was the third generation in a family of time travelers, Maisy conspires with Antonio to blow the whole thing up. She finally feels like she has answers for her misfit life, yet she has only scratched the surface.

Being involved with *The Company* has taken its toll on everyone, and Maisy is the young blood needed to lead the charge for this family to regain their freedom once and for all. While not fully abandoning the initial mission of trying to help save the planet, she, her parents, and grandparents set off to do collectively what one could not accomplish alone. One problem remains for Maisy, Antonio isn't part of the family.

Leaving the past behind, all three generations duly return to the twenty-first century as Trinkton and Christopher are finally able to share the truth about what had transpired during their absence. Both happy endings and love lost are inevitable.

"Fiction, and yet, very real. I was captivated. I was gripped. I couldn't put it down." — Sarah Edmondson, HBO's *The Vow*, Podcast Host, *A Little Bit Culty*

"A story that stays with you long after you've finished."

Morgan Conner had it all—until the words *cheating wife* appeared spray-painted across her property, turning her world upside down. Suddenly, her picture-perfect life is in pieces, and the whispers of her community grow louder by the second.

Caught in a storm of judgment and betrayal, Morgan must dig deep to fight for her truth and her survival. In a society where appearances often mean more than facts, can she rise above the scandal and find her own voice?

Dive into this powerful story of resilience, redemption, and breaking free from the expectations of others.